Take a journey into mystery:

"Regrettably the moon was in wane, a mere fourth of its fullness, and I found myself wishing, as we trundled along in the crepuscular darkness, that the *Goddess of the Night* had bequeathed us more of her nocturnal radiance. I carried with me–hidden upon my person–the revolver Lucien had instructed me to carry, and its presence gave me a slight reprieve from the ominous weight the darkness enclosed upon my wary frame of mind. I had questioned Lucien about the strange inscriptions I had seen upon the shells. He was somewhat elusive about the language–or symbols–that each bullet was inscribed, save to say that they were *apotropaic* in nature. This, of course, was hardly reassuring to my overtly rational self. I admit freely that I do not contain the capacity nor the experience and knowledge of the supernal arts of which his brilliant mind is so endowed."

-Excerpt from The Brassac Vampyre

The Profound Art of Omens

© M. E. Nyberg

www.menyberg.com

).(

Book design by Don Mangione

~

Cover photography by M. E. Nyberg

ISBN 13: 978-0-9970986-4-8
eISBN 13: 978-0-9970986-5-5

Library of Congress registration
Copyright #TX 8-234-067
November 14, 2014

~

To Karlyn

Other books by M E Nyberg

The Profound Art of Omens
The Man Who Would Be Coyote
The Wicker Woman

Table of Contents

Prologue

In the mid nineteen nineties I was hired as the Production Manager on a documentary project for a French production company in Paris. The subject of the documentary was the *rites of passage* inherent in certain indigenous and contemporary cultures throughout the world. The *rites* were concerning many varied subjects, birth and puberty, youth to old age, the concept of the *spirit quest* and of course *death and the afterlife*. It was from my involvement with this international project spanning many months that a broader circle of friendship (professional and personal) emerged. It was from this emergence and my subsequent travels that the following *'Tall Tales'* came to light.

Chapter *1*: *The Story of Loup Garou*
(The Strange history of Anton Corbeau)

My name is Willem Furey. I'm a business manager for the prestigious–albeit unsolicited–firm, *Karras and Corbeau: Investigators of the Strange and Occult* whose unmarked offices occupy the back rooms of the infamous *Riker Pub* situated deep within the bustling Soho district of London. I freely admit that I possess no ability or inclinations with what my employers refer to as *the invisible side of Nature.* In fact, it's an amazement that I work for Mr. Karras, my employer of record, a noted and published man of science with impeccable credentials and deportment. The only *blemish* on his accomplished career is his active involvement with the occult. His father was a member of the English scientific aristocracy, his mother a noted mystic, this apparently accounting for his interest and talents with *the other side of existence* as he refers to it.

I find Mr. Karras amiable yet mysterious. He is strikingly tall with dark piercing eyes that have a peculiar intense radiance, a look one might equate with creatures of the predator line, *the birds of prey* and the like; as if always engaged at a distance. His brow is often furrowed when deep in thought and his beard tinted with a slight brownish hue from his predilection for tobacco. He walks with a slight limp in the right leg using a gnarled old briar cane as a prop. He is generous with me financially and in friendship and has the penchant of sharing with me many of his rather remarkable theories and experiences despite my obvious lack of aptitude with the *nocturnal arts.*

When time and travel allow, we will sometimes sit at his reserved table in the rear of *The Riker* and he'll expound upon his adventures and ideas over pints of bitters and pipefuls of shag, sometimes with a strange guest in tow. The man never seems to waver from his convictions whether he's in the company of scientists, mystics, or clergy, all of who seek him out–however reluctantly–when strange and inexplicable events demand his unique and extraordinary talents. His clientele includes the extremely rich to the desperately poor, the atheist to ranking members of *the Church*; kings and queens– western and oriental–literally all members of society who's sudden, or chronic, foray into the inexorable and mysterious, demand a deferential and discreet effort of resolve. The company's record of success is quite impressive.

His ignominious partner, Mr. Corbeau, I freely admit, sends chills through my spine on those occasions we converse in person. He is shorter than his business counterpart and carries a somewhat unsettling aura. Animals shun him, and babies cry anywhere near his presence. The man's eyes possess an odd pallor as if he were perhaps blind, which he is not, and his skin carries an odd texture as if afflicted with some type of *lupus*.

He is always impeccably dressed, albeit old-fashioned, and his ancestry is distinctly French, his familial lineage apparently old and one of affluence. All-in-all, I must admit I know very little about the man except that he hails from the Sud-du-France and that his immediate family had met with some terrible tragedy that provoked his malcontented aversion to life and people. His dealings with Mr. Karras are both professional and personal, the two men sharing a devoted friendship.

When he chances to visit *The Riker*–usually on some type of business with Mr. Karras–he sulks in the dark rear recesses, more often than not alone. Through narrow eyes he watches the comings and goings of the pub in silence, sipping *absinthe* usually consuming sizable volumes at any one sitting before ambling out into the night through one of the rear portals, to wander the streets of the great city in a solitary fashion until the wee hours of the morning chases him back to the upper chambers of the pub where he'll retire until the evening of the following day.

Mr. Corbeau spends most of his time in France, residing somewhere on the Cote d'Azur and rarely visits the offices in Soho; possessing a strong aversion to travel. In my dealings with him, primarily financial in nature, I realize an acute intelligence; a member of a very old lineage indeed. His knowledge of history is immense and his understanding of geography and topography most accomplished. Yet within the gnarled framework of this man resides a very troubled mind. His nature is most always toward the darker aspect, quiet and reserved yet prone to occasional outbursts of the most unnerving magnitude. Although spare in frame his physical strength– so I've witnessed on more than one occasion–defies what one would ascertain as normal, and so it is with his senses. The man seems to possess markedly keen ocular and aural abilities, possibly due to his reclusive nature and the proclivity of moving about primarily by night, as he prefers the *quiet less obtrusive hours* and avoidance of *the harshness of the midday sun.*

Whatever the reason, reclusiveness or other, he is keenly aware at all times of the various *goings-on* about him. On several occasions our work within the offices have been interrupted by his proclamation that a certain individual of note was in proximity. Sometimes it's oblique references to persons within the pub, sometimes outside of it. Remarkably, on every occasion he is correct.

I once questioned Mr. Karras about his partner's amazing sense of sight and hearing. Oddly, his response was: *'Yes, but his nose is the far superior component.'* I laughed of course assuming a rare pun, but his demeanor was one of abject seriousness and the matter was instantly dropped.

Be that as it may, my curiosity was never quite slated and it was only after a terrible ordeal on a night in the month of June, marked by a strange and unusually violent episode–where Mr. Corbeau, for reasons quite unknown, ransacked the pub and sent two barkeeps and a local constable to the infirmary–that my employer, realizing my intense concern, took me into his confidence.

He sat me at his table, stoked his meerschaum and handed me a dog-eared envelope, addressed to him; postmarked Nice, France.

"Open it," he said quietly as he puffed the flame of a cedar match into his ornately carved bowl, exhaling a large volume of gray smoke into the room. I extracted several pages of crisp yellowed paper sandwiched between several more contemporary sheets. I took pains to carefully unfold them onto the tiny circular table; the crisp, yellow paper aged and delicate to the touch.

The sheets of contemporary letterhead contained a printed watermark unmistakably Mr. Corbeau's familial coat-of-arms, which I was privy to, but knew so very little about being reluctant to delve into the strange man's private affairs for fear of possibly igniting his peculiar temperament. The pen and ink looked to be a long and scratchy cursive unmistakably wrought by quill.

As I studied the body of the letter my gaze wandered inadvertently to Mr. Karras whose eyes were alight with that strange gleam I've often seen when he is onto something of import.

"Read it," he muttered through his pervasive beard, the fire from the small table lamp dancing upon his dark pupils. What I read–the following–was so amazing a missive that I have never spoken about it to a soul, content to relegate it to the strange and mystifying. The letter read as follows:

'My Dear Lucien,

'Let me state first-with-all, and emphatically, that you are as a brother to me. In my self-imposed exile from the graces of humanity you are the sole repository of my eternal faith, the lone sentinel of hope, hope and faith, that one day this accursed affliction will forever fail me. That perchance one day I might again walk amongst humankind as the man I once was.

'You have befriended me most graciously and despite my moments of torment and betrayal of civility you remain steadfastly immovable. It is for this reason I write this communiqué to you on this singularly portentous evening.

'Less an oration still more a confession, for a confession it is that naught an ear has beheld save yours upon this reading. Undeniably, I owe you as much. It is the least I can do to bring some modicum of light into the darkness that is my soul and how this darkness came to befall me.

'Be clear my friend, this is not the ravings of a salacious deranged mind or the illusions of a crazed imagination but the truth of my circumstances and all too very real.

'Be astute! Take heed what I depart and what these words portend, for that which laces its tendrils through my bosom is an insidious and malevolent thing, a vendetta against humankind that seeks no bounds but to undo everything of meaning, everything that is light and beauty and softness. The delicate ephemeral moment called a man's life, that the vanity of man so too often takes for granted—as if it were eternal unto him—is but an infinitesimal flame within a vast ocean of darkness, buffeted by an incessant unbounded wind, close upon him at all sides, like the very shadow that follows him about at every turn, there, yet naught upon the closing of the warmth of the day.

'My dear brother, I write you tonight not an account of the past several years of my varied travails, but this confession. Realize, I am no longer part of the multitude of humanity I gaze upon from my solemn retreat, but alas a shadow, prey to a curse that fathoms the darker nature of man, unyielding in its ancient manifestation. This, life of lies, will never die, but pass unerring onto the next a misery unimaginable.

'Tonight, as the silver orb rides full in the heavens, I write by the light of this thin candle my confession, my hope, that by some miracle I might find release from the doubt and deprivation my soul has floundered in these last wicked years. A confession to you dear brother for in truth, no church of the Christ of heaven could witness these words I impart, could quell the agony I speak of as the ancient sphere turns full and again my mind turns mad. Indeed, no priest nor holy man of the cloth, no cathedral, no holy place, could obfuscate this unwavering intent when the change becomes me.

'Mankind, the lambs of God. How I detest their feeble means to personify He in human form. This immense unfathomable thing! Lord of the night. Lord of fools and angels alike, the creator of this insidious duality, the creator of heaven and hell, sunlight and shadow both. Only Man could muster the hubris to think this monstrous immensity could be cast into such a shallow fragile shell that is Man.

'The ancient monoliths with their saints and demons, fan a rage within my soul, a foul wind within my dead mind, like houses of the damned run amok. Where is the slender hand of reason? Curse these imps that wrought me thus!

'On any average evening, perhaps in Bourges, perhaps some other solemn forgotten place, I will sit near them, a bench beneath a drooping bough of a great tree, and watch as they pass, deferent the ancestral stone and its myriad of secrets. Nary their attentions wander to the heights, the towers and belfries of these cloisters where the demons rage forth, forever frozen by the sight of God.

'I am that gargoyle with gnashing teeth and clawed fist, hiding within the gabled corners and shadowy recesses, casting evil stares outwardly upon a quiet green landscape filled with the art of Nature and growing things. I am that pale image at night poisoning the sleeper's dreams with nightmares of the nether regions that all know of innately. I am the monster that roams the great cathedral of life, a fascination and nightmare for the material earthbound mind with its multiplicity of desires, and soulless endeavors.

'It is a wicked and evil wind that blows through this empty villa where my body resides, where strange and sinister sounds emit their presence. The dogs howl in the distance and if you listen closely you will hear their low and sonorous warnings of the Loup Gare-ou. For it is his cry, the call of a soul lost forever in the blackness of eternity, endlessly wandering within a wild and desolate landscape, that sets them to frenzy. Frenzy it is brother, for no better a word can convey the fear and loathing that this animal in its age long ascension into the House of Man feels for the wild one, the half-man half-beast my countrymen have christened Loup Gare-ou, the wolf of war.

'They know of him, have known of him since the ages; for he exists daily as a man, a quiet and haunted man, who keeps to his own and darkly. A resourceful man, a survivor as his namesake implies, sometimes a loner, a sullen stranger prowling the periphery of a village, sometimes a wanderer of great distances, sometimes running in packs.

'This man, in the broad spectrum of the noonday sun, would appear as any other man, however reluctant at most festive and charming endeavors associated with the species. Yet when night settles her velvet hand and the light of far and distant stars sparkle on the horizon like diamonds on ebony, his mannerisms change subtly and more ill at ease grows he. When the darker aspect of his inner self pushes, nay claws, at the calmer exterior for dominance, then all the joys and diversions of mankind become hideously inconsequential.

'Then, if by some malicious coincidence of fate, the moon grows pregnant and full and the conjunction of the individual's astrology falls capriciously into place, beware! For nothing in this world of God nor men, of the sultry spires of contemporary science, can ward off the inevitable chain of events that Nature, in her mad and oft-times wanton ways, has bewitched into the wretched necromancy that is this misery of a man-animal. This creature is neither man nor beast, is neither beast nor man but a fruitless confluence of the human-animal nature. Alas it is so, since the time mankind first looked to the heavens and denounced his animal ancestry, his ascent from the earth and her creatures.

'These bad desires are carried like a curse by a reluctant martyr, a by-chance soul, desiring but uncertain, in the wrong place and too ill-prepared to rebuke the fated charge. That needlepoint moment when better judgment is thrown to the wind despite the shadows of omen that hang like an atmosphere, he will inexorably fall, not glorious before the gates of Hades, but desperate and filled to the skull with morbid self-deprecating fear.

'This strange intoxicating brew whispers the incantation and casts the spell condemning the soul to torment and misery, for a more miserable soul there cannot be upon the earth. Locked in mortal combat for eternity, two wills constantly under-minding the other, obsessed with strange and mysterious coincidences.

'Common place occurrences to any dull eye become acute subjects of foreboding, sudden shifts in the wind, the baying of a stray mongrel, the sudden released flight of birds, the twisted branches of a dead elder, the full moon, forms in melting wax, on and on, the mind becomes mired in an endless series of morbid thoughts. Common objects deft and mute of their own accord are given extensive and frightening attributes. Footprints in the dust attract unwarranted and disproportionate attention. The random movement of animals or birds create diversions in a projected path in lieu of larger more arduous circumnavigation. Fear is an aspect of the mind and where fear exists, exists the primordial door straight into the unknown. Open that door to an ill-fated wind on a day in a month when the guardian is away…

'I live in an ancient villa, built long ago to house gambling and other sordid human distractions. Thus, it sits situated high above the general clamor. The light of the city wavers through bands of rising summer heat and I can see the soft sporadic lights of ships on the sea as they quietly pull themselves toward distant ports.

'As I said dear Lucien, it is an old place with antiquated design. What things these walls would tell you, an Adept, of its history I could only guess.

'The old villa is filled to exhaustion with rooms, stairs and terraces, passages that lead to nowhere at all. The lower gardens are wild and overgrown and various species of ivy have choked the stone beyond recognition.

'Everywhere is chaos here. The interior has long ago been ravaged of its beauty except those things set in marble or welded into place with iron. There is no electricity, I, and my mute companion, content to use candles to see and to wash, whenever either might take such a notion, with cold water down below near the groundkeeper's quarters.

'My companion, I should mention, is a brown-skinned woman from the Orient, Madame Houri, a medium, and despite the danger, continues to live here with me. Her abilities in the occult practices are admirable. You would appreciate her Lucien. Her ancestry arises from deep within the ancient Persian Empire, where she comes from a long line of mystics and can forecast things of the future with incredible accuracy.

'As you know all too well, I have never embraced these notions of fate and forecast, yet the things this woman has seen in an ordinary deck of cards or the cracks in a ceiling or wall, or once yet in the movement of water over stone makes me surrender involuntarily to the notion that life is somehow predestined and in my case a hideous game played out; as the reading of a script, in the grand theatre of the absurd. I do my best to assume it to be some rather incredible insight on her part, some ability to conjure up phantasms in my already haunted existence. Yet the evidence inherent in her visions, her fathoming of these dark amorphous realms are unmistakable, undeniable, and so thusly only serves to fuel my discontent, my fury.

'But enough of this pathetic prattle and of my current state of decay. I am writing you to convey my story, my secret, or secrets I should say, and they certainly do not start here in this desolate villa overlooking the Mediterranean but at Provenceau, that accursed rampart, and my irrevocable encounter with its strange master.'

At this point in the missive the paper quality changed from the contemporary stock to the ancient and yellowed sheets of traditionally pressed paper, slightly larger in both dimensions and noticeably thinner and more delicate. In fact, it nearly crumbled in my grasp lest I handle it with the greatest care. There was no longer the watermark nor coat of arms insignia which marked the previous pages and the cursive was noticeably more elegant as well, unmistakably the same hand, but less of a meandering scrawl. I look up at Mr. Karras who is studying my expression with interest.

"Continue," he mutters, puffing on his pipe and stretching out his leg. I return my attention to the letter and continue.

'South of Paris near the town of Bourges resides the tiny hamlet of Levant, very calm and pastoral. Surrounded on all sides, save the east, which is wooded, by fields of grape and barley. T'was a serene day I recall when I arrived, tired and weary, onto those onerous grounds so ironically christened Provenceau.

'Maison Provenceau is a massive traditional manor with a good bit of land about her, ripe with fruit trees and framboise. Three large structures comprised the bulk of the estate.

'As I traversed the path leading to the maison principal, carrying my modest pack and note of recommendation from a professor of letters at the Sorbonne, I recollect a strange and mystifying feeling so enveloped my casual state of mind that I was forced to pause my gait and gaze about expecting someone addressing my approach, yet all was quiet. It was eerily silent, for not a bird was heard trilling in the numerous trees, though it was a fine summer afternoon. No animals graced the grounds, not a hare nor feline stirred, not even a mongrel, nor did I experience the sights nor sounds of children nor laborers, such the likes of farming hands nor barley maids.

'I continued upon the path, the mansion seemed to address my approach with large ebony windows for eyes and a gaping door for a mouth. I paused but a moment before sounding the iron, in the form of a great gnarled lion, and indeed the whole of the great house seemed to echo and reverberate. I waited patiently yet not a stirring arose. I surveyed the exterior of the palace. Vines clamored about the masonry and I chanced to notice numerous windows, queerly, had been stoned shut, a detail that gave the place an ominous and unsettling feeling.

'I have heard that in olden days, French law was such that an estate was taxed according the number of windows on the primary house. If true, this might account for the stoning of the portals at Provenceau, the permanent closure of those most likely deemed of less import by the master of the estate.

'This seemed to be the case, or so was my supposition. Other reasons for the permanent closure of windows, which at Provenceau numbered many, one could only speculate, the desire of its inhabitants to exclude sunlight for instance. My reasoning favored the former, which supposed–although the place and its ancient family were of noble blood–that perhaps at some point in the past the estate had suffered financial hardships, and the lord of the manor, in spite of the disfigurement, had the windows permanently stoned shut.

'Once again, my mind preferred the former postulation for indeed despite her traditional splendor, Provenceau somehow seemed to have fallen from grace, a grace sustained for probably several hundreds of years. Most of her foundations and bastions were in disrepair and crumbling, the well was antiquated and piecemeal, the numerous outbuildings were tired and broken and ravaged by the wilds. Thorny framboise bushes raged there and a variety of wood had begun to creep across what I assumed had once been a brilliant wide and verdant surround.

'No one had as yet answered my summons. I had resigned myself to lift the iron of the grotesque figure with its horrid gaping mouth when suddenly I could distinguish the sound of someone behind the door releasing a series of dry locks and bolts. The door groaned open, complaining all the while of the burden its hinges held undertaking this task, its single and solemn duty, carrying the bulk of that immense door. The smell of the great hall met my nostrils and held mute witness the seclusion and solitude of the inhabitants that resided therein.

'The withered and pale visage of an elderly man, undoubtedly the principal manservant, appeared from within the gaping black crevice of the door. His black eyes blinked several times apparently at pains with the morning sun and he requested my errand of business in a heavily provincial voice. I introduced myself, the nature of my arrival and requested the company of the master. The old manservant, his pale countenance unwavering, swung wide the great door and entreated me to enter.

'The main hall, within which I now found myself, was clad ceiling to baseboard with portraits of that distinguished family of which my commission was the last remaining member. It had been rumored within the Universite that he was a recluse and had not passed on the family heritage in the form of an heir. Indeed, all rumor reflected that no children had been bequeathed him. He had at one time–I learned–married, but little was known of this woman. One person at the school, the old Madame Secretary, had once indicated to me that she had gone insane and was housed in an asylum somewhere near Lyon.

'The manservant had left me gazing about the great hall of my own accord whilst he announced my arrival to the head of the estate. As I stood under those numerous eyes and faces, I was struck by the strange and persistent feeling of being scrutinized from deep within the inner recesses of that dark and gloomy domain.

'I began to notice all sorts of odd details. The woodwork, ornate and of splendid design and craftsmanship, lacked brilliance as if slowly dying from deficient care.

'The tapestries too were worm-eaten and deteriorating. A multitude of finely designed candelabras and statues adorning the numerous tables and niches had no longer the splendor they were created to possess. The reality of these details, the deleterious condition of the house, set me to wondering as the minutes began to amass.

'A remarkable old library packed with leather bound editions of great writers and scientists that frequented the numerous bookshelves were steeped in dust. I saw first editions of Voltaire and Balzac, Newton and Kepler's complete works and an impressive array of Shakespeare and Blake. Some of the editions were so old and withered as to defy recognition and many volumes were inscribed in gold-plaited Latin. There! An early printer's edition of De Revolutionibus Orbium Coelestium lying absently upon an ancient escritoire! Were the corrections along its ancient spine those of the grand inventor himself? The further I looked the more enchanted, more enthralled I became as the library adopted a more eclectic, and sinister facade, several old grimoires by long forgotten persons.

'The untimely arrival of the manservant pulled me from my reverie. I followed him, as he beckoned me thus, into a darkened antechamber beyond which I was shown an enormous dining room where stood, predominate, a large oaken table suited to accommodate a host of twelve persons, five chairs on each length and one chair at each extreme. The chairs were high-backed affairs and carved of the same solid wood as that prodigious table that stood resolutely empty save a small statuette of a nymph and faerie cavorting together.

'I was left in this massive room and seated at the far end of the table and asked to await the Master. No refreshment was offered, yet I was content to wait with anticipation, for I had travelled far from the teeming city to this quiet and remote place and the circumstances of my impending employment were of an uncertain nature to be sure. Much was being left to chance and if the prospect presented itself unfavorable, it had been my design to use what daylight remained to make my way back to Levant and straight on to Paris, back to my thin host of friends and colleagues and that most alluring city of opulence, grandeur and decadence.

'As I sat in the inner solitude of the dining room I was struck by the ornate display of its portentous environment–another vast wooden surround. On the northern wall and situated between two large shuttered windows hung a sizable portrait of a woman in blue. What I could make out in the dim light was a female of perhaps thirty years of age, with skin the color of ivory and ebony hair. Her lips were red and pursed evenly and a calm serene manner pervaded her entire appearance. The gown, a blue evening attire, hung elegantly below her shoulders being carried by the upper arms, her slender neck was richly jeweled suggesting a lady of high standing. Her countenance was enticing and in an astonishing moment of time, I wished to know her, to hear, with my own ears, the tones of her voice.

'I rubbed my eyes, taxed by the strain of the feeble light, forcing my attention from the portrait and resumed canvassing the domicile. The remainder of the room was filled with objects of art, sculpture and a continuation of family portraits–or so I assumed–that had greeted my arrival in the great hall.

'The air of the place was foul at best, a strange unbecoming scent not unlike the smell of wet mongrels with mange. I assumed some great old mastiff roamed the place but nothing other than a keenly foul scent supported the notion. Suddenly I could discern the sound of a door on the far wall being awkwardly fumbled with. I waited patiently, suppressing my anticipation. The door groaned open and ever so slowly in crept the hunched form of the Master of Provenceau.

'Instantly I realized with surprise–if not horror be the more fitting word–that the source of the odious proliferation was none other than he, for the old codger carried it about him like an atmosphere clinging to a raincloud. I forced my composure, stood and addressed the ancient personage with the proper respect due a man of his years and heritage. He took pause to stare at me, his drooping and sagging eyes possessed of some strange sharp intensity, reflecting a sliver of random light back towards me. A very odd and uneasy feeling crept its way into my bosom.

'He stood there a moment–though it seemed an eternity–gazing into me with those languid vitreous eyes with their pinprick of light and the mixture of that stare and the pestiferous odor emanating from his person quite set me at odds. Finally, the old devil shuffled to the chair opposite mine and sat himself down with a great deal of huffing and heavy breathing. His lungs seemed plagued with some form of consumption and rattled and rumbled all the while we sat together.

'The man had the obtrusively bad habit of hacking up phlegm and spitting it upon the floor seemingly without the slightest concern for the vitiating effect on his home. I felt completely repulsed and harbored the earnest desire to retrace my steps to the village from whence I had come, where birds were aloft in the bluest of skies and the wind with subtle tones carried the scent of lilacs and wildflowers upon its warm caress.

'We sat quietly for some moments when, in a harsh rattling voice, he asked me to excuse his current state, that he had fallen ill of late with a malady of the lungs, creating the loathe but necessary function of clearing his passages repetitively. I assured him that this was of no consequence and was pleased that he was healthy enough to entertain my arrival personally. He nodded, spat, and summoned his manservant by shaking a tiny iron bell near his left that I had failed to take note of earlier. Upon the butler's arrival he requested a bottle of very fine wine, a pressing I knew by name only, having never had the opportunity of tasting due its rarity and exorbitant price. The servant returned with two very fine crystals and served up a grape whose taste warranted a vast appreciation.

'We sipped quietly, I, delving the wine's bouquet which gained me an ever so narrow reprieve from the flatulent air that permeated the old man's body when suddenly and much to my surprise, he voiced his remorse about this problem openly with me. He attributed this foul odor he endured, pitiful as it was, to a rare disease he had acquired many years past while serving with the French military in the Orient.

'The diagnosis was that of a rare strain of lupus, said he, coughing and heaving more fluid, this time into a brass spittoon that his manservant had placed near his station at the table. The symptoms, he noted, were chronic and quite incurable. He indicated the necessity for darkness as another measure of the infection working its insidious tendrils inside him, causing a malady of the nervous system, in particular the eyes, so acutely sensitive to light as to render even the most overcast and cloudy afternoons completely unbearable.

'I pondered his dilemma, when he abruptly requested my papers and letters of recommendation. I produced these materials for him and in the darkness, he examined them and with a casual gesture returned them promptly. He then agreed to have me stay on and indicated recompense quite in excess of what I had been led to expect. Even the more generous as it was, an unmistakable feeling of premonition and foreboding permeated the moment and in spite of what I can afford only as my better judgment, found myself agreeing to the terms, upon which he rose and clasped my hand in a gesture of confidence and his hand, clammy and uncomfortable, held mine longer than I desired.

'It is moments such as these that the spirit or soul of every individual who considers himself a conscious being will undoubtedly define himself. The formulations of the mind and its fabrications are inextricably entwined between doubt and desire. The ego plays a vociferous role much in contrast to its more mysterious twin, that aspect one often hears termed intuition with its innate and primordial capacity to sense the invisible.

'Ominous or enlightened, the best intentions or malignancy of human nature and design; it is these polar interrelations of man that inevitably define the individual.

'Thus, was the case with me clearly in that singular moment, my mind with its relentless preoccupation with capital and worldly luxuries did indeed, I regret, sacrifice my being to torment and yes, a kind of living death, for not just this lifetime but indeed, I fear, eternity. I recall a complete and utter abhorrence deep within my bosom to the idea of remaining longer than a single moment within the dark confines of Provenceau. Yet the abstract quality of money and the frantic icy calculations of my mind devouring the figures of which the old man spoke overshadowed, regrettably, the fears and objections of my better nature. For as a young and naïve man in those days, I put no stock in the concept of a higher self, a guardian, if you will, though it was doubtless this self-same energy that attempted to save my pitiful life that day.

'Later that night as I lay in bed in a far recessed chamber on the third level I found myself utterly torn between the desire to stay on and count the slow rise of my fortune and that of packing my belongings and escaping into a dark but lovingly embracing night. For though I came from a family of wealth, my cruel and wanton behavior had exorcised me from the bosom of my family. I was set at ills with the father who begot me and though alas the schism was repairable, a deleterious and loathe conceit was at the core of my rebellious personality. My desire became absolute. To prove to the man that raised me as his son that I was the more substantial, and the acquisition of fortune was my ticket to self-worth and more.

'It was in this way I spent a long and tortuous night tossing and turning between the dream world and this reality until the morning when the sun extended its angelic head across a golden horizon of grain. By morning it was beyond further contemplation, I was lost.

'The sunlight colored the walls and an exquisite breakfast was served to me alone on silver and crystal. I walked the enormous grounds and smoked, idling for nearly most of the afternoon, finally sitting with my employer at about five thirty for not more than an hour of work after which time I was free to read my books or those from the library, or walk into town if I so desired. It seemed idyllic and was thus for some two weeks, until I became ill.

'What came upon me suddenly—a strange and inexplicable delirium—was without respite. I was drenched in sweat, floating between the dream world and reality; plagued by queer and unrelenting dreams, odd fixations on inanimate objects. A constant recurring sense of dread and loss of purpose, indeed spirit, permeated these days, their actual number of which I truly could not fathom to guess. In truth, I have never regained my original state of mind and body, that feeling of clarity and wellbeing. That feeling of youth and vigor that once so possessed my body and soul forever lost to disillusion and a caustic vitiated sense of self. What happened next was horrid.

'Some days after my fall—a week, two perhaps, again, I can only fathom a guess—I was painfully able to regain the stature of my legs and arms and enough of my sensibilities to rise and amble the grounds for short periods.

'I met with the local doctor as he was dedicated enough to journey the distance to Provenceau of his own accord and monitor my condition. Unfortunately, to my dismay, my condition completely eluded his expertise. There was no diagnosis of any kind that he was able to afford me and thus account for my illness. It was the general assumption held by all that a peculiar and rare strain of virus–that my body was at odds to combat–had afflicted me and so created this deleterious state.

'The doctor, true to his profession, offered the services of a more renowned physician of his acquaintance, yet this was considered overly exorbitant by the inhabitants of the manor–her strange and distorted cast of servants and keepers–and in particular the old man who in his concern for my health was subsidizing my medical expenses in whole. I was principally at their mercy without the financial means to afford a specialist myself and thus forced–however reluctantly–to wait it out. Then a very strange thing occurred.

'On one of my brief strolls, when I was well enough to do so, I chanced upon one of the gardeners, a particularly calm and delightful man named Paolo, whom I had entreated working and whistling on earlier occasions when he was contracted to render his artistry upon the voluminous vine-works of the grounds. He would work away merrily, only taking time from his tasks to eat the lunch he carried with him in an old canvas knapsack.

'Toward the end of his day, I had chanced to note, often it was his habit to pause and smoke his pipe–one of those long stemmed affairs one associates with the Eastern Slav or nomadic peoples–before tossing his tools across his shoulder to saunter off down the roan dusty road losing himself into the countryside.

'He was a brown skinned gypsy, perhaps Romanian or Bulgarian, with dark eyes that exuded a strange but friendly gleam. It was this man who whistled softly to me through the hedgerow that particular afternoon and caught my attention and surprise. I could see his dark round face–the eyes shining brightly beneath his straw hat–signaling me, unmistakably, to join him behind the thick wall of shrubbery. I did so, working my way slowly around to his side of the hedge thus obliterating all view of the house or its gloomy inhabitants.

'He looked at me intensely for several moments, smiling, before a strange and mysterious demeanor befell his countenance. He peered back through the brush as if concerned should anyone within the old mausoleum become aware of us. Once he was certain we were alone, he addressed me calmly yet with a dire necessity that it was of the utmost importance I leave the villa as soon as possible and with great urgency. I was more than surprised and inquired as to why he should advise me so. He hesitated, returning his attention to the house, passing his gaze up and down the grounds repeatedly before turning to me and uttered distinctly the words 'Loup Garou' his face accenting his words and I was nearly overwhelmed with a mortal dread! Again, he whispered these words carefully and gestured toward the house, an unmistakable, almost hypnotic glow emanating from his black eyes.

'I attempted to converse with him, shocked by his primitive assertion, that he was perchance confused by his ill-chosen use of words. There was no mistake. I was to leave that very night before the moon climbed into the heavens and coated the countryside with its full light.

'He spoke in broken French, yet his meaning was clear enough that certain stars were in alignment and the moon would play a dreadful role. As outlandish as it was, I became filled with a dread that evaded reason, for as I gazed into the man's eyes, I perceived the Spirit of Man that defines us as men; that innate self that puts one's neighbors before one's private concerns.

'Suddenly the sound of voices from the rear of the house startled my little informer and before I had the chance to stop him, he disappeared like an animal in its natural habitat. I could not retrace his steps. Then the nurse–as she was termed despite any practical knowledge in the art–ascended upon me with the aid of a manservant to help return me to my bed, for as I had been out about the grounds for nearly half an hour, she saw fit to keep me rested. I was unable to resist and was promptly ushered back into the bleak house, the old gardener's words ringing in my head, repeating their dire warning.

'Once back within the dark confines of the manor I was convinced of the gardener's good intentions for I had slowly become fatigued by the house's fastidious yet superficial doting. An evil air had encompassed the whole episode of my mysterious malady. Deep within my being an ominous feeling had slowly clawed its way upward into my consciousness.

'Even before the old gardener, with his mystical gaze, expounded his knowledge into my awareness, I had unconsciously perceived an impending doom. The house with its myriad of strange faces and whisperings from the hallway caused a great mortal alarm that rattled at the very fiber of my being.

'I decided that night, just before sundown, to summon all my available energies and to set out as far as I could from that house of the damned. I was delayed by the attentions of the nurse and an unexpected visit from the lascivious old dotard himself, who in his reeking presence I could feel myself becoming drained of my life's energy.

'Finally, at a quarter of ten, when things had quieted about the ancient manor–the house creaking on its foundations, slowly groaning out the pain of its existence– I packed what little I could carry, and silently descended the ancient staircase. Carefully groping my way in the blackness that permeated the house, I crept out through the arbor door and into the woody night.

'Instantly, to my surprise, I felt my mind begin to clear and my body become invigorated by the fresh night air, a damp perfumed moisture springing from the trees and fauna. I had decided my best chance of escape lie in taking the wood. I assumed that upon the discovery of my absence–which unquestionably would be forthwith as the old nurse was more a jailer than a medical practitioner– they would undoubtedly first scour the grounds then haunt the roads for indeed, to my firmest convictions, I now felt certain that my mysterious malady was premeditated, as if the warning of the gardener, and his reserve in their company, had awakened me to the obvious, that I was being deranged somehow for some unimaginable purpose!

'These thoughts passing through my mind quickened my pace and I began to feel a sense of relief surface through the cracks of my delirium with every step I made opposite the direction of that house of dread.

'I had travelled perhaps twenty minutes, the house now long behind me, swallowed by the teeming wood, when I was forced to stop and rest myself.

'I had entered a small clearing–a break in the heavy overhang–and the moon full in its placid radiance shone down and coated everything in a brilliant silver light. Slowly I became cognizant that no sound emanated from the night, all was a strange and inexplicable quiet. How odd, that none of the creatures of the night sounded forth but remained quiescent and still in their fastness. As I loitered, I was suddenly seized by a terror so real and so mortal in essence that I rose and quickly continued my pace in spite of my weariness. My head pounded with the pulse of blood being pushed through my veins by my racing heart.

'As I travelled onward, ever in the direction of the village, I became terrified to realize that something, or someone, in the blackness behind me, was pacing my steps. When I stopped there was the distinct sound of an after step, perhaps twenty or so metres behind me, that instantly died into silence. When I commenced my stride again, I could vaguely discern the tread of another –a crush of dried leaves, the snap of a twig or dried branch underfoot.

'I endured this disturbing routine for several minutes, constantly stopping and abruptly turning to witness nothing save the soft sway of the yew and laurel under the full moon. My mind raced frantically. An eerie feeling bristled the nape of my neck every time I turned to recommence my stride toward the village. I fought to contain the fear that was seeping into my heart, a mortal terror as black as the night that enveloped me.

'Suddenly, to my horror, the cat and mouse game ended. The predator, or whatever it was, ceased to shield its steps. I could discern the sound of a human gait working its way slowly towards me in the darkness. I crouched low behind a fallen tree. A solid branch I had secured sometime earlier from the forest floor ready in my hand to levy a blow. Yet the thing seemed to play with my senses, moving slowly in a circular pattern about the area that harbored my body. It would stop, change course and pace wide about me. I was left with only my imagination to torment me. It was insidious enduring this. All the while I was pressed to notice a peculiar scent, like the smell of wild dogs or sweating horses.

'The sound of a hideous breathing–a rasping or panting and occasionally low disquieting rumble of the throat–accompanied this charade and was truly dreadful for it seemed to have no relation to human physiology. Whatever was stalking me was not human at all but an animal! Yet why was the gait distinctly human, a creature on two legs? I was steadily being subdued by my own confusion and fear.

'More out of desperation than hope, I called out, my voice weak and breaking, demanding the person or thing identify itself forthright and the thought that perhaps this was a local hunter out on a midnight hunt under the light of the full moon–and assuming in my silence to be possible game–was in the process of trying to flush me out into the open for a clear shot. But alas, no response was forthcoming, only a deeper more dreadful silence than I had ever known. So quiet had the forest become that I could discern the sound of blood humming in my ears and felt the cold crawl of sweat despite the night's chill.

'Then without warrant the creature shrieked, a howl so evil and tainted with the blood-rage that I was struck to the very center of my being and the fire in my heart, what little still existed, was extinguished. I bolted, blindly, frantically clawing my way through the wood, each tree limb and branch suddenly turning against me, clawing at me, holding me back. To my horror I realized it was not the boughs and branches at all. I was being torn alive by a hideous and monstrous creature–a living hell, a spawn of the devil itself. Its eyes were blood red under the moonlight, and utterly fanatic. Its teeth and claws like yellow knives stabbed into me, ripping at my arms and flesh, and the sound it made, like the cavernous roar of hell itself, drove a searing shaft of horror, like a spike, into the brow of my skull.

'This is all I recall of the trauma, and for some insidious reason, I survived; for on that very same night– or so I was told–a woodsman, who had camped himself near the spot where I was attacked, was awakened by the hideous fight, and retrieving his rifle, hurried out into the wood to discover–to his horror I am certain–the vilest of creatures hunched over my sprawling form into which he emptied the barrels of his blunderbuss. It screamed, in what he recounted as a most horrific and numbing cry and loped off into the night.

'I was taken to a local medical facility then ushered off to Paris where I underwent days of surgery and months of recuperation. Only after the passage of approximately a year was I able to recollect myself, the use of my limbs, but I was horrid, deranged, a living nightmare. I was no longer, nor ever would be, the man I had been.'

At this point, the letter returned to its original contemporary watermarked stationary with its strange meandering scrawl and familial coat-of-arms.

'I left civilization as soon as it was feasibly possible, lost myself in the back woods of Aix-en-Provence, in fact the whole of the Sud-du-France and eventually to this lonely house, this decrepit and decaying villa that sits like a corpse on a hill overlooking the mass of humanity below as they swarm into the coastal towns looking for relaxation and delight.

'And so dear Lucien, as I sit here tonight overlooking the city below, like a constellation of tiny stars infinitely numbered and glittering amidst the blackness, the moon slowly works its way back into fullness. The stars—as they have for eons—rotate and form the conjunctions that move the wheel and the story resumes.

'For some, the stars harbinger great and glorious significance. Fortune and chance coincide, and luck plays its piquant hand. To others the lines and vectors and their primordial equations fall far short of fortunate. To those souls, the light of life will not shine or will be extinguished in the fraction of a moment.

'The patterns lay drawn and the spring of contracts— as it must—seeks desiderata. All the better for them, for in this world exists those who are tormented beyond death. Alas, for I, death—that ultimate restorer—remains forever illusive and a stranger. There is no rest for these souls of which I speak, but forever anguish, despair, loathing. Forth they traverse, lost and hungry, without respite, peace or resolve.

'Faithfully Yours, Anton'

As I quietly, with great care, closed the missive and returned it methodically to its envelope, I looked with a grand sense of awe into my benefactor's eyes. Their gleam was quite unworldly. He nodded to me with that silent understanding he was prone to exhibit when words were too thin a vehicle to contain rightful meaning. I shuddered involuntarily. One of the barkeeps–as if in response to some silent call–set a goblet of cognac before me and departed. I sipped the liquid and valued its grounding effects, for my head was swimming with the contents of the letter.

"Lucien, regarding the middle pages of the letter…why would he change to such old stationary and write in such an outdated form of cursive?" I silently watched as my employer slowly pulled his pipe from his mouth and peered through me with a most sublime expression on his face.

"My dear fellow, those pages were lent from the man's personal diary, from the early twentieth century. Anton Corbeau was born in Marseilles, France…in the year 1898."

Chapter 2: The Brassac Vampyre

I had been in Paris, residing at the company's office in the Saint Denis district. *Karras and Corbeau: Investigators of the Strange and Occult* maintained a small office in this part of the great city. More or less a glorified apartment sitting atop an old bar, *the Richleau*. This small innocuous complex had been my *home* barely a week before I received Lucien's telephone call from Kaza; brief and succinct. He instructed me to purchase a rail pass to Foix, to leave in exactly two days. He then instructed me to an address in the old quarter of Paris–the Marais–with instructions to pick up a package that would be waiting upon my arrival. I was to ask for a *Monsieur Renault* and in verbatim: *'Carefully conceal the package between the folds of your clothing within your valise and transport it with you to Foix. Emerald and I will meet you in the central Marche at midday.'*

Upon my return to St. Denis, I examined the contents of the package and was shocked to find an old, well maintained, revolver with ammunition. The apparatus was disturbing enough but the shells enclosed therein were even more amazing and mysterious. Each round was inscribed with a strange, rather mystical inscription. I puzzled over the thing for the next two days. Why would Lucien instruct me to acquire such a device and why was he cutting short his work in Tibet to journey to Foix? It was something of a mystery and a somewhat disturbing one. My sleep became fitful and my dreams took on rather strange attributes.

I worked to control my eager imagination and not let it run wild with phantom ideas. I surmised there was a logical reason for the odd request. Time reveals all truths.

Three days hence, I found myself on the platform at Gare du Nord awaiting the train that would convey me southerly toward the medieval town of Foix. I had elected to take the slower local route in lieu of the faster TGV, for I needed the chance to reflect and clear my head of the work I had just completed with Mr. Corbeau–namely, *the odd circumstances in Alesia*–before travelling south to this truly remarkable place deep within the Sud-du-France. I was certainly looking forward to seeing Lucien again and acquainting myself with his recent work and travels in Asia. My time working with Mr. Corbeau in Alesia had been difficult, due primarily the man's asperity.

It was early when I disembarked onto the station platform at Foix and commenced my slow meandering journey down the winding road, skirting the river that flows into town.

Sitting solemnly at the heart of this ancient village towers aloft the beautifully majestic *Chateau du Foix*. The castle resides amidst the currents of the river, the course of its stonework jutting up straight and slender like some fairytale castle of old. Having arrived ahead of schedule and having a modicum of time to explore the structure, I quietly eluded the throng of tourists and meandered about the labyrinth of passages, rooms, and dungeons.

Late in the afternoon–well past our appointed rendezvous–I'm startled by the rather abrupt appearance of my two colleagues, Lucien and the distinguished Emerald Montaigne–and a stranger–strolling up the busy thoroughfare.

It was not the intended meeting place at all but having tired of milling about the central square I had quit the bustle to repose beside an ancient stone church, complete with fenced in graveyard, neatly shaded by an enormous elm. It was in fact this enormous tree that arrested my attention from afar and wooed me to its shady retreat when rather unexpectedly they were there, walking abreast toward my place on the lawn as if taking a routine stroll about a common ground.

They were of pleasant countenance and eager to explore the *Marche* and obtain a taste of the local culinary crafts of which in addition to the legendary Foix goose included a blood sausage and exquisite regional cheeses.

The stranger, it turned out, was none other than Stanley Smalls, a rotund Englishman of approximately sixty years and a historian by rights. He had apparently travelled from Bruxelles–his home–with Emerald where they had been engaged in some sort of research. I had actually chanced to meet him upon an earlier occasion in London. He seemed quite surprised by my presence in Foix and expressed interest in lounging in the shade and *catching up* as he put it. Emerald, however, was quick to divert us toward the humming marketplace, her piercing azure eyes and radiant coal black hair glistening in the afternoon sunlight.

Emerald is something of an enigma. An heiress from the American South, New Orleans, of French ancestry, she now resides principally in San Francisco. She is a quintessential colleague and confidante of my intrepid employers, a person held in very high esteem within the company and its broader affiliations.

I find Ms. Montaigne at once both strangely alluring yet somehow vexing; some attribute about her eyes, their intensity, as if she were looking into a deeper aspect of oneself. Her manner is erudite, sophisticated and worldly and her very feminine nature, enchanting.

At a tiny iron table situated in the marketplace at the center of Foix proper–amidst the milieu of tents and vendors with their colorful assortment of meats, vegetables and woolens, we set about discussing the reason for our rendezvous this lazy summer day.

It regarded a somewhat mysterious communiqué, an invitation from an acquaintance of Emerald's alluding to odd events taking place in a small Basque community nestled in the foothills of the Pyrenees to the southwest. This man had invited Emerald–who happened to be residing with Stanley at the time–and she in turn contacted Lucien who in turn contacted me. Thus, we sat together, the four of us, in this very remote and picturesque place deep within the Sud-du-France.

It was all somehow timeless, a feeling of déjà vu about the moment and place. Something about the antiquated buildings and the rolling landscape; its people and those sitting with me at this tiny table, creating within me an odd feeling that I had been here before, this same place but within another distant time.

Having lunched on cheese and bread, sausages and goose–except Emerald who is vegetarian–we laid out our course of action. From Foix we would travel up the winding passage road that cuts a ribbon through the rolling landscape to the town of Brassac whereupon we would be retrieved by her acquaintance.

The fellow's name was Etienne and it had been arranged that he drive us by car, up into the recesses of the Pyrenees to the tiny hamlet of Le Plantaine, a very old and remote place apparently, with a population not exceeding a few dozen persons principally of Basque ancestry.

Unfortunately, *because of very unexpected circumstances* and the rural qualities of the town we were unable to secure a conveyance. Although it was late afternoon it was Emerald's decision to commence the trek up the meandering dirt road on foot despite Stanley's rigid assertions that we take rooms in town for the evening and depart the following morning. Emerald rejected this idea, informing us her friend had prearranged a specific time and place for our rendezvous, due to the fact that he lived a rather austere lifestyle and conducted his business, that of a botanist, without the aid of a telephone, or even electric current. Meeting him was also compounded by the fact he had no proper address of record, living in a re-conditioned *stable* as she explained it.

The trek proved slow and arduous on the ever-ascending road. The loose gravel became tricky under one's soles and the steady constant forward gait became rather taxing over time, especially for poor Stanley, a bit overweight and sweating profusely. To his credit, we paused our sojourn only once to rest and sample some tiny green apples in the overgrown confines of a forgotten country churchyard. The tired old cloister possessed a distinct northerly lean and its small congregation of out buildings–a long disused stable, a smithy, a tiny outhouse and a fallen nunnery–gave the place a peculiar but comfortable air.

As we sat pondering, I wondered to myself silently how many generations of hill folk had journeyed down from the mountain to pay homage and pray for a better, less austere, fortune.

Without doubt I had chanced to note as we climbed into the mists rising above us that everywhere seemed adorned with the remnants of the past–fallen houses with ramshackle fences decaying under the opportunistic growth, old machinery rusted solid where they had failed. Everywhere was a wild plethora of tired old country sheds, barns and houses, many abandoned and crumbling, the bones and skeletons of a previous time.

Moving amongst this decay–like tiny ships in a fog–were the pastoral animals of the highland farmers; cows, goats and sheep.

As we rose into the mountains and the mist grew heavier, one began to realize why these herders had the proclivity of tying bells about their beast's necks, for in the fog one could no longer distinguish their forms but the continuous echoing of their hand-wrought bells belied their obscured presence. Indeed, ingeniously, I could discern the various sounds of a given flock, each having its own distinct tone. I thought about the Irish fishermen who patterned a unique weave into their sweaters that in case of ill fortune whilst at sea their bodies might be borne home to their families. All was chilly and quiet.

Lucien, resting his briar cane across one of the split rail fences, filled his pipe and began quietly smoking while Emerald and Stanley bickered off to one side of the church–predominately about our current state of whereabouts.

The encroaching twilight was signaling the inexorable advent of night. Apparently, we were still some distance from Brassac. Emerald was resolute about pressing on while Stanley had come to the idea that it would be best to break into our resident house of God and within it, shelter the night away.

I puffed on a Gitane, content to let Emerald's good-natured assertiveness prevail. Contemplating the surrounds, I watched the smoke from Lucien's pipe mix in enigmatic swirls with the mist rapidly enveloping us when I chanced to sight an enormously rotund ewe and her bellwether companion skirt the rusty iron railings that outlined the church compound as they made their way upland. I surmised they were returning to the protection of their barn. It occurred to me that we could shadow the animals and visit their owner's farm for the evening and was voicing my observations to Lucien when we suddenly made out the soft muted chuffing of a tractor approaching from the distance, apparently on course towards a similar destination as our own.

Plunging forth from the fog like some gigantic monstrosity–probably sixty years in age yet junior to that of its antiquated operator–an ancient machine emerged, pulling an old wooden hay cart with hewn wheel-spokes and hand-wrought iron treads. I hailed him, and he brought the old iron to a stuttering halt. He peered down at us from his berth, his eyes studying us discernably from under his shaggy white brows. The old farmer gave us all a good looking-over before nodding his head in the direction of his cart and we were spared any further exhaustive marching.

Each sojourner quickly secured his place in the damp hay and the rest of the trip into Brassac was conducted in absolute silence except for the clatter of the tractor motor barely able to drown out the fatigued snoring of our tired and wilted Flemish sojourner.

Barely a town and more a crossroads with a few dilapidated buildings sitting about under the glow of a dull street lamp, we made *Brassac*–or what I surmised to be the outskirts of Brassac.

We bid adieu our reluctant taxi, stretched the bumps from our battered frames and peered about; not a soul in sight and *quiet enough to hear the dead breathe.* Emerald, small bits of straw interlacing her ebony tresses, seemed distressed, the soft azure eyes dilated and searching the environs; she feared we had missed our charge. Stanley fueled her discontent with incessant complaining regarding our collective failure to heed his better advice. A soft breeze thinned the mist about, us and we all tightened our collars to keep out the advent of the cold moist air and waited.

As Lucien packed his meerschaum with some of his English shag, I became aware that he was–discreetly, without being obvious about his manner–closely studying the shadows across the road.

He was obdurately silent, yet his eyes glowed with that inextricable inner gleam I have chanced to notice on those occasions when his senses were heightened. I was certain he was aware of something ulterior, but what he was attempting to discern in the twilight I could not fathom to guess except to say that this peculiar behavior aroused a strange feeling within my chest that crept up from my gut.

Of course, I had experienced it before, on previous excursions into the mysteries presented the company. My inner nature was to question him about his sudden change of mood, but something stilled my tongue and I remained quiet and detached, allotting him the necessary time and space in which to conduct his study. I withdrew the last of my remaining cigarettes from its weathered package, struck a flame and waited.

The antiquated old lamp, suspended by a wire across the dusty intersection, burned dimly, casting strange shadows, shadows that moved eerily with the soft swinging of the instrument. The thing was rigged between the two-story building to the southeast and its neighbor to the northwest of the intersection. I made out several dirty and bent signs advertising French products and services; tyres and the like. Nary a light belied the presence of human occupation in any of the rundown old buildings, only a single enormous lone moth buzzing the dirty yellow lamp held token to any other living thing save our small entourage. It was then that Lucien sided up beside me and re-lighting his pipe whispered to me under his breath.

"Don't react…do you see it?"

"See what?"

"A reflection in the darkness across the street? Don't look! Position yourself as if you're speaking to me. *Something is watching us from the shadows.*" This sudden revelation sent a thrill coursing my body. I did as he instructed. At first, I couldn't make out anything, then unmistakably, I could discern a tiny glint, a faint movement of reflected light that came and went in random intervals from within the darkness of the conifers.

It was an extremely minute detail but unmistakable; something was present in the shadows observing us from the obscurity of the darkness. I could detect a pinprick of reflected light, from a movement of glass or metal; *something, or someone, was watching us from the shadows under the trees!* Whoever, or whatever, the voyeur was, it seemed content to dwell within the obscurity of the dark, *not realizing the light of the lamp was revealing its infinitesimal movements.*

Lucien discreetly signaled Emerald to join us. It was quite obvious that Stanley's pugnacious nature was beginning to take its toll on our sensitive friend. Without revealing the knowledge of our observation, Lucien asked her to fathom the area herself. She quieted her emotions and almost immediately *sensed a presence under the exact same boughs.*

We quietly considered our position. However, before any rational decision could be procured, our clumsy English companion, who had joined our circle and having caught snippets of the conversation, took it upon himself to precipitate the situation.

Like Hannibal through the Alps, the Briton resolutely charged across the intersection and dove into the darkness leaving us to reluctantly trace his steps.

Before we could make the opposite side of the street, Stanley re-emerged from the wood into the light and waved us forward. We rapidly joined him in the darkness, surprised to see him bent over a beaten dark-green Citroen parked deep into the shadows. As we approached the vehicle out stepped an incredibly tall and thin person. I could make out the same reflected rays bouncing off his patchwork spectacles.

As he emerged into the light, he immediately embraced Emerald who introduced him to the rest of us. *It was Etienne, our host!* I was instantly at odds. If this man was our host, why then was he observing us from afar, under the obscurity of the shadows and reluctant to present himself? While I pondered this question, I heard Emerald voice the same concern. His oblique response was that due our tardiness he had fallen asleep in his car. He also made a point to confess that the rather removed location of the car was due principally to his acquaintance with the owner of the grounds and their willingness to allow him to reside there undisturbed. Something about the manner of his controlled and anticipated wording set me feeling a sort of contrived quality about it; similar in many respects to the dialogue of actors as they rehearse bits of a play seeking a realness never quite obtainable.

I was shaken from my meditations when Emerald formally introduced me. My initial impression of him was his pallid countenance, a peculiar pale color, blued ever so slightly by the blood in his thin veins. He shook all our hands and I must admit to a subtle involuntary revulsion to the damp languid touch of his limpid grip. The second impression–by no means the inferior–were the large dark eyes like a shark's eyes in the depths.

If first impressions are often correct, then our gangly host moved rapidly to dispel these notions. Although apparently taken by our number, he immediately cast himself into active and earnest conversation. I was surprised by his pleasant and eloquent voice. His command of English was good albeit heavily laden with that particular southern Gaul inflection so evident in that great expansive range.

It became immediately obvious that this was a man of great intellect and sensitivity. In fact, within minutes of embarking upland in the cramped Citroen, my friends quickly engaged in vivacious conversation with him. I soon began to doubt my earlier apprehensions altogether, relegating them to the imaginings of a tired mind within the bewildering and unaccustomed landscape. I soon felt very weary and longed for a decent place to lay my tired bag-of-bones and get a little sleep before imparting on the work at hand which no one in the car seemed in any great hurry to address; their conversation dominated by past experiences and travels.

A curious thing I began to notice during our nocturnal drive up the mountain was a peculiar lack of lighting. What I'm referring to is the ever-present lighted window or doorway. I could make out the houses–ebony silhouettes like black monoliths against the dark indigo night–but seemingly not one lighted window or open door on the entire drive. *It was as if the entire community was boarded and sealed in for the night.*

During a break in the conversation, I chanced questioning our guide about this queer observation. He mulled it over silently a moment before dismissing it passively. Before I could press him further, Stanley stammered on about some ridiculous topic oblivious to the nature of my query. I pondered Etienne's response and found it somehow evasive. Surely someone within this gentle expanse of community *burns the midnight oil* as the saying goes, yet try as I could, *I saw not one single lighted window along the entire road.*

Lucien coughed softly from beside me in the backseat; exchanged a knowing glance. The observation hadn't gone unnoticed by his keen eye. When I started questioning him about it, a mere gesture of his finger had me instantly silent, left to ponder my thoughts alone as the auto wrenched itself up the steep winding roadway cutting into the mountainside. The Citroen's headlights, like knife blades slashed at the stone embattlements of the homes and stone buildings, silently witnessing our passage in the darkness. Ever onward we climbed, ascending into the absolute darkness of the Aquitaine night.

Le Plantaine was a surprise to me. It was nothing more than a smattering of derelict houses and stables that hugged the spur of a dusty dirt road. Etienne pulled the car before what looked like a glorified chickencoop and began wrenching open its sagging doors while the rest of us stretched the kinks from our bodies. I canvassed the entirety of the village, sullen and eerie in the moonlight. Perhaps a dozen structures–of a variety of shapes and questionable derivation–hugged the dirt-track like a huddle of solemn strangers.

The largest was a home of perhaps a century of years and possessed a distinctly gloomy air. Its adjacent looked younger to me, or perhaps an old carriage house that had been expanded upon with brick and mortar. Further along the cul-de-sac sat a low beige stone structure I was certain had been perhaps a small foundry at some point early in its existence. The smithy's old furnace stack was still in use, exuding a thin vaporous smoke; the smell of burning firewood permeated the midnight breeze. It was into an ancient and weathered stable that Etienne directed us and which he referred to as home.

Prior our arrival, a soft rain had begun to fall, coating everything in a patina of crystalline webs. We waited in the dew while Etienne parked the Citroen in the withered old outbuilding separate from the house. I surmised his home had once served as the estate's horse stable.

We sheltered our heads with our satchels, except Emerald who had procured a small, compact bumbershoot from her pack that telescoped out smartly.

"From Japan," she said in response to my thoughts.

"Indeed," I replied, mimicking my employer and studies the bleak house. Emerald's dark eyes wandered the structure and I could see plainly her concern. However, once inside, we were all collectively surprised to find the place quite the antithesis of its outward appearance. The interior of the old barn was cozy and warm, the wood floors and surrounds entirely reworked by skilled craftsmen. I was further surprised to learn that the craftsman was none other than our emaciated host. The flooring was highly detailed tongue-in-groove oak planking with dovetail jointing and an almost Moorish hexagonal patterning at the corners; masterfully executed.

A large cut-stone fireplace stood dominating the southern wall. An antique iron stove occupied the kitchen to the north, pleasantly warming the place. Upon this ancient device simmered a huge pot of potato soup with the bouquet of wild chives and basil. A solid oak table with two heavy benches comprised the only furniture in the room and created a sort of natural divide between the assumed kitchen and the fire hearth. Upon this wooden behemoth our ever-attendant host placed a basketful of provincial pan, olives, fresh greens and a bottle of aged Bordeaux.

Etienne proved remarkably generous with his *personal cellar* and we drank several excellent bottles of wine past supper and well into the evening. I must admit to his general change in character upon our arrival. A sort of glow–to profoundly misuse the word–became etched upon his lean face and he lavished what little he apparently had upon us. A sort of impetuous glee and interest in the idle chatter of the world was quite evident. It wasn't until the hour became quite late before his hold on our attentions waned.

After this spree of drinking and conversation around the hearth, we were directed to our beds in the upper loft. A single large room–entirely void of furniture, the floor comprised of ash wood, ornately fashioned–greeted our sight and we all quietly turned in for the night, sleeping in woolen blankets–locally made–upon the floor while Etienne retired to a small room behind the north wall of the kitchen below and not a sound we heard from him the remainder of the evening.

The rain had dwindled to barely more than a patter on the old slate roof when something afoot that night awoke Lucien and I simultaneously. Strange as they were, the sounds were distinct; a shuffling of dirt and grit upon the road near the house. There was a queer repetition of steps, and labored breathing, back and forth for several minutes then a sudden and unearthly wail that could put *the fear* in a person.

Emerald bolted upright, her slender ivory shoulders glowing in the candlelight, her countenance one of utter shock. The three of us sat straining to hear while Stanley snored on in an apparent drunken stupor.

A sense of dread and foreboding laced those emanations from the night. I struggled within myself, pushing my better half to somehow manage my fear while we collectively acknowledged the strange sounds from outside. Without doubt there was the animal scent about, coupled with a vague sort of grunting or disharmonious breathing and the lurching of steps in the gravel. This went on for several minutes then as abruptly as the sounds had occurred, they vanished into thin air.

Our quaint trio was left to consider this bizarre occurrence without the assistance of any visual aid. Strangely, not a single window adorned the entire building and it was quite some time–I'll admit freely–before any of us were in any mood to sleep.

Not a sound or movement from below belied that our host was cognizant of the weird events that had transpired within such close proximity of his domicile and Lucien's attempt to raise him by first knocking then trying the locked door of his bedroom did nothing to arouse him. We had no choice but to return to our makeshift beds and attempt to return to our previous slumbers while Lucien was content to sit by the flame of a kerosene lamp he had procured from below and work on his notes from Tibet.

Even with his cavalier effort, it was a long and fitful night, deplete of any real sleep and in the feeble light cast across the room from Lucien's flickering lamp I could see Emerald awake, her eyes like shards of obsidian, staring blankly into the room as if through it, out into infinity.

Early the next morning and well before our companions, neighbors, or enigmatic host arose, Lucien quietly woke me bidding me to dress and join him downstairs.

I soon joined him and followed him outside to investigate the perimeter of the abode. This is what he had already discovered.

In the moist sandy gravel of the road that skirted the home were the imprints of a large four-toed animal about the look and size of a large dog, or possibly a wolf, if such a breed still existed in the area.

Mixed within these tracks, but beneath them and softened by the previous night's rain, were a variety of human tracks, neighbors and such, with one singular exception; a long thin narrow human track, bare-soled, distinctly male–that Lucien took careful pains to note– over-lapped several of the animal's tracks and vice-versa; both crisscrossing back and forth and meandering up and down the sandy road.

"This poses an interesting conundrum," he whispered.

"What do you mean?"

"The animal tracks were laid in the early hours, sometime between two thirty and five in the morning."

"How do you guess that?" I asked incredulous.

"No guess, it's certain due the sharp distinct outline of the imprints. It's obvious they were laid after the rain had ceased falling."

"Yes, I see, but the conundrum?"

"So, the question arises, who is this nocturnal visitor who left his prints atop *and beneath* the animal's? Why are they mixed in such an odd fashion and what was the meaning behind this apparent tracing and retracing of steps? What could possibly be the purpose of this strange late-night vigil?" I looked at him, his eyes keen, glowing with an inner excitement.

"What might the answer be?" I asked.

"*What* indeed. Wait, it only gets more mysterious; see here." He led me off a distance further up the road to a particularly sandy area and began to point out with the stem of his pipe. "Look closely," pointing to one track after another, then another etcetera for a length of perhaps three or four meters; approximately the length of the sandy patch of lane. I began to realize–to my horror–that the two superimposed each other, *in fact they blended into each other.*

"What is this?" I hissed beneath my breath and Lucien's eyes were like two coals burning in the night.

"Yes, quite. *What* indeed?" he echoed, stroking his beard. "I dare say I've not seen anything like this for quite some time…not since *the experience in the American Nevada desert, on the Piute reservation north of Spirit Lake."* I studied him a moment. This *experience* must have been prior to my employment. I returned my attention to the tracks again and studied them in more detail while he packed his meerschaum and stoked it.

"How can an animal take stride with a human being in such perfect fashion?" I asked and he smiled; his eyes pulsating.

"It can't, a mongrel is a quadruped. Man is bipedal."

"Of course, but…"

"You're trying to fit a square peg into a round hole my friend, it cannot be done," he said. "However, the round peg may oft-times fit the rectilinear."

I was about to ask him what he meant when a shout from the stable arrested both our attentions. It was Stanley. Like the proverbial *bull in a china shop* he was walking up the road through the very center of our study! I started to shout when Lucien's grip upon my arm silenced me.

"No," he said. "Not a word of this to anyone in the house, not even Emerald."

"But the tracks, he's contaminating the evidence!"

"I have the evidence here," he said tapping his temple. "Discretion is the essential ingredient right now. We mustn't tip our hand prematurely."

"What on earth do you mean?" I asked mystified.

"There isn't time right now. Stanley is upon us. Listen, I need you, as diligently as possible, to trace these tracks north as far as you possibly can. See where they go. It's a tall order but I need you to do your very best."

"Of course, but for what reason?"

"Tracks are living things, marking time and space. At the end of all tracks resides something that tells its story." I was aghast.

"Are you suggesting I confront this thing?"

"Obviously not. Willem use your eyes. The thing returns here. I want you to find out where it went, what it did, if it has left some kind of mark."

"Of course. I understand."

He quickly shushed me as Stanley approached and stood amid the delicate evidence of this most astounding phenomenon that we had so deliberately taken pains to address only moments before. We exchanged pleasantries and I took care not to wince as he shuffled his feet about, *obliterating nearly all traces of this most extraordinary record of events*. Lucien cordially asked Stanley to join him for morning tea. I said I wished to take a walk and enjoy the dawn.

As the sun was rapidly rising and light now filled the placid sky, it was easier to follow the tracks in the direction of the forest.

The large animal had apparently set out on a north by north-easterly course. With slow methodical observation I was able to follow its trail quite some distance until I uncovered *a most grisly sight.*

Perhaps a kilometer northeast of the village, and deep into the wood, I came upon a small meadow, a break in the solid growth of trees. Approximately some sixteen or seventeen meters into this tiny clearing I discovered *the mutilated body of a sheep or lamb*; it was difficult to discern, for the wretched thing had been *ripped apart and gutted and major parts of the body were missing.* Entrails were strewn about the area in wild abandon.

I carefully surveyed the scene detailing the behavior of the tracks. Oddly, there were none of the sheep's tracks leading into the area. It seemed rather obvious to me that the beast–for by now I was certain the *animal* I was tracking was not a mere dog–had carried the unfortunate prey to this sheltered spot for this specific purpose.

An extremely unsettling bit of evidence that presented itself all too clearly was the horrific realization that the wolf–or whatever it was–had seemingly abandoned its natural quadrupedal gait *and had taken to walking on two legs!*

These new revelations were disturbing, to put it mildly. A rapidly ensuing sense of dread began to grip my consciousness and a pervasive feeling of alarm and foreboding tainted the spot. The dark crevices between the conifer boughs seemed suddenly menacing; faint sounds from the wood, birds or the shuffle of animals now possessed sinister intent. I worked to control these wild thoughts and resolutely concluded my study.

Retracing my steps back toward the village with a livelier gait than of which I had come; I kept a steady even pace, glancing over my shoulder frequently to ascertain there was no one following me, for in truth I could not shake the odious feeling that *something was following me back in the direction from whence I had come.* Nothing supported this impression, no sounds or sights warranted such trepidation other than the feeling itself; perhaps the macabre scene still reverberating inside my head, yet it was a keen sense of relief that flooded my soul when I broke the wood and at last saw the stone encasements of Le Plantaine. Smoke wafted from the ramshackle chimney and I surmised–correctly–that my companions were in the process of preparing breakfast. Inside, the smell of cakes and sausages greeted my arrival and the fear that had wrapped its tendrils about my heart diminished somewhat.

After breakfast, while we were outside, I voiced my observations to Lucien who became quite transfixed as I detailed my early morning sojourn. It was decided we would investigate the situation at our earliest opportunity. When that chance came, under the flimsy guise of a mushroom hunt, I was appalled to discover that the *sheep's corpse had been removed!* Infinitesimal amounts of blood splatter remained to verify my account, but I was greatly disconcerted to find that *the tracks had seemingly been erased.* Lucien and I commenced to discuss these new findings in great detail, however our canvassing of the wider area produced nothing remarkable, we were temporarily stymied. Voicing my concerns openly, he concurred that something extremely odd–sinister in fact– was in play within this tiny pastoral hamlet lost deep within the rolling foothills of the Pyrenees.

Upon our return to the house our three colleagues were having their afternoon tea. As we somberly took our places at the table, I was quite taken aback when Etienne asked a very direct and unanticipated question.

"Have you seen it?"

"*It?*" echoed Lucien. Remarkably, Etienne commenced to explain the current state of affairs as we knew them; all the while, his deep-set eyes darting about, from behind their piecemeal spectacles. Lucien confided certain details about our discoveries, being careful–I noted–not to disclose too much. The Frenchman brooded over his words quietly for a moment before continuing his oration and what he had to say was beyond extraordinary.

He confirmed our observations, and that our conjectures were far from fantasy. He confided that for some time now the local inhabitants of the community had been disturbed, in the wee hours of the morning, by strange happenings. He said that several of the local farmers and herdsmen had complained about losing livestock in the eeriest fashion. What I had witnessed, he said, was very much the pattern in previous instances with the occasional exception *where the goat or lamb's artery had been severed and blood drained from the animal!*

His discourse had an unnerving effect upon my mind and Emerald grew noticeably quiet and rigid. He went on to note that a number of local canines–finely bred and adequately trained animals–that had been set out to watch over the flocks, had either disappeared or met with similar grisly fates. The situation had raised much concern and speculation from the immediate community. Correspondence had been delivered to the various local and regional authorities, yet nothing had come of it.

The conversation had a distinct and profound effect upon Emerald, the pupils of her eyes dilating, her demeanor growing darkly. Lucien queried our gangly host as to what possible animal–or creature–could be causing such ominous loses to the local herds, at which point, he stared fixedly at us from behind his cobbled wire glasses, with his piercingly black eyes, and stated that the locals had begun to refer to *the monster* as *the Brassac vampyre.*

I was stunned. Etienne elaborated that the *thing* had been witnessed on more than one occasion and that several of these reports spoke of seeing the shadow of a man at or near the scene of the horror; other reports indicated that of an enormously large mongrel or wolf-like creature.

A morose and muted tone instantly permeated the room. We all fell into a kind of stupor, for indeed, this was an unexpected–and morbid–postulation, especially from a person such as our host, an educated and learned man of science. All grew introspective. He had touched upon those occult and ancient concepts, primordial instincts we all possess as wont our species. Fears, so old and antediluvian, as to exist even today.

I suddenly recalled Lucien's words from a previous time. '*Despite contemporary science and modern thought, deep within the inner workings of the human psyche, exist the Mysteries. So profound and unexplainable that even men of science and scholars deem it necessary to embrace them conceptually rather than simply dismiss them as farcical.*'

We sat dumbfounded for several minutes, each lost within his private thoughts when the quietude was suddenly and inexplicably broken by Stanley.

"See here," he mumbled under his moustache. "Are you trying to say that these back-wood residents actually believe that this...panther, or wild hound, or rogue wolf, what have you, is none other than our infamous old friend Count Dracula, risen from the grave?" He huffed and looked to us for support in his vituperation. Emerald remained stolid, deep in thought, her delicate ivory hand laced before her scarlet lips set in a most saturnine expression, while Lucien was obviously calculating these striking details within his brilliant and deductive mind. All grew eerily silent.

Etienne offered me a cigarette from his pack while Lucien withdrew his meerschaum and deerskin tobacco pouch from the pocket of his coat, all the while staring fixedly at the tabletop–*through it*, would probably be the more accurate description.

"Well, what say you all? Cat got your tongues?" I looked at Stanley, unable to grasp his sudden exhortative tack. I felt a distinct sense of fear in his behavior–or was it my own? He seemed to note these features in our faces. "Come, come now, not you three? Surely educated people as yourselves can't give in to such a ridiculous notion as to believe this wild, warped individual, or rabid dog, whatever, is a damn vampire?" He then struck the table with the flat of his palm, startling Emerald who physically *jumped*, glaring at her boisterous friend. He seemed not to notice her dismay as he carried on, his voice growing in volume. "Good God man," he said directly at Etienne. "This is the bloody twenty first century. Vampires went out ages ago. A hunt with a few good bird dogs will solve your problem, not wooden stakes and garlic!"

"You think that hasn't been attempted mon-ami? How naïve do you think we are?" Etienne replied, sipping his black coffee.

"Well get on the blasted tele and call in a professional. An experienced huntsman will have your posey little monster skinned and mounted before you can-"

"We have already done it!" Etienne snapped, not controlling the irritation in his voice. "This year...a man from Nairobi, seasoned, equipped." He grew quiet, suddenly deep in thought.

"Well, what of it?" Stanley inquired, his voice exhibiting impatience with the Frenchman.

"He too disappeared. Not a trace of him, nothing...vanished, and is still missing." He looked up at us all one by one, and it was difficult for me to hold his piercing black eyes.

"Hum," huffed Stanley. "That's odd...very odd." He twisted at his moustache a moment. "Say, perhaps he's one of those odd fellows who stage their disappearance for some kind of personal gain?"

"Think what you want," Etienne answered. "This has been going on for nearly two years. It has the communities down the valley, locked up tight." He withdrew his crumpled pack of Gitane cigarettes and struck a wooden match at the edge of the table.

"Etienne?" Emerald interjected softly. "I'm curious about something."

"Oui?"

"Has there been any other persons attacked or killed?" Etienne paused, folding his hands together as if to pray, the smoke from his cigarette circling about his face and head.

"Difficult to answer," he replied and sighed deeply. "About, oh, two years ago…a man, a stranger to the area, claimed he was attacked by what he described as a large animal, but on two legs, on the road between Brassac and Le Plantaine. However, when the authorities arrived to substantiate the story, he could not be found. No one had seen him leave the medical clinic, and there was no record of his name or an address or from where he had come."

"What happened?"

"It was written off as a hoax. Shortly after this, the shepherds started to notice damage to their flocks."

"How many attacks upon livestock have occurred?" Etienne raised an eyebrow as he thought it over.

"Many. I'm unsure the number."

"Have the attacks all taken place in and around this area?" Lucien questioned further. "Have there been attacks up the mountain? Perhaps further down the valley?"

Etienne shook his head. "I don't believe so. I believe the mutilations have been primarily between here and Brassac."

"Then your assailant resides in the area." Etienne only shrugged, saying nothing.

"Has your work suffered Etienne?" Emerald asked.

"Suffered?"

"As a result of these-"

"I can't allow it to compromise my work," he said waving his cigarette through the air between us. "Of course, fortunately, there is little I can do in the wood after sundown so…" He shrugged again and remained silent.

"You're implying that no one goes out after dark?" Lucien queried. Our host seemed to hesitate before responding.

"I'll step out to smoke, or take a short stroll on occasion, but here, when the sun sets…everyone retires." His eyes were intense darting back and forth between us as if to take in our reactions to his report.

"That's madness!" Stanley bellowed. "That's bloody preposterous!"

"Stanley, please," Emerald said bringing her index finger to her lips.

"Oh, come down off it will you! You're a bloody scientist, what?!" he continued, and Emerald took hold his arm.

"Stanley do shut up," she said in earnest and quickly redirected her inquiry toward Etienne. "Let me ask you…this creature…could possibly be, as you said, a man…an individual with morbid tendencies perhaps? Has there been thought given to that?"

"Absolument," he nodded. "But there is one problem with that theory."

"Problem?"

"Oui…this same problem your friends have spoken of earlier." She frowned.

"Je ne comprends pas," she whispered. He stared at her blankly.

"These odd formations of animal tracks…on two legs. This is repeated again and again and even stranger…reports of beast tracks…" he paused, searching for the proper English word, "…you say, *metamorphose*…into the human tracks." We all exchanged looks and I felt a distinct gloom permeate the room like wildfire.

Silence.

"Well I don't believe it, not for one damn minute," spoke our portly friend rising to his feet and pacing the room. "It's all a product of some lunatic mind with a bit too much available time, and too vivid an imagination. The sooner someone puts a bullet in the bugger's arse the sooner you people will sleep at night."

"And who'll put the bullet to him Stanley?" Lucien asked in his calm manner.

"Bloody hell right!" he answered with conviction. "And tonight, I should say, the sooner the better," he stammered ungraciously.

"Oh, come Stanley, sit down before you hurt yourself," Emerald retorted, which annoyed our man further.

"No, I mean it, damn it all, right now! Tonight." He slammed his fist hard upon the table. "Etienne, I wager you have a gun about, surely?"

"Oui. A shotgun for goose but-"

"Then get one of these superstitious peasants to donate a goat. We'll stake the bastard in that damn meadow Lucien found earlier and I'll put both barrels to the devil for good." He smote out his chest and seemed quite pleased with himself.

"Stanley, stop this right now," Emerald insisted but our rotund colleague remained steadfast and belligerent.

"No Em, I mean it. I'm for going tonight." He turns upon our host. "But, if I shoot some crazed fool and am called before the magistrate, I'll expect the good people of this village to take full responsibility of the whole bit. I want it in writing."

"I'm quite sure," Etienne said demurely over his spectacles, "that under the circumstances, you'll have their full support."

"Good, it's settled then. Now…who's to go with me?"

The question was nearly like a death warrant. Stanley gazed at us all, his eyes resting on our lean French host, somewhat contemptuously. "Not I," Etienne was quick to say, and his eyes reflected the seriousness of the situation.

"What?" Stanley snorted. "Show some backbone man!"

"I've been privy to this all before. I'll not step foot into the wood after dark," the Frenchman countered. Stanley stood as if struck or dumbfounded.

"You're mad!" he announced, spitting his disdain openly and turned his eyes upon me next. I must admit I paled at his gaze, not considering myself as reckless as he. Sensing my consternation, he looked to Lucien who addressed him amiably but reservedly, speaking not a word but contentedly smoking and thinking.

"Bloody pansies!" Stanley said vindictively and Emerald quickly interjected, perhaps wishing to avoid an unnecessary conflict.

"Stanley, you need to calm yourself," she interjected in her erudite feminine manner. "You needn't concern yourself so."

"Oh yes I do indeed Em. If for no other reason than to prove to these damn provincials that this is the bloody modern world!"

"Please Stanley, do calm down, I implore you."

"No, I mean it, I'm going tonight. You blokes can hovel together here in this cow barn if you like. I'm up for a bit of sport myself." We all exchanged dour expressions. What was he trying to prove I wondered to myself, the imbecile! It was as if some strange sort of obsession was overtaking his common sense.

Something in the man's rhetoric seemed vaguely delusive. Emerald addressed Lucien directly, placing her svelte, jeweled fingers atop his.

"Lucien, what do you think? Would it be time well spent? Perhaps you could go…perhaps you both could sit with him…if only for company's sake?" To my utter amazement Lucien consented, albeit gravely.

"As you wish it," he murmured. Something in his voice set the hair on my neck on end.

Stanley was surprised at this sudden admission and quietly grunted his approval. All faces then turned toward me. Emerald's soft azure eyes were simply impossible to ignore. I found myself reluctantly consenting, despite an ominous sense of dread at the idea of it all. Damn, I thought silently. The bombastic fool had us at rope's end.

Later that evening, after a hefty three-course meal, oddly reminiscent of meals served to convicted criminals prior their march to the gallows, we geared up for our nocturnal vigil.

Lucien questioned me about the pistol with the mysteriously inscribed bullets. I confirmed that I had it stowed safely in my satchel. He nodded approvingly as he got into his weatherproof.

"Bring it with you but tell no one. Keep it close in hand," he whispered. I excused myself and quickly procured it for our journey hither.

Earlier, Etienne had secured the assistance of a local farmer–Laurent by name–who was willing to supply the *sacrificial lamb* and it was this, the most innocent of beasts, that had been staked out in the aforementioned meadow.

Regrettably the moon was in wane–a mere fourth of its fullness–and I found myself wishing, as we trundled along in the crepuscular darkness, that the *Goddess of the Night* had bequeathed us more of her nocturnal radiance. I carried with me–hidden upon my person–the revolver Lucien had instructed me to carry, and its presence gave me a slight reprieve from the ominous weight the darkness enclosed upon my wary frame of mind. I had questioned Lucien about the strange inscriptions I had seen upon the shells. He was somewhat elusive about the language–or symbols–that each bullet was inscribed, save to say that they were *apotropaic* in nature. This, of course, was hardly reassuring to my overtly rational self. I admit freely I do not contain the capacity nor the experience and knowledge of the supernal arts of which his brilliant mind is so endowed.

We had travelled to many strange and remote places under the employ of *Karras and Corbeau*. In those travels I have come to experience many weird and inexplicable things. Extraordinary and supernatural events cannot simply be dismissed.

Indeed, I am sure that the bones of the unimaginative– those persons whom despite the omens, plunge headlong into the heart of the unknown, without the necessary means to accomplish the end task in hand–litter the entrances and egresses of what my employers refer to as the *Twilight Kingdom,* spoken about in verse and prayer; that strange ethereal plane between this world and the next.

These poor migrants of which I refer are simply not equipped to interface with the amorphous entities that occupy the thin margins that divide life from death, darkness from light.

To journey forth into the midst of the *Legions of the damned*–as it were–with naught save curiosity and hubris is like stepping into a maelstrom unadorned, without shield or fabric, tool or compass to navigate the secrets of the mysterious.

Never was there a more fitting example of this sad individual, than our friend Stanley Smalls on this singularly portentous night. I contemplated the man's dire situation with a morbid sense of dread as we positioned ourselves within the fallen trunks of several large trees, near the periphery of the meadow. Oddly, Lucien was quick to station my focus into the shadows behind us.

"Do not take your attention from the umbrage for any reason, except to look about from time to time. Don't strain your eyesight. Allow your peripheral vision to take in the complete expanse of wood, if you see something moving in the shadows, resist the urge to focus your eyes upon it. Use your ears, which is the stronger sense at night, and keep your hand on the revolver in your coat pocket. Be attentive and stay calm, don't fatigue yourself and if you value our lives, do not fall asleep."

A soft film of silver light coated the meadow in a crystalline mist as moisture began to condense in the night. The poor lamb bleated in the distance, clearly distressed by its situation. A chill mistral arose and soon the meadow was cold and strangely silent under the Aquitaine moonlight.

The entire meadow was as quiet as a tomb–with the exception of the lamb calling for the ewe. No one spoke, nor did anyone smoke or move about as the minutes rolled into hours.

Stanley, who initially remained focused and intent upon the bait–rifle ever at the ready–now huffed his warm breath into his chilled fists allowing the shotgun to lie beside him at arms-length, as he tried in vain to compress his corpulent body as tightly as possible into his coat. His collar was pulled up over his ears, blocking his radial hearing and blinding him to his flanks and rear. More a target than the hunter, I bemused, only this time the stakes were higher than a quail hunt. In the pit of my stomach, I feared for all our lives, for the fact remained, I had witnessed first-hand the evidence, and the *Brassac legend* had taken on horrific proportions within my mind.

At about two o'clock in the morning, Lucien woke Stanley from a sound sleep to focus his attention on the wood opposite our position on the meadow. It had been a long sullen evening and the lamb had quieted considerably. The moon, riding high above–now that one's eyes had fully adjusted to its light–cast just enough of an aura to completely bathe the open space in a dim eerie glow.

At first it was more *a feeling* of a presence than anything I actually saw or heard, for everything was quiet and still. The mistral had dissolved to barely more than a thin breeze and the pine boughs minutely trembled.

I suddenly became aware of Lucien's demeanor. Something had locked his attention upon the woods on the opposite side of the break. I could literally *feel* something within the shadows at the edge of the tree line, watching, contemplating. I scrutinized the shadows for any sign of movement or sound, but there was nothing, only an unsettling silence.

After some twenty or thirty minutes, I began to tire and relax; our stalwart rifleman soon returned to his slumbers. I found myself considering waking Stanley, retrieving the lamb, and returning to Le Plantaine *when suddenly it happened!*

Deep within the darkness, just on the edge of the moonlight, I could make out an indistinct shape *moving within the undergrowth, slowly traversing the edge of the woods.* As Lucien had instructed, I could actually see it better in my peripheral sight; a peculiar *ashen figure bobbing up and down within the moonlight and the shadows cast by the tree boughs.* It moved in a most bizarre fashion, bobbing up then down, then disappearing for a moment only to reappear askew its former position much the way a large predator stalks game while gaining proximity to its prey. This activity sent a bolt of energy coursing my body setting all my follicles on end. I reached for Lucien to garner his attention and his sudden and fierce grip upon my forearm confirmed that he was keyed upon exactly the same object. Before I could roust our slumbering companion, the thing sprung forth from the trees with such a malevolent howl that I was truly frozen with terror; its peal of animal-like rage sufficient to raise the dead.

Poor Stanley was instantly awake, disoriented and petrified to the core. He scrambled for the rifle, but in his haste while retrieving it, unwittingly unloaded both barrels randomly into the night with an enormous thunderclap, sending the weapon careening from his trembling grip. What this accomplished was to alert the *man-devil* to our presence. It flashed its *large nocturnal eyes directly at our hiding place.*

Never in all my years of living, nor experience in the darker aspects of life, have I ever beheld so terrifying a countenance as those eyes–sheer brutal rage coupled with a foreboding essence of evil; large, glassy and without reserve, thirsting for blood, *a living nightmare!*

The large bipedal form–but barely human–sprang toward us, howling like death itself as it closed the distance between us with a bounding speed that no mere human being would be capable! Stanley simply crumbled, whimpering in the darkness as those dead eyes shone in the thin beam of moonlight. I will admit that I was literally *swallowed* alive by the thing's uncanny piercing stare as *our quarry* rapidly moved upon us.

What I remember, thinking back, was the realization that the revolver was in my limp useless hand; I had somehow extracted it from my coat pocket. I remember someone shouting but was it my colleagues, myself, or the terrible sounds of the beast now merely a few dozen meters from our camp?

Suddenly, there was a familiar iron grip upon my wrist and the sharp pulling of the pistol, and following its path in the moonlight, I witnessed Lucien holding the apparatus above his head, silhouetted against the indigo night sky. I recall an odd thought; that he looked exactly like a statue of Mercury I had once seen in the garden of a villa on the slopes above the French village of Saint Paul du Vance; the ancient messenger God holding aloft his scepter in the mystical twilight of the Mediterranean night. I remember standing transfixed as Mercury stood poised overlooking the ancient sea, the quality of his image so real, so precise, that I imagined the thing to move–infinitesimally–or had it been the trees or the mist or my imagination?

However, this time Mercury did move. I watched in awe as my companion lowered the pistol, took aim and fired directly–nearly point blank–into the heart of the onrushing shadow that was enveloping us like some enormous dark-winged *angel of death.* There was a scream that sliced through the night, reverberating off the distant trees, a sudden rush of evil-smelling wind that brushed us both onto our backs and within the flash of an eye, was gone; the night immediately returning to its former somber silence, save the distant barking of a dog. I looked down at poor Stanley staring back at us under the moonlight, his eyes wide and wild, were rigid and unblinking, his face a deadly white pallor. The poor fellow had suffered a heart attack. He was stone dead!

I must admit surprise–but not amazement–the next day when I learned of Etienne's abrupt and unexpected departure. He had left quite early, sometime before dawn, ostensibly, on research somewhere deep within the Basque country of the southern Pyrenees. Emerald had phoned us from a neighbor's home while we were down the mountain with the local authorities, seeing to Stanley. She had indicated that Etienne had left some kind of a note. I felt disdain regarding this news, what with Stanley's corpse stretched out upon a conference desk at the local municipal hall while Lucien struggled with his limited use of the native tongue. I castigated our absent host to my companion but to my great surprise he wouldn't indulge in conversation about it. Perhaps it was in respect to the dead that closed his mouth, I surmised. It wasn't until our return to the house, that things became clearer to me.

When we returned to Le Plantaine, I was saddened to find Emerald in deep mourning regarding the events that had transpired. Her beautiful cerulean eyes glistened with a profound sadness as we took our places solemnly around the thick oaken table that only hours prior had been the platform of much mirth and merriment.

I was deeply shocked at what my ears beheld. Emerald was in mourning not only for our friend Stanley *but Etienne too!* She criticized herself severely for allowing Stanley to come on the journey, and for: "*letting Etienne disappear again into the world, lost and wounded."* I was confused by my colleagues' conversation and spoke as much openly. Emerald seemed unable to respond Lucien reluctant to do so. I pushed the matter more intensely.

"Certainly, you were aware, at least on a subconscious level, of what was going on around you?" he said with conviction; less a question and more a statement. I had to admit that I didn't understand his meaning. "Why, the omens were about you like signs on a roadside," he said. I could only ponder his meaning. Emerald sensed my general confusion and took my hand gently in her lithe fingers.

"Surely you realize that I, so subsequently you all, were brought here under false pretenses?" she questioned softly. I admitted– rather reluctantly–no such knowledge. She exchanged a quick glance with Lucien who puffed on his pipe staring at the hearth. "Etienne and I are very old friends. We studied together at the Sorbonne many years ago."

"So?" I muttered and her eyes locked with Lucien's.

"You better tell him the story Em."

"Several years back, while studying plant biology in the Congo, Etienne became very ill. It was his belief he was being bewitched by a native sorcerer. I went there, to administer to him but he had gone. Several times, through the course of our various travels our paths nearly intersected but always, for some reason, some *happening* intervened until his call a few days ago while I was in Brussels working on an old manuscript with...with Stanley." She stopped, placing her hand across her mouth, the eyes tightening with remorse as she wept for her departed friend. Lucien gently took the top of her hand.

"Go on."

"I implored him not to come. I insisted he not, but he was always so...so stubborn headed," she murmured quietly through her hands. Lucien and I waited for the pain she felt to subside. At length, she regained her composure and continued. "I knew, the minute I received Etienne's call that it was *the end of life as I knew it*," she said mysteriously. "Not death per se, but *a living death*." My mind tried to grasp her meaning. "I just couldn't," she said emphatically to Lucien. "I knew it was the end...*and I so much want to live.*" She looked imploringly at Lucien who took up her hand in his. "I'm so sorry to have put you all at such risk...it's unforgivable."

"There was no other way Em," Lucien answered. "Stanley's impetuousness killed him, nearly killed us in the bargain, certainly not you. His recalcitrant nature was his undoing. If he had only exercised patience, things would have turned out much differently. You mustn't torment yourself." There's a tender moment shared by my two companions. He then looked at me strangely, reading the confusion upon my face.

"I'm wholly unsure what you're talking about," I said and my employer and friend smiled, tamped his bowl and addressed me directly.

"You know, I would have never asked you down either Willem, but there simply wasn't the time for me to make Paris…and Renault would never travel outside the Marais. He simply won't do it, the old cynic." I must have looked like a deer in the headlights for he quickly pointed his pipe at my chest. "Without those shells…well, think such things as you will. I believe we'd be feeding the worms. I do thank you for coming…and showing such courage." His eyes glowed. I wondered silently if he was poking fun at me for freezing at the crucial moment. As if reading my thoughts, he continued. "You showed extreme valor my young friend. My sincerest thanks."

"And mine Willem, thank you."

"Remember, if we had failed in the wilds, Emerald would have been subjected to a living hell, and quite frankly…I wouldn't wish that upon a single living soul, not even Etienne," he said looking at Emerald, her eyes locking with his and I sensed the affinity between them.

"I'm sure I don't understand…really, at all…what either of you are talking about," I blurted. Emerald gave me a long solemn look. Her delicate eyes were like looking into a deep blue mist.

"It's called *empathy* Willem," she whispered. "You mustn't close that part of you that knows. You're not the physical material *thing* your mind believes you to be, but the eternal *conscious being* your spirit knows you are. How else does the concept of *eternity* make sense unless we end where we begin, and begin where we end?"

"*Begin where we end*…what does that mean?"

"We know this intuitively, have known this since the beginning, but alas men want to control the lives and thoughts of his fellows, and his religion–that which should bind him with *Universe*–all too often separates him from it, *our very source*. Politics, that should serve mankind, enslaves him. *Love and fear*, our ancient companions: love opens it, fear condenses, contracts it." She paused and studied me closely for several long moments and I was unable to avoid her radiant tranquil gaze. She suddenly grew intent as if looking through me, the pupils dilating noticeably, and as if in a trance, spoke to him through me. "You *are* that energy Etienne, the energy that makes your wound will mend you." The moment she said these words, her eyes clouded over, and her tears began to fall once again, like rain.

Chapter *3*: *Eye in the Keyhole*

While closing the offices of *Karras and Corbeau: Investigators of the Strange and Occult* on an inauspicious rainy evening in the month of July, I'm startled by the sudden intrusion of a tall dark shadow that had gained access through the rear doors. The figure loitered in the darkness of the room and I was awed by the silence of the moment, held captive by the black silhouette, lacking any distinctive features save the outline of a human form. The *thing's* slow methodical approach created a sharp primordial fear within me, for indeed there was an otherworldly quality in that singular moment. The greater shock was when I realized the shadow visage was none other than my very own employer, Mr. Karras, newly arrived from the Orient! As he came into the light, the feeling of menace dissolved rapidly. He studied me intently with dark piercing eyes and laid his hat upon my desk as I labored to regain my breath.

"What is it?" he questioned with a knowing look.

"You startled me...why...I thought you were still in Tibet."

"Finished," he said laconically, removing his weatherproof and shaking the rain from his beard. His face seemed to have somehow weathered. He looked me over curiously as one surmises a vendor pedaling wares. "Well?"

"Excuse me, but you look a bit careworn." His eyes locked with mine and for a moment I felt a tinge of angst regarding my expostulation and quickly changed the discourse. "How was your trip, successful?"

After an exceedingly long and uncomfortable pause, his expression lightened.

"Yes, I've no doubts that I do," he said unbuttoning his waistcoat. "Yes…we were successful," he said grimly. I puzzled over his inflection. "How are things here on the home-front?"

"Routine," I answered implacably. "Not much out of the ordinary I'm afraid."

"Consider that fortunate," he said as he loosened his collar and something in his voice made me realize the sincerity in his statement. I wondered to myself what things he may have witnessed on this most recent and mysterious trip.

"Would you care to discuss it perhaps?" I asked. "I was just closing and thought I might take a drop before heading back to my flat." He stuffed his meerschaum with shag from his beaten deerskin pouch and lit the bowl puffing profusely filling the room with a gray haze, then gestured toward the doorway into the pub.

The Riker Pub, the frontispiece of the company's iconic business endeavor, was abuzz with life and not an eye seemed witness our entry. We quietly took our place at the small green table in the rear that served perpetually as Mr. Karras' private table. Philippe, *the Riker's* vivacious manager, was quick to join us, waving off the barmaid.

"Good evening messieurs, how were things abroad Boss?" Philippe was Basque, his accent steeped in the particular inflection endemic of that vast mountainous area.

Lucien nodded. "Fine. How's business Philippe?"

"She's good," he said, gesturing toward a packed house full of dart and chess players sporting mugs of brew; a guitar player sat in the corner crooning ballads to the preoccupied revelers, drinking and laughing. "The usual Boss?" he inquired, already knowing the answer and was immediately off to pour two pints of Guinness. We sat quietly until the drinks were served. It was only after his first hardy draught that I chanced to question him about events in Tibet. He was steadfastly reticent.

"I'm afraid I can't discuss it, please don't be offended." This was a rare response indeed for Mr. Karras was wont to confide with me, often, about company business. I had begun to fashion myself a sort of *sounding board* for he continually sought my impressions regarding his exploits and travels. I came to believe that it exorcised his mind to speak of the strange and varied experiences his art–or trade–had delivered him. The stories were often quite incredible, and as often as not, quite unnerving. I baited him one last time, certain he would acquiesce but amazingly he remained firm in his assertion that whatever had transpired in Tibet on this particular trip would quite probably remain unspoken. I was sullen. He obviously took note and chuckled at me from behind his pipe. "Your sense of disappointment seeks no bounds," he quipped. I frowned, taking a long slow drink of my ale, knowing his eyes were fixed upon me, as if studying me under a microscope. He withdrew the pipe from his mouth, exhaled and queried: "Tell me, have I ever spoken to you about *the Wicke affair?*"

"The Wicke affair?" I echoed. "I'm afraid you have not."

His dark eyes gleamed with that strange inner glow when he's onto something of import or of fascination to his intelligent and active mind. He then tamped out his bowl in the ashtray, produced his pouch and refilled his pipe as he commenced to recite the tale.

"Doubtless, one of the oddest experiences of my professional career originated from a certain estate in Knightsbridge, from a noted financier who had newly acquired a property, a brownstone, situated on a *cul-de-sac* near the East End, an area particularly devastated during *The Blitz*. This building, remarkably, suffered no damage whatsoever during the melee despite the fact that all of its immediate neighbors had been razed or severely damaged by the incessant bombing and ensuing firestorms. Somewhat baffling, wouldn't you agree?"

"I suppose," I muttered not entirely certain about the point he was trying to make.

"To date, there had never been an adequate explanation why the old dwelling, built near the turn of the century, was spared the bleak fortune of its adjacent structures. It was assumed to be just another of the many oddities of that dreadful chapter in the history of our human legacy for indeed similar stories reverberated the whole of London after that loathsome time and not much thought was accorded it."

"A terrible episode."

"Assuredly, yet consistently, many strange inexplicable occurrences haunted the various inhabitants and owners of the property over the course of many years. Some of these *disturbances* were reported, others purported, over the course of time giving the old home a rather maligned reputation within the immediate community."

"Odd."

"Witnesses had reported seeing and hearing strange inexplicable things within the abode and one tenant, a Miss Lucinda Crain, was said to have vacated the home in the middle of a winter's eve in 1919 in naught save her nightshirt. She apparently refused to return to the dwelling but instead solicited the services of a moving company to gather up all her earthly possessions, unsupervised, and had them delivered to her sister's residence in Essex never to set foot in the place again."

"That's rather notable."

"Other accounts proclaim weird ethereal visitations during the early hours of the morning. Many of these *incidents* fail to describe exactly what was seen or heard. Mostly, persons report the strange behavior of animals while within the house. One particular individual, a Mr. Cornelius Petra, was purported to have sold the home at a distinct financial loss, and after a very brief tenure as owner, due to, and I quote: '*a constant and unexplainable sense of foreboding within the domicile,*' end quote. The subsequent buyer, a suffragette by the name of Claudile Chissit, complained to her neighbors that she was incessantly awakened during the night by the crying of a baby, yet the mysterious wailing was completely unexplainable. She soon vacated the building as well and the following year it was sold; however, the records at this point are fragmented and inconsistent primarily due to the war."

"Fascinating," I said taking another draught from my pint while he took a moment to rekindle his pipe, exhaling a large volume of gray smoke into the already hazy environ.

"Between the years of 1954 and 1956, the house was acquired by a rental firm and the upstairs shoddily renovated into multiple units. The firm subsequently sold the property and I state verbatim: *'Due to complaints of the tenants of constant nocturnal intrusions of an undisclosed nature.'* The police reports of the time fail to substantiate any evidence of foul play and dismissed many of the various reports as *fraudulent*. The following owner, a barrister from Wembley, went to great lengths, and cost, to return the property to a single dwelling for the purpose of bequeathing the home to his eldest daughter who by all apparent accounts simply refused to stay in the house and returned to live with her parents. The barrister prudently rented the house to a schoolteacher by name of Clarence Easton who lived in the house, apparently without incident, for the next dozen years, until his retirement took him out of London." He paused to indulge in his stout.

"That was the end of it then?" I inquired. He laughed softly and the laugh was somehow unsettling.

"Not quite. After this, a mix of tenants, for the next decade, complained about minor discomforts, inexplicable noises during the night, missing objects rediscovered in inappropriate places, cold chills during the heat of summer, things of this nature but nothing that stands out in earnest until the purchase of the home by the financier, Mr. Anson Wicke and his wife Amelia."

"The client."

"Quite. A fine upstanding English couple with impeccable credentials. The dossier on them excluded anything *of the fantastic* about them in the least."

"Interesting."

"Now, of course, you know of my work, so you understand I give credence to the bizarre and mystifying events that the *unseen world* plays upon that of the material. Whether a person believes it probable or not that the *disembodied spirits of the dead* reign upon the world is immaterial. For the fact of the matter is *I know*, without the shadow of a doubt, that these *ghosts* or *spirits*, as they are termed, do indeed occupy this world with us but explicitly in an *ethereal* form due primarily the fact they are naturally parted from the material in all bodily ways save *the memory* of their former self. It is this *energy stamp* that may linger, due to the tremendous and mysterious nature of the eternal spirit, for an extended period of time or until the *soul* relinquishes its grip, or more appropriately, *its obsession*, with the material world. For, in fact, time exists *uniquely* within the spirit world in stark contrast to this material plane with its checks and bounds of weeks, months and years, with its rotation and equinoxes of days, nights and seasons. So, with this said, you can understand my utter amazement and fascination when I witnessed first-hand in the stately brownstone at Muirgarden, the ubiquitous *Eye in the keyhole.*"

"I'm sorry, did you say *eye*?"

"I did," he replied. "Perhaps I should start at the beginning."

"Please do."

"I had been called into Knightsbridge, by Amelia Wicke, the wife of the aforementioned financier. She was sister to a woman whose life had been plagued by the relentless intrusion of a malicious entity since the time of her youth."

"How dour."

"We had successfully exorcised the clearing of this unsavory situation with the assistance of a certain Catholic priest of my acquaintance, a man of ability, and in turn the sister had advised Mrs. Wicke about our company's qualifications. I was cordially welcomed upon my arrival at the Knightsbridge estate by Mr. and Mrs. Wicke both. Mr. Wicke informed me that because of the gravity of the situation, he wanted to be present and meet with me personally. Due to the particularly sensitive nature of the Wicke's *problem* it was crucial to him that the matter be addressed with the utmost confidentiality."

Lucien stopped deep in thought and I sensed his reliving those early moments. I waited patiently as he puffed several times on his pipe, apparently gathering his thoughts.

"Go on," I pressed him.

"As in most cases of this nature, it took the Wickes time to come around to addressing the issue at hand, namely, the strange circumstances at the recently acquired property at Muirgarden. In fact, neither of the two, obviously proper and practical people, actually addressed any particulars, but remained aloof in their assertions *that a weird unexplainable occurrence* had taken place at the property and they wished to secure our services, to which I readily agreed. Terms were negotiated quickly and a rendezvous at the property in question was arranged for the following morning." He paused as if suddenly frozen in time.

"What happened?" I asked to shake him from his reverie.

"The next morning was cold and heavy with fog and rain, as I prefer it frankly despite the discomfort it tends to cause my leg," he said rubbing his right.

"Indeed."

"I arrived fifteen minutes early to discover the house empty and dark. I filled a pipe and smoked while I looked the house over under the cover of my bumbershoot and considered its demeanor. A lovely old brick home built by masons of caliber, its panes and cornices exquisitely composed. Nothing about the structure would portend that something was amiss. As I smoked and contemplated the house, *a distinct sense of loss and sadness* began to creep into my consciousness. I took down my perceptions, as you know, in my notebook."

"Of course."

"At fifteen minutes past the appointed hour, the Wickes arrived by auto and with very little formality showed me into the house. A quick tour of the main floor was accompanied by Mr. Wicke's disclosure of the circumstances of his obtaining the home. Eventually we made the kitchen. Here was a classic in the tradition of the English culinary station. The floor was composed of ash showing its years in wear, but polished and maintained, with naught a peg out of place, each tongue and groove as tight as the day it was lain. All about, in walnut, clamored the shelves and stow encased with leaded glass doors, also composed in walnut bracing, so well-built that very few sagged. The stove was not original but obviously occupied the original spot designed for it. I could still distinguish the firebrick foundation that was common in the days of firewood and gas. In fact, the original gas spigots and valves that would have fed the stove and lights their gaseous sustenance had been left in place despite the absence of any of their companions throughout the rest of the home. Fascinating yes?" he queried me.

"Yes," I muttered, once again, unsure the point he was trying to make.

"I questioned Amelia about the state of the kitchen and enquired if they had remodeled it, for I surmised that it was still of original décor. They readily affirmed this notion and added that despite the various owners and tenants over the years, the kitchen had basically remained intact and suffered few to little changes whatsoever, quite incredible wouldn't you agree?"

"Yes, I suppose," I said obliquely. He gazed at me several moments with dark inquisitive eyes and I wondered why such an apparently trivial detail seemed to impress him. After a short pause, he continued his tale.

"There were three portals in and out of the kitchen, one wide archway on the south wall that connected with the adjacent dining area and an oak door directly opposite the arch on the northern wall that opened into a private study with an adjoining half bath. The third portal was a door on the west, leading directly out into the narrow of the side yard; more of a passage than a yard, it was undoubtedly designed to allow access to the carriage house in the back. It was this door I quickly discerned was the object of my current employer's concern for once we had set foot within the confines of the kitchen, I became acutely aware of a drastic change in the couple's naturally composed demeanor. They became noticeably pensive. I chanced to note Amelia Wicke's inordinate attention to the western door. In fact, she could literally *not take her eyes from it the entire time we were within the room.*"

"Odd."

"I was more than cognizant of her behavior and found myself inadvertently glancing back and forth between the two. Mr. Wicke raised his arm and pointed accusingly. '*Well, there it is,*' he said gesturing towards this same lone door. I looked it over from my vantage and noticed nothing out of the ordinary, with the possible exception that it was quite old and therefore seemingly rather out of place."

"What was strange about it then?" I asked.

"The Wickes stared at it from a distance as one looks upon an abyss or *the portal to an unimaginable darkness.* I went to the door, paused a moment, and opened it and saw nothing but the greenery of the narrow side yard and nothing more. I closed the door and questioned the couple as they stood together at *the furthest point in the room from it."*

"Interesting."

"'*I'm afraid I'm at a loss,*' I had said, when Mr. Wicke, with a distinct tremor in his otherwise composed voice requested that I *look into the keyhole.* Astounded, I knelt before the door, put my right eye to the antiquated lock and was quite unnerved, I must wholly admit, to discover *an eye peering back at me from the other side of the latch!* I was so shocked by this unexpected sight that despite my better intentions, was forced to recoil from the aperture and my body involuntarily shuddered, as when catching a sudden cold draft of wind or stepping into a frigid body of water. I blinked several times to clear my sight and had another look. To my utter bewilderment I was awed to distinguish clearly *an eye of faded blue tone, with a deep piercing stare, looking back at me through the keyhole.*"

"Incredible."

"Indeed. I felt a strange cold sensation run the marrow of my back and almost without thought quickly yanked the door open, half expecting to see some person, for whatever reason, observing us from the other side of the door, but of course as I knew, there was absolutely no one there."

"Unbelievable."

"I glanced up and down the length of the building just to be sure no one was within the grounds; all was quiet save the dripping of rain from the gables and eves. I looked back through the latch in the direction of the kitchen yet there was nothing but the dim shape of the Wickes carefully avoiding any proximity with the door. I stepped back inside, took a deep breath before returning my attention to the latch; again, as before, there was *the unwavering eye intently staring back.*"

"My God," I whispered, and Lucien's dark eyes pierced the smoky environment.

"I was rather shaken by this, I'll admit readily, for the thing had a definite eerie quality about it. I took several moments to compose myself and to contemplate this remarkable phenomenon. The Wickes seemed to exhibit a sense of relief that I had witnessed what they dreaded to be all too real. I assured them that I was in concert with their observations and that the ocular aberration was numbing to say the least. However, I was at a complete loss to immediately explain it."

He paused as Philippe reappeared with two more pints of ale followed closely by none other than Beryl Collins the company's indomitable financial controller. As Philippe exchanged the spent glasses, she addressed Lucien in her very proper English manner.

"Welcome back fearless one. So very nice of you to say hello before stampeding off to the bar."

"Hello Beryl, how are things?"

"The same Lucien. Over half our clients owe us money," she stated matter-of-factly. "You do tell them we are a *for profit* business concern?"

"Indeed," he huffed beneath his breath taking a long draught from the fresh pint.

"I need to gather your receipts from this most recent trip oh hallowed one."

"They don't issue receipts in Tibet Beryl. I believe we've had this discussion a number of times."

She scowled. "Lucien…they certainly would if you simply ask, which obviously you seem incapable of."

"I'll write you a chip," he said offhandedly.

"Lovely. I'll add it to the collection," she said succinctly and glowered at me. "Now then, not that answering the primary telephone is in my job description per se…" she added glancing at me sideways, "…there's a Mr. Gittes on the wire. He says that it's urgent he speaks with you immediately and that you're expecting his call."

"Gittes you say? Calling from America?" Lucien inquired. "A haunting I believe?"

"Yes, indeed it most certainly is," she said looking squarely at me then the pint of ale in my hand. "I swear the man is nearly hysterical. He's called a number of times while you were away. I would sincerely appreciate your looking into the matter forthwith."

"Take his number, tell him I'll call him within the hour." Beryl clicked her tongue and winked at me. We both watched placidly as she weaved her way back through the crowd to the offices and slammed the door.

"I admire Beryl very much," I said beneath my breath. "But she can be really annoying at times."

"A unique personality most assuredly," Lucien said. "However, her candor pales in comparison to her financial acumen; a brilliant pecuniary mind. I dare say without our gifted Ms. Collins, I'm quite certain this institution would have gone bankrupt years ago."

"Right…" I waited patiently for him to continue.

"The latch was one of those old-fashioned contrivances, operated by what was referred in olden times as a *skeleton key* and open to both sides. I surmised that the thing was original equipment when the house had been initially built. I puzzled over why a door and lock so outdated as this could have possibly been allowed to remain affixed for such an extended period of time, being an exterior portal as it were." He stared fixedly at me as if expecting some sort of response.

"Go on," I said, and his eyebrow raised and lowered a fraction as he leaned back in his chair, extending his bad leg and took another long draught from his mug.

"I examined the latch further *until I could not endure the thing's gaze a moment longer*; for indeed there seemed to be a *presence* about it, intent upon the interior of the kitchen. I found it nearly impossible to engage it for more than a few seconds at a time. I disclosed the necessity of further investigation into the matter with Mr. Wicke who readily procured a latchkey so as I could access the building at my leisure. We parted company shortly thereafter. I commenced my examination of the entire house, head to foot, taking notes about the entire building and its grounds for any possible clues to the mystery of *the Eye*."

"Anything of note?"

"Nothing. When I was satisfied with my work at the property, I set about the tedious grind of collecting data on the history of the house and the various occupants over the course of its lengthy existence. After a week of this drudgery, I was no nearer in solving the riddle of what it was or how it came to be lodged in the orifice of the kitchen's west door."

"A dead end? Surely there was some sort of physical evidence?"

"My technical examinations of the substance of the door and latch all produced negative results, as if nothing but the air itself existed within, yet every time, over the course of the entire week, that I ventured to peer into the keyhole, I was astounded to see *the Eye* always present, inexorably, without the slightest trace of movement steadfastly peering back at me."

"Uncanny…and unnerving. I mean really Lucien…I would be quite at odds over the whole thing. What did you do then?"

"Upon the closure of the second week and with naught but a lengthy and somewhat fragmented history of the house as proof of my pursuits, I decided it was time to bring in some very potent assistance in the form of a *seer* I had met a number of years prior, on one of my many travels abroad. This remarkable person is an *Inuit medicine woman* from an extremely remote area of Canada."

"Inuit? You mean an Eskimo woman?"

"In the parlance of the West, yes. It took two days before I could finally reach her by telephone. I explained the conundrum and with the kindly financial assistance of Mr. Wicke, she agreed to travel with her daughter three days hence."

He paused while he knocked the spent ash from his pipe into the ashtray, reamed it and refilled it.

"Evangeline Kill Hennepin and her youngest daughter Nora, aged a mere sixty-two years, departed their aeroplane at Heathrow with nary an eyebrow raised about them. Those in attendance could not possibly know that this short, plump woman, whose years on the planet had escaped record, had amongst her impressive talents a unique ability that set her quite apart from most the rest of humanity; Evangeline could *die at will*."

"*Die at will*? You mean...kill herself?"

"She had been *dying* repeatedly since the age of twelve years when the elders of her tribe became aware that Evangeline could *travel to the Spirit World*. Even more incredible, *interact* with this mysterious world and bring back platitudes of various sorts for the benefit of her people. As a pure *healer* of the afflictions of humanity, Evangeline, I should mention, acknowledges none of the barriers of race and religion that all too often effectively sets our species at odds with itself. She has grown fond of travel, and *healing,* on a more worldly scale. Subsequently, she has become renown within certain circles. Her exploits are indeed impressive, could easily fill volumes if the medical profession would in the true essence of healing embrace the art of traditional medicine."

"Indeed."

"As a *shaman*, she is to a professional medical doctor what Francis or Teresa would most probably be to a Cardinal of the diocese. Doctors, much like their spiritual counterparts, have in our modern times become more akin to administrators, obligated with the task of administering medicines and medical protocol."

"I quite agree."

"Evangeline, like so many others of her kind, whose education doesn't come from the prominent schools of healing with their cadavers, scalpels and sutures are *bequeathed their knowledge directly from the Source.* Unfortunately, her medical and spiritual accomplishments will most probably go unrecorded for the benefit of humanity due the ignorance and fear of the supposedly *learned and educated.*" He paused again and lit the new bowl exhaling a long thin film of smoke into the air. I sipped on the fresh pint of ale and quietly waited.

"Please continue."

"She seemed in good spirits and quite unchanged since the last time I saw her in Toronto two years prior. She smiled profusely and patted the back of my hand, reluctant to relinquish our handshake. This was her norm, for in fact what she was doing was communicating with my energy, my spirit, in the same way two persons converse verbally. It was a quicker method for her to reunite ourselves."

"Interesting."

"We made our way to the baggage claim, her eyes aglow with that special inner fire that was hers, she hinted that my liver was complaining somewhat about my penchant for the bitters. The woman was abhorrent of alcohol consumption, having witnessed its icy effects on her native community. We quickly secured a cab and made good time to my flat near Hyde Park."

"Your previous apartment prior the move into Soho?"

"Indeed. I made the women as comfortable as I could granting them the use of the living room and front lounge overlooking the street; pulling back both of the massive sliders that normally separated the two rooms."

"I recall the place fondly."

"I left them to unpack while I was off to put on the kettle and prepare a meal. In respect to her culture, I decided to let Evangeline get around to the subject at hand, that of the primary reason for her visit. I was content to sit with her and Nora and catch up on *the news* at Tlingit, Kolosh and the various tribal groups that Evangeline is so much a part of. She inquired about mutual friends and acquaintances and such was the conversation for the better part of the evening when suddenly she placed her cup before her in both hands looked me straight in the eye and asked: '*What ghost is haunting you now, eh, Lucien?*' I commenced my account of *the Wicke affair*. The women were both noticeably enthralled and exchanged dialogue in Inuit on numerous occasions throughout my discourse. I was convinced they were quite impressed and was relieved when Evangeline announced we would inspect the property the following morning. Having been a long and tiresome trip, my companions were then quick to turn in. I bid the ladies good evening shortly thereafter and soon they were quietly dozing away leaving me uninterrupted with my books and letters into the early hours. As you know, I rarely sleep more than four or five hours per night."

"Yes, undoubtedly."

"The next morning began in earnest. The women were up at six and finished their morning prayer by six thirty. We had a quick breakfast of tea, kippers and bread and were on the street by seven o'clock. A thick pervasive fog greeted our departure from Hyde Park. By the time we arrived at the East End the fog was so thick you could cut it with a dagger. I opened the front door of the house and turned to witness Evangeline and Nora standing before the stoop discussing the house."

"Discussing it?"

"Evangeline made large gestures with her arms and hands above her head as if mimicking a tree or umbrella. She pushed by me and made her way inside while Nora still contemplated the area of the roof. As she ascended the stair, I questioned the daughter about their discussion. She smiled and hesitated as she usually did when addressed directly. This was her particular mannerism when questioned directly. *'There's a spirit around the house, protecting it'* she said and entered through the front door. I took a moment to gaze up through the heavy mist where the gables ascended into the fog, then turned and entered."

"What did they see?"

"Patience my friend. Inside, the ladies were pacing about the old structure talking quietly in their native tongue. They seemed to be looking–actually *feeling* would be the better word–the energy of the place. Eventually we ended up in the kitchen where their talk quieted considerably, nearly to a whisper. They both sat down astride the west door and talked together; their words in Inuit, soft and rhythmic. Oddly, neither took the occasion to look into the keyhole. Eventually I took the liberty to address the problem where upon I was quickly chastised for doing so. *'You mustn't look into the Eye, The Mother dislikes it.'* Evangeline informed me. I was puzzled and tried to voice my confusion. Evangeline cut me off. She then said something in Inuit to Nora and the two had a rather hearty laugh, at my expense I surmised, Nora covering her mouth with her hand as she chuckled, Evangeline not bothering to do so. I was content to watch and remain quiet. Obviously, I had recruited the right persons for the task."

At this point in Lucien's narrative, two young people, a man and a woman probably in their mid-twenties very casually dressed, approached our table and introduced themselves cordially exchanging handshakes. I gathered from the conversation they were related to someone Lucien knew well. They wished to speak with him regarding something they were obviously reticent to discuss in my presence. He advised them to return to the pub the following day and inquire for him at the bar. "Who are they?" I asked upon their leaving.

"The daughter of one of the Countesses," he said. I chanced a quick look back at their fleeting forms exiting the front door. They looked young and carefree.

"What's wrong?" I inquired as he withdrew his notebook jotting something down in it. He closed the book and returned it to his vest pocket.

"We'll know tomorrow," he said, taking a drink from his glass, deep in thought.

"What happened next?" I asked, anxious to return to our dialogue and he took a moment to recollect his thoughts.

"The two sat there for what must have been the better part of an hour staring at the floor and conversing softly with not a glance into the latch. At one point, Nora reached into her carry bag and removed a large beautiful fan made of Spotted Eagle feathers. The handle looked to be elk skin with some marvelous bead work in red and white, the national colors of Canada, and began to fan the area between them with waves of her arm, accompanied by an occasional flutter of the fan as if simulating the bird in flight."

"Interesting."

"Evangeline produced a small flat earthenware bowl and lit some cedar with a butane lighter. She then produced an odd bent stick not much larger than a full-sized pencil *and began tapping at the orifice of the lock* with what seemed random intervals. This went on for about twenty minutes when suddenly and abruptly the ladies began packing their implements as if to leave. I questioned their intent to do so but was quickly hushed. I helped them with their coats and carried Evangeline's bag and without a word we left the house taking care to lock the door tightly behind us."

"That was it then?"

"Hardly. Once outside, I broke the silence and stood waiting for a report concerning their impressions. Evangeline scratched at the hairs on her weathered chin, looked at me then the house, then back at me and asked where we might secure a good cup of strong coffee. I suggested *Penders,* a few kilometers away. Minutes later we were seated amidst a throng of tourists in the aforementioned establishment, Evangeline and Nora both sipping chocolate flavored beverages from large cups while I nursed an espresso, wishing like hell it was a Guinness."

"Indeed. Go on."

"Not a speck of conversation had anything to do with the morning's adventure and I was–however reluctantly–forced to tag along with their rather esoteric conversation about shopping and various clothes they were planning on acquiring when Evangeline abruptly drained the last drop of her coffee, sat back, burped loudly enough to draw the attention of our immediate neighbors."

"Humorous."

"She patted my forearm and said: '*Hah! Have you got a live one over there!*' she said and drew up near me, lowering her voice considerably and waved her withered index finger at me like a parent scolding a child. '*Don't you dare look into that Eye, not if you value your eternal soul.*' Her manner was so severe that I recall a tingle bristled the base of my skull. '*The spirit inside that tiny little hole is so powerful it protects the entire house. It won't let anything remove the door within which it lives.*'

"'*It resides within the door?*' I questioned her.

"'*The hole. This is very common in our beliefs, you know Lucien, which is why you've brought me down.*' I admitted to her that I was unsure about her last point. '*The orifice…in Inuit mythology…oh you know damn well what I'm talking about!*' I insisted I was still somewhat in the dark regarding her point. '*Your higher self certainly knows,*' she said, her eyes possessing a strange unearthly quality. I asked her to elucidate. '*It's a wayward soul,*' she said, Nora agreeing, her demeanor turning solemn. I questioned her term. She took my hand in hers and gave a quick glance about to be sure we would not be overheard, then looked me fixedly in the eye and my attention was completely locked with hers. '*You call it a lost soul down here, but that's not it. She's not lost, she's wayward.*' I questioned her use of gender. '*It's the wayward soul of a woman,*' she said, and Nora nodded emphatically. I asked about the identity of the spirit, completely absorbed. '*Won't know until we cross over.*' I must have looked thunderstruck for the daughter was quick to intercede and recited a series of statements as to the process loosely followed by the shaman."

"Do you recall her exact words?"

"Yes. Her precise words were: '*Mother leaves here and travels to the other side. There she speaks with an ancestor, or sometimes a volunteer…waits there in the spirit lodge while they send the Eagle…sometimes Wolf…sometimes Raven goes. They talk with the spirit to find out what's wrong, then they come and tell grandfather, mother's father…he died a long time ago. Grandfather tells mother…mother tells us.*'"

"Truly incredible."

"I recall I sat in silence for some time taking this in. I inquired if they had any notion as to why this spirit was in the door latch. Nora eventually answered my query. '*She's looking for something,*' is all she said."

"Ominous."

"The women continued their trance-like communication. I could tell they were conversing together silently. I was acutely aware that they knew more than they were willing to talk about. '*You intend to return to the house tonight?*' I asked. '*Oh, hell no,*' Evangeline blurted out loud enough to draw attention. '*You watch too many movies Lucien. Only the stupid go chasing spirits of the dead around at night. That's askin' for it. We'll go over tomorrow morning, same time. Meanwhile baby and I have shopping to do. Do you have a good mall around here somewhere? Not no dime-store operation.*'"

"You're paraphrasing the woman nicely," I quipped.

"I gave Evangeline the proper directions to *Harrods* and some of the money owed her from the client. '*Don't wait up for us, we'll find our way back,*' she said and the two started off leaving their bags for me to drag back to Hyde Park."

"That was it for the evening?"

"No. She then returned and whispered in my ear: *'Lucien, we've got some dangerous business tomorrow. I'm going to need some things. I'll need the name and address of your very best person, and not some sideshow hoaxster, a serious apothecary with experience in native plants.'* I pulled the name and address from my book and presented it to her. Andrea Beckwith, an herbalist with Third World Collectibles. *'Is she one of those hippie chicks?'* she asked. I assured her that Ms. Beckwith was as serious as they came and could locate immediately, anything she might require. *'I hope you're right,'* she informed me. *'We'll need all the help we can get. That's powerful medicine over there,'* she said and with that was off."

"What did she mean by *dangerous*?"

"I'll admit it caught my attention. I was left entirely with my own thoughts as to her meaning and the strange events at Muirgarden and the rest of the day passed in an odd sort of way."

Here he paused and spent time refilling his pipe. I looked about the bar. The dart players were having a spirited game of Cricket and the balladeer had taken a break to converse with a lovely blonde patron who sat alone at her table near his station. A small skirmish was taking place at the front of the bar between Philippe and an overly intoxicated man who was demanding another whiskey and water. When the man loudly referred to the lively manager as: *'a damn bloody froug,'* Philippe gestured across his throat with his thumb and two of *'the lads'* barmen in clean white aprons, had the fellow by both arms and he was efficiently escorted out of the premises. Lucien relit his bowl with another cedar match.

"Please continue Lucien, I'm fascinated."

"The following morning arrived and the three of us were soon upon the stoop at Muirgarden. Hardly a word had been exchanged the entire morning; the women surprisingly reticent compared to the previous day's excitement and Evangeline's jocularity. This morning they were sullen, or perhaps I should say, pensive."

"I certainly would be."

"Once inside, the women quickly unpacked an assortment of wooden, feathered and botanical accoutrement. Several small clay dishes were stocked with a variety of herbs and plants. A small elk skin drum was placed in the center of what was quickly becoming a semi-circle of natural ingredients and objects circling the west door. I noticed seal rib bones and the talons from an osprey or some other predator bird. They lit cedar and another herb that gave off a rather obnoxious aroma in stark contrast to the wonderful scent of the cedar. A handwoven blanket was placed near the circle and was the approximate length of a human person. When all was ready Evangeline turned to me. *'Lucien, I need you outside, you mustn't allow anyone to come in here under any circumstances, understand?'* I was more than surprised. Surely my services were needed here. I voiced this opinion openly. *'Lucien, don't act like a hurt schoolboy and get out there and make damn sure no one comes barging in here while I'm away from my body.'* I sat numb for a moment then rose and walked out the front door."

"She sent you away? Why?"

"We'll get to it soon."

"Go on."

"Outside was a soft drizzling rain and nothing more. I gazed down the street and not a soul was to be seen nor heard. I withdrew my meerschaum, filled it to the brim with my best Virginia shag and sat sullenly in the drizzle and smoked. My disappointment was acute. I have yet to witness this mysterious native process in action, my understanding of it, through secondhand sources only. Imagine, this incredible procedure at my fingertips and I'm relegated to watching the rain falling across the cobblestones of a lonely forgotten cul-de-sac."

"Regrettable."

"Approximately an hour had lapsed. I was knocking the ash from the second spent bowl when a loud fuming lorry trundled down the lane and parked in front of the house next door. I watched quietly as three motley dressed men ambled out, stretching and yawning all the while. By all accounts it appeared that the neighbors were in the process of a move when quite unexpectedly they popped open the rear doors of the truck and with as much clatter as possible extended a beaten old metal ramp down to the drive directly before me. I watched in earnest as the men marched up to the stoop where I was stationed and *introduced* themselves. '*Mr. Wicke perchance?*' the largest one inquired. '*Karras, is my name,*' I responded to which he simply moved to pass me by, extruding a full ring of keys and began to sort through it. '*Excuse me sir, may I inquire as to your business here?*' I asked. He never raised an eye in my direction but continued his hunt for a key to fit the latch. '*Our business is with Mr. Wicke,*' he said from behind his shoulder."

"What happened next?"

"I repeated my question in earnest. He slowly turned his face toward mine with an incredulous look upon it. *'We're here to carpet the three upstairs bedrooms mate, if it's any business of yours.'* He shoved an invoice, dated two months prior, into my face and continued his search for the proper latchkey."

"You do a splendid Cockney accent I should say."

"*East-End* rather, but thank-you. *'My dear fellow, this house is currently unavailable. No one is to be allowed in,'* I said pocketing my pipe. At this point the man looked me square in the eye and not a pleasant gaze was it. *'Says who?'* he asked. *'As per the wishes of Mr. Wicke himself,'* I answered. The fellow exchanged looks with his mates and squared himself before me, his hairy knuckles resting on the girth of his waist. *'And who might you be?'* he queried again. *'As I said, Karras is my name and I'm currently under the employ of Mr. Wicke. You're welcome to contact him directly.'* He poked a stubby finger into the lapel of my coat. *'Listen mate, I don't care if yer Queen Victoria, I got a lorry full'a wool and these blokes on payroll standin' 'ere and I aims to lay this rug this bloody afternoon.'* He rattled the invoice before my face to emphasize his point. *'You call Mr. Wicke.'*"

"Splendid rendition. Lucien, I believe you missed your calling in the Theatre."

"Hardly Willem. My line of work all too often requires the use of costume as well as subterfuge. Acting goes hand-in-hand with the mystic. Shamans are as much actors as healers and vis-à-vis."

"That sounds a bit underhanded."

"Not in the least. There's no misrepresentation of the truth in our line of work, merely the garnering of moments."

"Please go on."

"He folded and pocketed his paper while his cronies chuckled, then withdrew a key from the ring and inserted it into the lock at which point I laid the handle of my cane gently but firmly across the top of his wrist. *'Excuse me sir but let me reiterate emphatically, no one is to go into this house at this time. I advise you to contact Mr. Wicke and he'll explain everything satisfactorily.'* The man's eyes blazed with an inner rage pent up from years of bad living and a penchant for fighting, his nose bent slightly to one side from some previous trouncing. His chin twitched as did his left eye and he inched his way as close and as intimidating as possible. I remained calm and kept a tight grip on my briar." Lucien presented me his cane, twisting it in his grip. "A very lightweight but incredibly durable stick that grows rather straight and hard. I favor it for its convenient weight and strength. Excellent for travelling and a most appreciated companion when confronted by an adverse situation of which, woefully, I've had my share."

"Indeed."

"*'You got a helluva nerve for a little feller,'* he said and spat on the stairs of his employer. As you know, I'm six foot three inches in height, about five inches above him so I imagined his remark was directed towards my thinner build. He pulled some of the weight from his belly and worked it upward towards his chest and breathed his rather sour breath directly into my face, but I was committed to stand my ground. *'See here fellow,'* I exhorted. *'If it's a row you want then I'll oblige you but understand it's the wish of our employer that no one enters this house at this time and that's simply the last word on it.'*"

"And then?"

"I whacked the side of my boot with the lower part of my briarwood to drive home the point and readied myself for whatever attack the clumsy oaf might allay. He looked about for several moments back and forth between his mates, the house and myself, apparently uncertain what to do. *'What's going on in 'ere that's so bloody secret?'* he enquired indignantly. I stood my ground unflinching and answered him not a word. *'Cheeky little bastard!'* whined the jackal at his side, a slight fellow barely half my weight in stone. *'Take 'is bloody 'ed orf, Luther.'* Luther seemed more angst ridden than ever, running his sleeve across his mouth and began palpitating."

"Oh-oh."

"At this point the other fellow, an older man with tired eyes laid a hand across the big fellow's shoulder and pulled him gently aside and began whispering something in his ear. What was said I care not, but the men—as loudly as possible—tossed their beaten old ramp back in their sagging yellow truck and slammed the doors. Luther gave me one last look over his shoulder. *'We'll be back shortly enough and you better not be 'ere! Bloody punter.'* They climbed into the lorry, the monstrosity roared to life belching smoke and was off."

"Thank goodness."

"It was several minutes before I felt myself calm enough to enter the house and see if the disturbance had affected the proceedings inside. To my great amazement, in the kitchen, Evangeline was laid out on the floor adorned in a feathered blanket completely still, as if in a trance, while Nora, also trance-like, beat softly in four-four time on the elk skin drum and sang a beautiful song in Inuit."

"Astounding."

"They seemed oblivious to my presence. I simply stared at their process for several minutes, awed into a quiet submission, before I regained my senses and withdrew outside to continue my vigil for what would become several hours of patient waiting, smoking and contemplating."

"What happened?"

"When it was all over, Evangeline and Nora walked out into the rapidly approaching twilight, bags packed and in hand, as if they had just returned from a tour of sightseeing. I recall Evangeline looked up into the clearing sky, dim stars just appearing on the horizon, and took in a deep breath and exhaled. '*We're done here Lucien. You can tell your client he's all set to move in or whatever. Let's get something to eat.*' The ladies headed down the walk while I locked the front door and followed them up the lane. When I caught up with them, I inquired about the evening's proceedings but neither of the two would say a word until after they had eaten. I inquired what they might be in the mood for. '*What have you got?*' Evangeline responded. I contemplated this a moment, stating there was a wonderful Indian restaurant I was quite partial to, not far away. '*Perfect,*' she said, sitting down on the bus stop bench. I didn't bother with the bus but hailed a taxicab."

We're interrupted by Phillipe. "Another round Boss?"

"Please. Thank-you Phillipe and put the drinks on my tab. *The Maharaja* is a small innocuous place that advertises not in the least. In fact, its marquee is nearly invisible to the untrained eye. As a result, the proprietor's clientele is nearly handpicked. Do you know of it yet?"

"I believe you've mentioned it. Wasn't its proprietor in about a month ago? Something about a haunted mask or…"

"A head. A haunted shrunken head. He's a peculiar man. I met Mr. Nare in Rangoon on one of my odysseys to the Orient. Shortly after this time he introduced me to his quaint little restaurant in London. Subsequently, I dine there on a monthly basis, when I need to get away. As you know, I've a penchant for Indian curry and a remarkable friendship with the entire Nare family; all highly educated and interesting people who frequently travel abroad and are full of news from other parts of the world."

"Yes, he came in with his wife and son. Delightful people. Extremely well-spoken."

"The tiny restaurant is narrow and long, done in beige stucco and adorned in the colorful fabrics of India herself. Many brass-plated *objects-du-art* of Indian craftsmanship are placed about in an appealing design. Often on weekends a Sitar player with Tabla accompaniment, grace the narrow confines of the hostel lending an exquisite air to the place. The bill-of-fare consists of all the glorious dishes that India has developed over the centuries into a fine art with a particularly keen array of curries; which on this evening we indulged in heartily."

"Why haven't I been there yet?"

"Mr. Nare paid a visit to our table and invited me for a smoke in his private lounge, while his lovely wife Preethi conversed with Evangeline and Nora; the women instantly carrying on a spirited conversation like old friends."

"I can imagine that."

An elderly couple stopped to shake hands with him and chat briefly. I casually waited until their departure.

"Nare's back lounge is infamous among the initiated. It's somber in tone, mostly dark teakwood, with the vital exception of his incredible collection of masks *and authentic shrunken heads*. Many of these heads are garish and rather frightening, and quite illegal. Most are from Borneo and possess a dark brown complexion with hair as black as ink. However, there is one rusty-haired exception and I often wonder what poor chap found himself in such straits as to lose his head in such a way. I asked Nare about it once. I remember his response word for word: '*That one's old, very old, very well preserved. Probably done by an old master. I imagine he was some rogue sailor, early eighteen-hundreds, who lost his head gambling, committed rape; some capital crime or some such rot,*' was his response and that's been the last word on it."

"You do a splendid Indian accent as well. I'm impressed."

"As I said, I dine there monthly and Nare talks my ear off, as they say in the vernacular."

"Quite."

"In the middle of the room sits a low table with floor pillows about it. In its center is a large ornate hookah. This pipe is the center-piece of the room and many a company of world travelers have shared tales and adventures here. We sat and puffed on a fine blend of Turkish and caught up on things. '*Who are these old women carrying on with the wife so?*' he asked pleasantly. I explained most of what had transpired that evening–for, once we had sat down to eat, Evangeline and Nora explained the remainder of the mystery, the *loose ends* if you will, that fit nicely with the research I had accomplished previously."

"Oh?"

"I used the opportunity to tell Nare all about it. I'll reiterate it for you if you like?"

"Please do."

"The house at Muirgarden had been built in 1906 by a man named Montclair whose occupation was in textile manufacturing. He built the house and lived in it with his wife Lena, a Danish immigrant, who was twenty years younger than he and who died at the tender age of twenty-three, shortly after the birth–and death–of their daughter child. The circumstances of her death were most tragic."

"Go on."

"A child was born to the couple shortly after their marriage and was barely a year old when shoddy police reports from the time indicate a tragic accident occurred within the house and that the infant had died. The report I obtained indicated, *'Death by asphyxiation'* and said nothing more other than there was no criminal intent and the death ruled accidental. More out of curiosity, I investigated the death of Mrs. Montclair and learned her demise was self-inflicted suicide. I was unable to procure any details other than the death took place in the home. What Evangeline told me was shocking. Evangeline had *died*–if you will–and travelled in the *astral* to the *spirit lodge* of her ancestors who commaned with the *wayward soul* of Lena Montclair, *the Eye in the keyhole.*"

"Astounding."

"When Evangeline returned to her body still endowed in the *astral light,* she was able to witness *the tiny form of the Montclair's infant daughter still sleeping before the stove, the object of Lena's eternal vigil.*"

"Why, that's nearly unbelievable. What on earth happened?"

"What had happened on a cold December night so many years prior was truly misfortunate. Lena Montclair had the habit of placing the bassinet of her child in the proximity of the great stove in the kitchen. Heating was rudimentary in those days and it was of course sensible to put the child in the warmest room, namely the kitchen, where Lena was so prolific. On this particular night while Lena's daughter lay sleeping by the stove, for whatever reasons, the flame was extinguished and the gas poured forth within the room, which had been closed tightly to keep in the heat. By the time the mother realized the error it was too late, the child was–by earthly standards–dead. However, through a rare set of circumstances the soul of the child remained fixed in the warmth and familiarity of the kitchen with its proximity to the stove where she had lived a goodly portion of her short life."

"But for heaven's sake why?"

"Perhaps it was the spirit's desire to remain near her mother, perhaps it was another explanation more mysterious, but the fact of the matter was, the child simply did not pass on to *the Eternal* but remained, forever an infant child, swaddled in its cozy nest and too content or naïve to know its predestination. What Evangeline discovered further was that the mother, bereaved beyond all rational thought by the death of her precious infant child, simply could not endure life further and died in very much the same manner, by *self-inflicted asphyxiation* in the kitchen. Once her soul departed its body it became aware of the child's spirit still bound to the earthly plane and simply refused to leave her, but instead–incredibly– resided within the aperture of the western door where it could *watch over the still sleeping baby."*

"Good lord Lucien…"

"Thus was the state of affairs at the house at Muirgarden for over a century, the baby asleep by the stove, the mother looking over its wellbeing simply not allowing anything to disturb her eternal slumbering."

"My goodness Lucien. Truly remarkable!"

"Nare said nearly the same thing upon the conclusion of my tale. He then procured a bottle of Martel, poured two glasses and downed his neat before filling it again."

"Astounding. But…what's become of it? The child and the mother, are they still there?"

"Evangeline saw to it that the two…passed-on together, shall we say. We both sat silently caught-up in our own thoughts about the matter until Preethi entered. '*Ms. Hennepin would like to retire for the evening. I'm going to have Auden drive you.*' I thanked her, and my host, finished my drink then cordially excused myself. Nare merely nodded, deep in his own thoughts. I exited into the gay atmosphere of the restaurant and caught-up with my charge as they were donning their coats. I attempted to pay the bill but Mrs. Nare, very uncharacteristically, refused to accept it. Soon we were out into the brisk London night and into a fine black BMW driven by the Nare's eldest son, and smoothly and quietly, we were off down the avenue and into the misty London night."

Chapter *4*: Pissing in A Graveyard

Is a thought alive? Does it possess power? Can the power of a thought set into action a chain of real events? Can a word, or the assemblage of words and utterances, such as prayer, a mantra or a wish create a series of circumstances, sometimes with disastrous effects?

An odd situation occurred during a recent visit to the Japanese islands–during the course of our work there. It all started with an observation and my proclivity in voicing it. It had become something of an obsession and revolved about the topic of what I perceived as Japan's inordinate number of crows and ravens, predominately the ravens, huge ebony and brazen creatures, that permeate the entirety of Japan.

If one travels to the Kanto or the Kansai, Kyushu or Shikoku or as far north as Hokkaido, they will be there to greet your arrival and entertain your stay. They are literally everywhere. If one explores the confines of the great cities or the remotest coastal regions, one needs only to look over one's shoulder to witness the intrepid fowl. From the mountains of Kai to the plains of Musashi, they adorn the trees, temples and telephone wires. Throughout Gifu I often witnessed them in groups of three or four, in the small seaside village of Atami they seemed to wander in a more solitary fashion.

It doesn't take one long to notice a rare intelligence the animal possesses of the ways and habits of human beings. They shadow their human hosts and successfully thrive on society's midden.

I've witnessed the bird's qualities–and turpitude–not only in Japan but nearly the world over and find the creature enchanting yet somehow disturbing. Their eyes possess no color whatsoever save an absolute black, as dark as night, except for a curious sort of inner luminance that seems to pour forth an aura of mischief and curiosity. They watch and observe the behavior of other animals and mimic those traits best serving their tireless natures. They study and consider and thus secure their place in the hierarchy of intelligent life upon the planet, for in fact any soul, great or small, that ponders and creates must surely take its place in the pantheon of sentient creatures.

I had questioned several of our Japanese colleagues about the bird's apparent abundance. Most were at odds as to how their numbers proliferated so. One individual considered it his opinion that these creatures were clever enough to manipulate the waste systems of the cities and outlying areas to their advantage. He had taken note of their keen sense of smell and cited the bird's ability and intelligence to extend energy only on those bags and boxes containing foodstuffs. Other opinions ranged from the animal's inexorable abilities of procreating to a distinct lack of a suitable predator.

By and large, it seemed the general consensus painted the talented fowl in a less than favorable light, the majority according the ancient animal's behavior opportunistic at best, to parasitic.

There was, however, one distinct voice amongst the company of persons I had entreated with this concern; a strange old man named Ozawa.

I had met Mr. Ozawa while travelling by boat to rendezvous with Lucien and an old indigenous acquaintance of his–Mr. Mori–a Japanese scholar who resided on the island of Hachijojima, one of the distant tiny volcanic islands that extend from Tokyo harbor several hundreds of kilometers due south into the vastness of the Pacific. Mr. Mori was the purpose of our visit and it was in the evening after my departure from Tokyo Bay on route to Hachijo Island that I made Mr. Ozawa's acquaintance.

I had stowed my bag below in the common before returning up on deck. The ferry was crowded with people, families bound principally for Oshima Island, one of the larger islands of the Izu string of which Hachijo is a member.

This particular individual stood out amongst the throng in two distinct ways, his rather rhapsodic nature–upon my arrival aft–and his ability with the spoken English language. He was a radio technician recently returned from South America; friendly and interesting. It was only after a variety of topics that somehow the conversation turned to the matter of crows.

He evidently delighted in this topic and surmised that crows were no ordinary bird but in fact were *the disembodied spirits of the dead*, whose demise on this earth had cast them into dubious and unanticipated fortunes!

Incredibly, it was his considered opinion that the reason for Japan's excessive number of crows and ravens was due entirely to Japan's rather bloody history. He spoke in a dry matter-of-fact tone that rather awed me.

Quite sincere in his opinion, Mr. Ozawa stated that throughout *the warring states period* the animal had the proclivity of feeding on the scattered bodies of dead warriors and civilians, one ghastly conflict after another. This *cycle*, he said, continued century after century, starting with the Jommu period and not ceasing until well after the bloody escapades of the vibrant Oda Nobunaga when–at last–Tokugawa Ieyasu and his descendants were finally able to put an end to it all and launch Japan into several centuries of quintessential peace and solitude.

It was his considered opinion that the souls–he used the word *tamashii*–of some of these dead warriors had transmuted into the fowl and a *cyclic unbroken chain of insight, intelligence and intrigue* was the result. He insisted it was the same the world over. The ebony bird had the endemic ability of *soul transmigration with the human species.* This old person was so convinced that his postulation was correct that I found myself pondering this rather ominous perspective and it added even stranger more mystical dimensions to the already remarkable fowl.

I found myself recollecting past encounters where certain *individuals* within a murder were in fact exhibiting behavior that was highly questionable at the time; watching and anticipating my actions, following me about, actually *shadowing* my work or meanderings. The more he elaborated, the more I began to find this notion unnerving. I bid my companion adieu retiring to the recesses of the ship below.

Perhaps it was the trepidation this discussion put into my mind or perhaps a matter of coincidence that shortly thereafter I was to encounter a most strange and fearsome set of circumstances on that tiny island deep within the expanse of the *Kuroshio,* Japan's *Black Current.*

Because of the encounter with the old man, I had retired to the sleeping lounge below deck well in advance of the crowd. The Japanese ferry was void of the single room cabins common on Western boats but came stocked with large open, carpeted rooms that serve to bed groups of forty or so persons each. One is issued a small pillow and blanket and expected to secure his own place on the clean floor–no shoes allowed past the entry–and rest or sleep as the person desires. There was a smattering of persons already staking their place about the room, families with small children mostly. I had no trouble finding a corner and laid myself prostrate upon the floor and prepared myself for slumber.

The strange old signalman had forced his words firmly into my imagination. I puzzled over the possibility he was putting one over on me for amusement. Yet why would he do so? I considered he might be mentally off balance, yet his prior didactic manner was extremely civil, intelligent and interesting. No. His intense embrace of the subject of the crows was neither fancy nor fraudulent but sincere, at least to him. His postulations and lively and intense look shone clearly from behind my closed eyes as I struggled to quiet my thoughts for sleep, and sleep did come, eventually.

When I awoke at dawn, I was shocked to find the compartment filled nearly beyond capacity with the bodies of sleeping people. I carefully threaded my way through this human maze and made the gangway topside to have a smoke and clear the cobwebs from my head.

Once on deck, I was startled by a vision quite beyond my comprehension. I still see the sight clearly within my mind's eye; three massive and ancient *junks* entirely the color of old chocolate with massive tined sails, sailing opposite ours in a clean nautical line extending into the mist.

The closest in proximity was very clear and distinct yet not a soul did I chance to see upon her quarterdeck, nor lights from within her galley. Its immediate companion was visually half her size and less distinct, perhaps several hundreds of meters to her portside and a third ship was just barely visible on the misty horizon. Not a light was evident on either of these dark sojourners. I wondered with the best of my rational mind if I was actually in fact seeing an aberration, an Eastern version of the *Flying Dutchman*.

As swiftly as they were there, they receded into the misty womb of the ocean and were gone leaving me standing and pondering alone on the aft deck as the dark swirling waters bounced and tossed our craft on further southward.

At Oshima Island, the boat nearly emptied and the rest of the journey to Hachijo was more peaceful and sedate. I never saw my curious old radioman again.

Upon arriving at the small utility port on the west side of Hachijo island, I rented a tiny truck from a local gas station with the goal in mind of circumnavigating the entirety of the island before meeting up with Lucien and Mr. Mori at a prearranged location and time, somewhere near the center of the island.

Barely more than a glorified golf cart, I maneuvered the conveyance south along the coast road that winds along the jungle skirting the black lava beds that comprise the island's western coast.

Hachijo-jima, I should mention, derived its name ostensibly from being the eighth primary island in the Izu chain of islands that cut a direct north to south axis from Tokyo Harbor. *Hachi,* is the word for *eight* in the Nihon language. Hachi also is the word for *bee* and from above the island possesses an eponymous connection. Additionally, the island has the rough outline of the numeral eight due to its twin volcanoes, Mihara-yama at the southern extreme and Hachijo-yama to the north.

Regarding the latter, I learned Hachijo-yama is affectionately referred to by the islanders as *Kofuji* meaning *little Fuji* due its amazing likeness to its mighty brother on Honshu, the main Japanese island to the north.

The long and narrow two-lane road, without shoulders, went on kilometer after kilometer with no practical turnouts or rest spots whatsoever. Obviously, this road was more utilitarian than tourist oriented for it was also deplete of shops or vistas nor any visible homes that I could discern. I began to wonder about the purpose of the road altogether. It seemed almost pointless with such few interruptions as it snaked under the tropical canopy on and on to the point of exhaustion.

Eventually a flat clearing opened, and I pulled in and stopped the truck to alleviate my bladder. It wasn't until I had turned off and exited the vehicle that I realized the spot at which I had stopped was none other than an antiquated graveyard.

It was ancient and moss covered with very few new *toba* markers–the tall thin planks of wood with the *kaimyo* (family name) written on them in Kanji. It blended-in so well with the jungle foliage that the stone gravesites looked more like the natural rock than a place of rest.

Japanese graveyards are quite different than their Western counterparts–with the possible exception of cemeteries like Pere-Lachaise in Paris. Japanese graveyards are literally stone on stone with very little greenery between the markers or graves. There is very little that is pastoral about them. I had visited gravesites and shrines in the northern part of Japan near Sendai and had visited sites in Tokyo and Kyoto as well. These graveyards were well manicured, rather austere and sterile, while this one rambling into the trees and growth was like nothing I had ever seen before. It seemed nearly *alive*, filled with green and living plant life. I surmised the jungle was too inexorable and probably the place was little used anymore, most likely forgotten.

I was suddenly startled from my meditation by an awkward cackling from the canopy above that engulfed the entirety of the site. I gazed about the foliage, surprised to spy a *murder of crows* staring down at me from the branches directly overhead, five perhaps six animals in all, watching me inquisitively.

One of the birds sounded out again as if asking a question and they silently scrutinized me as if expecting an answer. I studied them closely a moment. Curiosity seemed to emanate from their black eyes. I must admit surprise.

I'd grown used to seeing them on the main islands but now I was several hundred kilometers across some very vast and turbulent ocean and here sat an amazingly large group watching over an abandoned graveyard. Somehow, I thought it rather unusual.

My body–and its needs–suddenly regained control of my attention and the birds were quickly relegated to fancy. I was concerned that the place I had chosen to alleviate myself was a graveyard, however, there really was no other course of action left me.

More out of a sense of modesty, I chose one of the larger granite monoliths and commenced to expel water when my peaceful state of mind was abruptly compromised by the sudden clatter from the fowl overhead. Something had surely roused their wrath and several more birds alighted and joined in the chatter. *What on earth had stirred them so?*

Having concluded my objective, I was just returning to the truck when I was startled by a voice in the distance.

"*Oye...oye,*" someone was calling out, a common Japanese exclamation to gain a person's attention. I was surprised beyond words to see a bent old man working his way toward me from the jungle. Only a moment ago I thought myself the sole proprietor of that solemn piece of ground. Suddenly here was a bent old bone seemingly as old as the jungle from which he came.

He slowly made it to where I stood reluctantly waiting for him and looked me over apparently shocked to see a foreigner this far from the cities; the birds continuing their clatter above.

The old man uttered several words in Nihongo. I shrugged, indicating that I did not understand. He brooded a moment rubbing his grizzled chin and glancing at the foliage above. I gazed up to see what he was looking at, *the murder of crows watching our every move.* I felt a tug at my sleeve and returned my attention to the old man bent beside me. Although ancient in years his eyes shone brightly, a strange inner gleam that denoted interest and intelligence.

"*Tatari,*" he eventually said, pointing at the *murder.* "*Fuko.*" I didn't recognize these words but took note of them in my mind. He repeated the words, pointing at the monument. "*Inoru*" he stated resolutely and looked up at the crows then at the gravestone then back at the crows still cackling and carrying on. He then held up his palm, "Chotto-matte-kudasai," and was immediately off in the direction from which he had come. At a distance he stopped and called back, "chotto-mate-kudasai" before disappearing over the crest of the hill.

I was familiar with this last phrase and understood that it was his desire that I wait. I kicked at the pebbles under my feet, wishing I had used better discretion, and looked about. The old cemetery was completely deserted.

Soon, my imagination began to fabricate all sorts of wild ideas as to why the old man wanted me to remain. I could suddenly envision a group of angry locals coming over the hill and assailing me verbally–or other–for my lack of foresight. Eventually, I couldn't contain my imagination any longer and quietly sliding behind the wheel and turning the key, I was off down the small drive and back onto the meandering two-lane road heading south.

Later that evening we were having dinner at Mr. Mori's home; an exquisite traditional wood frame Japanese house replete with paper shoji doors and a wood-fired *furo* bath. Mr. Mori is a fascinating and interesting individual. A writer and lecturer on Japanese antiquities, he had befriended my employer on one of his trips to London where Lucien had acquired his services in connection with a mysterious case involving an old silk kimono that was purportedly *haunted by one of its previous owners, a distinguished courtesan from sixteenth century Kamakura.* The story is certainly unique. The experience cemented the relationship and the two men have remained steadfast companions in all things mysterious and ancient.

I was surprised, and somewhat disappointed–I'm embarrassed to admit now–to find Mr. Corbeau in attendance; my greeting less than cordial. I had no idea he had flown into Haneda airport and then on to Hachijo the previous evening from Shanghai where he had been visiting with an English acquaintance in *The Bund.* He grunted his salutations upon my arrival and seemed preoccupied with his own inner thoughts while consuming large amounts of beer and sake. Mr. Mori and Lucien seemed to take no notice of his self-absorbed aloofness, completely engaged in their conversation while Mori's beautiful wife Yuki graciously made us comfortable. Mori's wife was several years his junior and an accomplished Koto player and Ikebana specialist. Her grasp of English was far inferior to her husband and she participated little in the conversation except to pause in her activities from time to time before finding something to do elsewhere within her lovely home.

We were sitting at the *kotatsu*, a heated table with a thick skirt where a person could warm himself by the radiant heat underneath; discussing the island. I learned that Hachijojima was renowned for a particular tropical plant, a small tree an ornate shrub, they grew on tiny plantations on the island and imported to the cities up north. The other major export–now in decline on Hachijo Island–was its silk, a particular pattern and color referred to as *Ki-hachijo,* that was apparently quite coveted and expensive. Mr. Mori suggested we take a trip down to *'the works'* as he referred them, to see first-hand the traditional process of harvesting and dyeing still in motion on the island.

"It has not changed over the centuries," he said through his cigarette. "They still grow the grass here to produce the dye, a greenish yellow hue with a little bit of red weave. They dye the silk then hang it on long poles to dry. This they use to make the particular color and pattern we see and know as *Ki-hachijo*. Very beautiful, very rare…very expensive," he noted. "Real Ki-hachijo is only made here on Hachijo-jima."

"Interesting," I said sipping from the beautiful hand-made sake bowl.

"Of course, like many things made in Japan, you can buy fake," he added tossing a few peanuts in his mouth and sipping on his glass of beer. "But the real thing is very much desirable." With cigarette jutting from his teeth he hopped up from the floor and withdrew a large hardbound volume about Japanese silk kimonos from one of his many bookcases. He flipped through several pages before spinning the massive book in my direction and pointing to a picture of a beautiful woman wearing a lemony colored kimono.

"See? Key-Hachijo silk has a pattern of thin intersecting reddish-orange bands throughout. Very beautiful."

He returned to his cross-legged position on the tatami and snuffed out his cigarette while Lucien puffed on his pipe nodding softly. Mori then spoke in his native tongue to Yuki in the next room and she began to set the meal.

As we went about having dinner together, I asked Mori about the cemetery and my encounter with the old man came up in conversation–with the exception of my having urinated on the grounds. I sought Mori's advice about a couple of the words the old man had used.

"Which words?" he inquired.

"I was curious what the words *tatari* and *fuko* refer to?" I asked nonchalantly and Yuki instantly grew rigid with a rather shocked look on her face. Husband and wife exchanged a strange look and he asked me to repeat both words, I did so. There was a noticeable change in the room and Lucien seemed to be studying them closely. Mori spoke quietly with Yuki before addressing me squarely.

"This man, at the graveyard...this man, he was the caretaker?" he asked wide-eyed.

"I don't know, but...I would guess perhaps that he was," I stammered and noticed Mr. Corbeau was now staring fixedly at me from beneath his furrowed brow.

"Why would he say these words to you? What reason please?" Mori pressed. There was an excruciating pause and sensing my discomfort, Mori suddenly said: "To answer your question, *tatari* means...curse."

"*Curse?*" I asked incredulous.

"Hai, so...*curse*," he repeated. I laughed but it was a small nervous laugh, not full and vigorous. "Are you certain he said *tatari*?" Mori asked. I quickly sensed a way out of my predicament and said that it was very probable I was mistaken. Mori didn't seem convinced.

"What is it Mori-san?" Lucien questioned him.

"Well," he mused, scratching his chin, "the other word...*fuko* you say?"

"I believe that was the word," I answered, and his expression grew quite severe.

"*Fuko* is Japanese word for different things. For instance, it can mean, scenery, scenic views, like that, but...in context of *tatari* it would most likely mean misfortune, disaster...and..." he sat thinking.

"*And* what?" Lucien inquired.

"Death."

There was an instant pall over the room, *and I must have looked like the Devil had walked in*. Again, there was a quiet exchange in Japanese with Yuki. I noticed a distinct change in her manner. Mori scratched his temple becoming thoughtful.

"What is it?" Lucien queried in a quiet voice.

"Both words together is...ill-omen." The following minutes seemed like eternity, when Mr. Corbeau broke the silence with his raspy voice.

"See here old boy, what exactly were you doing in that cemetery anyway? If, you don't object to my asking... robbing graves of their corpses?"

Slowly, painfully, I confessed about my indiscretion. The men seemed somewhat amused, however Yuki remained detached failing to share her husband's humorous perspective.

Mori chided her softly, but her manner didn't waver in the least. She seemed to be taking the matter quite seriously and apparently said so openly which was a departure from her previous quiet and innocuous manner. Mori only shrugged, scratched his grizzled chin and lit another cigarette.

"Well, did he say anything else? What did he do next?" Lucien questioned me after an agonizing silence.

"He asked me to wait and then left."

"And did you?"

"For a while, then it began to seem an absurd waste of time...so I left."

"Hmm..." he mused rubbing his long nose, deep in thought. "What do you think about all this Mori-san?" Mori gave a short little shrug.

"I wouldn't worry. Some of these old islanders are full of superstitions." He gave a short glance at Yuki. She grasped his meaning and quietly excused herself disappearing somewhere inside the house for the remainder of the evening.

"I'm sorry Mori-san, I seem to have ruined our evening," I said. He waved his hand exhaling a stream of smoke.

"Don't worry, you've made the evening very memorable," he said and chuckled. "However, next time, pick a better place." This brought more levity and abruptly the conversation turned to other things.

The next day was spent exploring the island. While Yuki taught Koto lessons in town, Mori, Lucien and I took a hike in the jungle and climbed to the summit of Kofuji– Mount Hachijo–the younger volcano that comprised the northern half of the island.

Mori was in fine physical shape, quite athletic and even Lucien, despite his bad leg, kept up a nice steady pace to the summit.

Upon arriving at the top of the volcano, Mori tied a prayer to an old wind-blown tree that seemed to be a favorite for this purpose as there were numerous prayers tied to its withered branches. He also chanted for several minutes, as he was a devout Buddhist.

The caldera was nearly symmetrical and dropped fifty meters or so. We hiked around the rocky rim; all sorts of pathways had been laid well before us. From the top of Mount Hachijo one could see the *lay of the land* quite nicely on this fine sunny day. The airstrip was plainly visible resting amid the low ground connecting Kofuji with its older twin, Mihara to the south. The entire island was completely surrounded by the vast Pacific Ocean. From the summit of the volcano one realized how small and insignificant the island seemed, lost in the grand expanse of ocean.

Before journeying back down the mountain we ate lunch in the nook of two craggy outcrops of rock and Mori-san spoke about the history of Hachijo Island. The small population that inhabits the island could trace their ancestral roots back hundreds of years, since the first settlers arrived, predominately outcast samurai that had been banished to the island in lieu of death or as an alternative to other less favorable fortunes.

"These persons ranged in status from nobles to outright criminals and their bloodlines still exist on the island," Mori informed us. "At different times in history, small groups of warrior clans ruled the island and prayed to a *kami-god* who still *witches* the island to this day,"

"Fascinating," I said.

"There is still a shrine on the island and some of the people still maintain it," he said while he munched on a piece of *onigiri*–a rice ball wrapped in seaweed. "Traditions die hard in Japan."

"I'd like to see that," I said and both men stared at me.

"Really? We could go there this afternoon."

"Let's," I said and caught Lucien's dark eyes scrutinizing me from above his pipe. "Sounds interesting, you agree Lucien?" He took a long time in replying.

"If you like."

A short car ride later–after picking up Anton from the village pub–we were on the edge of the jungle which appeared to have been cleared several years prior, possibly for planting. A thick heavy tropical grass had grown but the big trees and heavy canopy were cut back several hundreds of meters. Mori parked his tiny Peugeot on the shoulder of the road. We followed a thin winding pathway that snaked through the tall grass–well over our heads–in a westerly direction. Soon the grass gave way to a small clearing and as we rounded the stand of trees that obscured it, we all stopped and stood face to face with *Him*.

Who *He* was exactly, not even Mori seemed to know precisely–a great surprise to me since his knowledge of Japan's history and her supernatural beings in the various pantheons seemed immense–yet here *he* sat, this enormous orange-skinned *god of war*, with curled yellow teeth and dark blazing eyelashes adorning wild and angry eyes. Festooned with scant clothing and wielding a fierce scimitar above his head, this *god* posed a formidable and rather frightening visage.

The grounds about him possessed a variety of accoutrements commensurate with his role as a warrior-god. Massive stone *toro* lanterns–perhaps a ton each and centuries old–stood the grounds like sentinels. A fairly large *torii gate* twenty feet in height and painted in a similar orange color as the god, composed the basic elements of the shrine. Mori indicated he believed the torii gate was a much later addition and not part of the original shrine.

"The torii is a Shinto shrine, I believe added much later, probably by priests. It's painted with lacquer from the *Rhus verniciflua*, a tradition. The kami-god is painted with a crushed rock pigment, I believe. Japanese people are very traditional in process and art. Once a certain process is set it never changes, very rarely."

The place was nearly engulfed by the jungle, yet it was obvious that someone was maintaining the site for enough was revealed of the grounds and as such, we were able to circumnavigate the entirety of this rather impressive statue.

The god sat upon an enormous stone block, vaguely in a squatting or *lotus* position but active, not sedate or serene like the *Amida*. It was as if his brilliantly colored body was set to pounce, nearly leaping forth like lava from the pit. The god's arm was raised above his head and in the mighty hand was clenched a large curving scimitar–not the thin elegant symmetrical curve of the Japanese *katana* sword but a thicker heavier version more akin to the Indian or Moorish blade. I sensed a rather Oriental look about the thing and found it grotesque.

To me, the garish apparition seemed oddly out of place on the island–in Japan in fact–with its fierce wild eyes, the eyelashes exploding forth about its enormously dilated pupils floating within putrid yellow eyes that bulged nearly from their sockets. The most unsettling thing was the gnawing feeling that *those eyes were looking right at you*. Wherever one moved, the eyes seemed to follow.

There comes a time in everyone's life where a constant vigilance of life's rhythms and symmetries may reveal inner mysteries. Indeed, it is the mediums and prognostics over the course of history that exploited this careful study to suit their own ends and those of their clans. Chance and coincidence blur and omens present their meanings obliquely, sometimes clearly and direct. In fact, most persons simply refuse to acknowledge or dwell on *omenistic* events when they transpire for fear of being swept into the maelstrom of the *unseen* and *unknowable*, as if life walked a tenuous balance between fate and free-will.

The events that followed fall into these categories, and simple conjecture cannot dispel for me the knowledge that the sinister was afoot and spectral designs were in motion; for the very split second that I stepped beneath the mighty left arm with its colossal blade, *the damn thing came toppling down!*

I recall an awful sound, like the howling of some great beast or enormous wind, followed by the wrenching pull of a great force upon my collar–that I was to learn was Mr. Corbeau–pulling me backwards from certain injury, perhaps death.

Lucien said later that the sound it made was more a shriek than the sound of splitting wood; and thunder when the colossal arm broke apart upon the flagstones. The first words from his mouth, I recall distinctly, were: *'You're alive,'* and then, as he helped me to my feet: *'If Anton hadn't pulled you away...'* I turned toward Mr. Corbeau, picking himself up from the ground, Lucien quickly taking his arm.

"Are you all right Anton?" he asked. The man nodded, all the while keeping a suspicious eye on the statue towering above.

"Ca-va...bien," he muttered under his breath examining his ruined hat and expounding expletives in French. I looked at Mr. Mori, frozen, an unfathomable expression etched upon his lean face. His eyes then locked with mine and the utter shock upon his face imbued a feeling of mortal alarm within my chest.

"How on earth did you accomplish that Anton?" Lucien said in earnest. "It was but a fraction of a second. The bloody thing would have surely killed him!" Mr. Corbeau remained reticent, continuing to give the fractured god an extremely dour look. Lucien then addressed Mori who remained motionless, as if frozen in time. "Are you all right Mori-san?" Mori seemed as if unable to speak and the moment lapsed much longer than I feared I could endure. "Incredible. Look here."

As wont his nature, Lucien was instantly kneeling, examining the broken remains. He had taken note of the shattered arm, examining it closely with a pen from his breast pocket. The wood was wormy with thousands of tiny interlacing tunnels and pustules.

"Why, it's worm eaten through." We gathered about being careful to keep a healthy distance from the thing.

"Let's take leave this bastard lot Lucien," Anton said tossing his spent chapeau aside.

"Yes, quite," Lucien agreed. "The thing's saturated with worms. Amazing it hadn't failed sooner." We all stood back a moment looking up at those grotesque eyes, the war-god staring down at us with its sinister curling smile and spiteful expression.

"Encroyable," Anton said, and they all looked at me simultaneously. Then without another word spoken we quietly left that sullen and gloomy place.

That afternoon we were preparing to dine at Mori's home. Yuki was setting a lovely table of deliciously smelling food upon the low table in beautiful hand-made *yakimono* dishes. The men all sat cross-legged on the *tatami* mats. With the customary formal bow, we proceeded to dine in silence. Yuki suddenly became aware of our sullen dispositions and questioned us about it.

I felt reticent, reluctant to discuss it. However, Mori eagerly began to describe the afternoon's proceedings. When he got to the part about the shrine's arm falling, she inadvertently gasped and dropped her bowl of miso, spilling its contents across the table.

How long she actually sat there with her delicate hands across her mouth I don't remember, but the incrementally slow turn of her eyes to mine seemed like an eternity. She silently stared at me, into me, her dark eyes searching mine, and it was as if I could read her thoughts; like picking the words one by one from the gentle basket that was her soul.

When evening sullenly arrived, the four of us men decided to go to the *onsen* on the west side of the island.

An *onsen* is a natural hot spring endemic throughout Japan. Hot mineral water is forced to the surface by geothermal pressure and pooled in natural or man-made ponds. They are refreshing and exceedingly healthy.

The onsen on the *nishi-kaigan*–western beach–on Hachijojima Island is a grouping of man-made structures, interior and exterior pools, and a series of natural ponds that stagger slowly down the black volcanic rock in a winding pattern to the sea. Near twilight, the ocean's waves create an astonishing effect as they hurl relentlessly onto the ebony rock causing brilliant translucent blue and white hues cradled in effervescent misty foam; the smell of salt on the breeze.

We had taken the furthest-most pool from the building that, its torch lighted vestibules welcoming the local guests. We busied ourselves dipping into the mineralized waters until the heat would chase us back out again, then sit on the edge with only our legs submerged and drink sake from the several large bottles we had brought with us that lent itself perfectly to this type of engagement. The light playing off the Pacific was near mystical, the waves, in fact the very air itself steeped in the deep rich tones of twilight.

Mori sat on the stone rim with a small white cloth atop his head and a cigarette between his teeth, engaged in conversation with Lucien. Anton seemed lost in his private thoughts–and drink–while I tried to relax between the heat of the pool and the crisp coolness of the rapidly approaching night. I study my colleagues; Mori as I described him, Lucien smoking his pipe engrossed by their conversation and Anton, whose heavy hairy body–*with an incredible array of scars*–was in stark contrast to the other's lean frames.

I gazed down the black shoreline out toward the horizon. Small specks of light on the water, ships, blended with the first stars to create a surreal landscape and I found myself, strangely, wishing I could journey there, into the ethereal blue mist of the mighty endless ocean for an eternity.

Mr. Corbeau drained the last liquid from one of the large brown sake bottles and tossed it to one side. He drank to soften the pain he felt–physical and mental–*he was a man out of time, lost in the modern world.* I felt pity for him. His eyes locked with mine and I sensed the rage within him; always just behind the thin gossamer plane that was the dichotomous reality of his life. He seemed to be looking through me.

"Not to alarm you mon-ami but how do you feel about what transpired today?" All conversation ceased as if all had been waiting to address this sensitive issue but reluctant to speak of it.

"What do you mean? The statue's arm falling?"

"Of course that's what I mean you idiot!" he snarled procuring another bottle of his sake and wrenching the top from it. It was as if *the furies* had suddenly been released and the dark night became alive; shadows leapt from their hidden recesses and the waves pitched and crashed violently on the rocks below.

"I'm not sure," I murmured.

"Well, I've been thinking about that. What you said about the old dotard in the graveyard...your desecrating an ancient tomb and then buggering off before making amends...and Mori's wife reacting as she did. She's a native islander isn't that so Mori-san?" he asked our congenial host.

"Hai, so desu," he responded nodding. "She is very concerned."

"Of course she is. She knows this island's history. The legends. Islands are peculiar. They're different than the mainlands. Their energies more condensed, intensified." He paused a moment staring. "A blind man could see your predicament with his fingers."

"What do you mean?"

"What do I mean?" He looks at the others. "What do I mean gentlemen?" He laughed, a loud cruel laugh. "Your head was nearly split wide you damn fool! Oh, and certainly not inauspiciously. Why no. Not a loose rock or an old tree limb; a burning auto wreck. No...*by the blade of the holy pagan god himself!*" he snorted and drank deeply from the bottle. All remained silent while he wiped the side of his mouth with the small white towel around his neck. "You're in quite a predicament I should say my arrogant young friend, and I'm curious to know what you intend to do about it?" I suddenly began to dislike his tone and felt a sudden anger rage within me.

"If you're trying to get a rise out of me," I said loudly, "it won't work." He began to laugh–that same vitriolic laugh–staring at me with dark wolf-like eyes.

"That's right, that's all this is...a jest...a bit of malicious fun for the amusement of our illustrious little group. Nothing more than a mere game...like mumbly-peg...except there's more than a stuck finger at stake dear boy, wouldn't you agree?" I said nothing, glaring at the man with disdain. He took an enormously long draught from the bottle and rising, tramped off naked toward the surf.

Later that night back at Mori's home, as I slept atop a soft billowy futon, my troubled mind meandered in and out of a restless half-sleep; something kept buzzing in my ear. Mosquitoes?

Suddenly I found myself back on the deck of the ferryboat that had brought me to Hachijojima. This time all was dark and grey, not the early painted dawn I encountered on my earlier voyage. I was quite aware that I was dreaming and verged on waking myself or staying on to experience the dream. Three chestnut-brown junks were sailing in tandem–just as I saw them in real life–however this time they were treading the waters in the same direction. This time, the ships were peopled with a host of dark grim warriors on their bow and aft decks. They wore old trappings from a bygone era and their countenances were stark and severe. Something about the look of these men was upsetting to me. I tried to go below but could not move my body from where I stood. I awoke just before dawn, drenched in a heavy sweat.

That morning, after Mori had finished working in town, we decided to slate a curiosity we all shared regarding the tunnels constructed by the islanders during World War Two.

Shortly after a noonday lunch, the four of us geared-up and went *spelunking*. This warrants a brief introduction. During World War Two, as the American forces began their inexorable advance upon the Japanese homeland, Japan commenced an enormous defense program throughout her string of islands. Hachijojima was not spared this aggressive campaign of tunnel building and fortification.

The island's population was purportedly conscripted to cut a web of underground tunnels and rooms, hewn from the lava rock that comprised the ground between its twin volcanoes; an area that presented the best–in fact only–option for an amphibian assault.

It was into this subterranean morass of passages we delved that afternoon. At first it was difficult to find, despite Mr. Mori having been there on dozens of occasions. Eventually, on the backside of a small plantation that specialized in exotic tropical palms, Mori was able to locate a small rather innocuous entrance in the rock, nearly obscured by grass and hanging vines. This proved to be an old machine-gun emplacement. The hole was just large enough for two, possibly three men; the tunnel quickly descended nearly a dozen feet before levelling out into a horizontal passage.

We gathered around this tiny orifice to the underworld excited but nervous. It was at this juncture Mr. Corbeau confided his disinterest in joining our endeavor. He had brought along a book–Camus–a flask, and his filter-less Gitane cigarettes and prepared himself for a quiet vigil at the entrance. Mori offered him his keys to the Peugeot suggesting he'd be more comfortable back at the car but he declined, saying–oddly–that it was better he remain at the portal.

As I mentioned, Mori had taken this adventure previously. He belonged to a sort of makeshift club of amateurs; tunnellers and war enthusiasts, who had set about mapping the entire system. We had come equipped with a number of ingenious devices, none of which proved more valuable than the head lanterns; lightweight plastic caps that held small battery-operated lamps to one's forehead allowing the freedom of both hands.

This device proved invaluable because the tunnels under Hachijo Island were anything but level or uniform. They meandered about in a multitude of directions; some requiring climbing up or down extreme vertical inclines. Many slick with moisture.

What struck me the most was the intricacy of the tunnel system. It traversed an enormous amount of space and was hewn, by hand, from the living rock; the chisel and hammer marks still evident in the stone.

Most of these tunnels were about four to five feet in height, some taller. Here and there positioned strategically about were rooms cut out large enough to berth a company or platoon of soldiers. There were several of these rooms and the entire tunnel system must have spanned kilometers.

Occasionally an upward vertical shaft would lead to a small overgrown opening to the outside. Closer inspection usually revealed these holes to be machine-gun and mortar ports, for they were generally built to contain two or three men at most and constructed to afford the best possible protection and accessibility; if breached, it was obvious, by design, that the tunnel opening could be sealed off with hidden charges, detonated from below.

These vertical *pinch-points* were so tight that an average sized man would be required to twist and turn his body to make the shaft below. I nearly got stuck, which I must admit is an unsettling experience when one is underground in literal darkness. In fact, the longer we explored underground the more nervous I became. I suggested to my colleagues that we return to the surface and quit the tunnels for the day.

However, Mori was like a child with a new toy. His sense of adventure and thrill of exploring this alien world, replete with the debris of war would not be quelled, at least not until we had penetrated an area of the system that was still relatively unexplored; nothing but vague outlines on a hand-drawn map. Regrettably, I agreed to go on.

This area proved to be much more strenuous than the tunnels we had already visited. This series of subterranean channels seemed to take advantage of natural anomalies in the lava beds, for parts were hewn out and other passages seemed to follow a more natural pattern; not following any particular symmetrical design save those dictated by Nature herself.

Again, I found myself pleading with my stalwart companions to quit that dark dank place and return to the sunshine and fresh air above. Mori then got the foolish idea–in an effort to save time–to separate at a particular junction where the tunnel split left and right. He was certain that the two rejoined further ahead, creating a loop, and was adamant about confirming this on his map. I disliked the idea but when he agreed to quit for the day if we proved his theory correct, I agreed to pursue the endeavor and be done with it. I chose the right, *on an impatient whim*, and proceeded into the bosom of the unknown.

It was perhaps ten minutes into the tunnel when I began to realize that it was not circling back toward the left, as it should if Mori's prediction were correct. Instead, this bleak passage continued a slow but steady descent ever downward. I began to wonder exactly how deep I was going. Then, just at the point I decided I would turn back, *my light failed!*

Try as I would, I could not get the damnable thing to relight. It simply quit and there I was, in utter darkness, without even the ability *to see my hand before my eyes!* I also realized, morbidly, that Mori possessed the emergency hand torch we had brought along as a spare. My heart began to race, and a profuse sweat began to drip from my forehead stinging my now useless eyes. It was with a great effort that I was able to calm myself and return my breathing to anything close to normal.

The air was suffocating, stale as a tomb. I began to call out for my companions, my voice reverberating harshly off the stone. I strained to hear a response but there was none. I repeated this ritual a number of times until it became quite evident that Mori and Lucien were entirely out of earshot. I would have to retrace my steps back in the darkness to the fork of the main tunnel where hopefully they would hear my calls.

I commenced to crawl my way back from whence I'd come, inching my way in the absolute darkness; and I will tell you that this strained my courage to the brink. I cannot begin to explain the variety of thoughts, sensations and fears–verily, the sheer sense of dread–that one encounters when *lost in the darkness underground.* The knowledge that one is entombed underground, deep within the bowels of the earth, beneath tons of rock and dirt–lost and without the aid of one's sight or navigational accoutrements–sends an ice-like terror coursing throughout the body and torments the mind with primal fear.

As if *buried within a coffin alive,* the stone closed in on me like a cold steel trap and ebony phantoms emerged from the rock, painting phantasmagoria upon the canvas of my fertile imagination.

This slow inching trek back from the land of the dead, finger by finger, was truly the most horrific experience of my life, and it was about to get worse.

I proceeded back up the shaft, in the direction of the main tunnel, favoring the right wall, using its rough surface and the ground beneath as my guides; however, something had gone amiss. Suddenly, to my astonishment–and abject terror–I found that I was at a dead end, the rock-face blocking my forward progress, *as if I had been purposefully entombed!*

Panic began to surge wildly out of control. I moved quickly to collect my wild emotions and channel my energy, calling out repeatedly for Lucien and Mori but, alas, to no avail. A thick pervasive silence and welling sense of despair swept over me, engulfing me. I felt as if I were losing my faculties. It took several minutes of concerted effort to calm myself again and consider my dilemma.

Obviously, I reasoned, I had veered from the main ascending tunnel and inadvertently taken a sidetrack. I cursed my lack of attention and realized that the stress I was feeling of being underground so long was clouding my analytic abilities, for normally, I'm very observant when travelling in new and unknown places. Somehow, I had missed this sidetrack, a hidden off-shoot on my way down. I reasoned to myself, if I continued back down, holding my right, I would regain the ascending tunnel, which would lead me upward toward the primary where I had parted company with Lucien and Mori. Once at the fork I could wait it out until they found me. I certainly would have a better chance of being heard.

I inched my way back downward, leaving the wall of stone behind; using my fingers as a blind man uses a cane. In an effort to make up lost time–or perhaps falling prey to a gnawing sense of panic–I began moving faster than before, taking steps rather than crawling. Suddenly my feet gave way from underneath me and I felt myself falling down a vertical shaft and *plunging into the blackness of frigid fetid water!*

Like an animal suddenly snared in a trap, or being devoured alive, I was instantly swallowed by a chilling aquatic terror. I began to frantically thrash about, scratching and clawing at the walls, seeking a hold or toe-hole to secure myself and free my body of the icy grip around my throat. After several minutes of this fruitless pursuit, and through an enormous effort of personal will, I attempted to collect myself and set about circumnavigating the walls to gain an exit from the pit. Eventually–*to my horror*–the reality of the situation began to thread itself into my consciousness.

I had fallen into *what must have been designed as a trap*–or perhaps it was a storage cache that, seventy years ago, would have been covered over with heavy wood planking, now rotted away. It was a vertical shaft definitely hewn by hand for I could discern small chisel indentations but there seemed to be no cracks, nooks or portals of any kind for which to escape. I began to panic, shouting at the top of my lungs and the sound that issued forth was vulgar and wild, like an animal bellowing in the darkness. This use of my air sent me down into the water like a lead weight.

I was in over my neck in water but also knew there was a bottom, for I felt its touch when I submerged. I realized–to my utter horror–that I was trapped in a rectilinear stone box of sheer walls.

Trying–fruitlessly–to access an upper ledge, all seemed in vain. By holding my breath and floating, I continued to feel the walls for any type of hold, anything to leverage myself up and out of the pit's icy grip. However, it became quite clear very quickly that I was desperately trapped, and that my only hope was Mori and Lucien. Again, I began to scream at the top of my lungs but all this accomplished was floundering and a lung full of fetid water. I began to panic, caught in a nightmarish grip of terror.

It was extant that if I didn't get possession of myself– and quickly–I would undoubtedly drown. With a mammoth effort of will, I was able to control my fear and breathing. By taking in a large volume of air and laying my head backwards I was able to float momentarily in the pit and rest my rapidly tiring limbs. Then, by exhaling and allowing myself to dip below the waterline a moment, I could again re-emerge, take air, float and attempt to collect my wits and search for an escape. Soon enough it became increasingly evident that it was impossible to scale the walls. There were no niches to grab and the shortest width of the trap was too wide to leverage my body to scale the walls.

I was in over my head and tiring quickly when by sheer chance upon one of my failed attempts to leap up grabbing for roots, or anything I might get hold of in the dark, my foot knocked against something on the pit floor.

By *submerging myself into the dreaded ebony water*, I realized that a large rock, probably fallen from the roof of the cave, sat upon the pit floor and by repeatedly submerging and moving this toward a corner of the pit, I was able to stand and keep my head above water.

Thus, had become my state of affairs; trapped in a sarcophagus hewn out seventy some years prior by indentured servants. There I teetered, standing precariously upon a rock in utter blackness, up to my neck in water; hovering in a corner like a frightened creature awaiting the inevitability of hypothermia. *It was a nightmare from which I was unable to awaken.*

Bellowing repeatedly at the top of my lungs, I waited, praying for a sound. All was utter stillness and solitude. I repeated this over and over again, for how long I cannot say, but nothing, save blackness and the omnipresence of desperation and fear, answered my calls.

By placing my feet against one wall and my hands on the opposite, I attempted to *walk* myself from this hellish dungeon, but the trap was too well prepared and its dimensions too far apart for my six-foot frame. No matter what little progress I could make I inevitably fell back into that sickeningly vile pool of stagnant filth, only to emerge gasping and grasping for a foothold. Eventually I became too weak to continue this hopeless process and could only stand on my rock in the corner and pray.

Continuing to call out for help until my voice became hoarse and began to falter, I slowly succumbed to a harrowing thought; that I would die like this, perched on a rock, water lapping at my neck. I realized by the time a rescue party could be amassed I would fall prey to the chilling water and drown.

More out of desperation, I began to attempt to climb out using the small indentations left by the hammer and chisels. This only proceeded to bloody my fingertips raw until I could no longer stand the pain. I recalled morbid stories of persons who mistakenly–or other–*had been buried alive*, only to be exhumed by the living and found with their nails and fingers torn and shredded by their futile attempts at freedom. I began to imagine all sorts of horrid visages of my dead bloated body floating like a balloon or shrieking like an emaciated skeleton, mouth held wide with the terror of death in such a place.

Had I been down in the pit for many hours or was it only minutes? My mind seemed to have lost the ability to reason, for reason flees from such places.

Despite my innate fear of dark water, I plunged down repeatedly to feel the bottom for any kind of tool or implement to assist my cause, perhaps an old bayonet, but only a conglomerate of loose rock and gravel greeted my touch. Eventually, I could no longer endure submerging myself in such a foul pool and could only take my solemn position atop the rock in the corner and call out into the abyss.

My voice began to echo strangely; I began to imagine I could *hear the rock vibrate as if alive.* Each crescendo of my voice created a distinct cascading effect that rippled down the course of the stone as if it were flowing with the vibrations. The sensation was mystifying. I played this game for quite a period of time, nearly forgetting the pit that held me in its grip until my voice grew so hoarse and vulgar, I could no longer endure the sound of it.

Was it my imagination or was the stone aglow? Small infinitesimal specks of light that seemed to outline my prison in a feeble light; but as I stretched out my hand to touch the light my numb feet inevitably would slip from the rock and I would plunge once again into a frigid darkness, like the icy grip of eternity, all returning to blackness and silence once more.

Slowly, my legs, in fact my entire body, became numb, void of sensation. The ghastly realization that I would soon be unable to keep my head above the water arose a feeling of morbidity within me so deep and profound that in the darkness I began weeping. Strangely, it was as if listening to someone else mourning; a strange feeling of total detachment most likely brought on by my rapidly deteriorating condition, for my body was now completely numb and only a minute shaking caused by the cold water and fatigued muscles gave me any impression that I was still alive. *Then I heard it.*

Was it my imagination creating illusions in my tormented mind? Was I becoming delirious? Then I heard it again, somewhat louder, but what was it…the baying of a hound, in this underworld? Such a thing could never be. I was losing control of my mind; this was insanity setting in. I shouted out my rage at the top of my lungs and it sounded like a pitiful wailing, as an injured beast gnashing and clawing in the wilds attempts to stave off death. I waited again for the silence to enfold me but this time, there *was* a response; louder, clearer, *coming closer with a heavy horrid breathing, a deep guttural intonation, and it was staring down at me from the darkness above!*

What was this thing, a wild animal come to devour my corpse? I expected the worst when a most amazing thing happened. In a loud growl nearly more animal than human, *I heard my name.* Frozen and silent, unable to fully grasp what had befallen me, I could make out a deep guttural breathing; then again, as before, my name, albeit louder and with animosity.

"Who is it? Who's there?" I croaked. My voice barely audible. There was a moment's pause then an animal-like growl.

"Reach me your hand!" I was afraid, indecisive. "Reach me your hand you sniveling coward!" the voice boomed in the darkness.

"Anton? Mister Corbeau?" I said into the darkness above me. "Is it you?" It was as if a savior had arrived *in the guise of the devil himself.* I feebly tried to raise my arm, but it was as if it were dead; weighted and useless.

"You slimy little bastard, I said reach up here! Reach man, or by *Hades* I swear I'll rip your bloody heart out!" Was this just another strange outlandish delusion? How could such a thing as this be real? How could he be here in this cavernous darkness, without light or a guide? Again, I attempted to throw my arm up above my head; pain shot through my shoulder, but I was just able to grasp at the wall above me and stretch out my fingers. I could hear him straining from above, cursing horribly, but try as I would, I could not grasp his hand, nor feel his grip upon my sleeve.

Then, my arm failed of its own accord and went limp crashing back into the cold water. There was a terrible commotion above as if he were wrestling with some demon in the dark.

All went quiet for a moment and it occurred to me, I was waking from a dream. I called out expecting only the silence and the darkness spit and howled.

"Listen, you pitiful miscreant. Do you want to die down here, like a rat in a trap? If I return to the world above, you'll never get out of this filthy pit alive. You're at the end of your noose my friend."

"Yes…" I groaned.

"I could just as easily return empty handed. Who would be the wiser?" he sneered in the dark and a bolt of dread coursed my soul.

"Don't leave me here." He laughed and it was that vitriolic laugh I had heard from him on other occasions.

"Why? You care not to help yourself, why should I risk falling into your snug little dungeon and join you?" His guttural breathing was like a saw against wood.

"Please, just light your flame so I can see about me. I'm sure that would help me navigate."

"What! And show you my hideous face?!" he bellowed and it was like the sound of a tempest. "You vermin! Don't you realize what it has taken to find you? You sorry wretch! How else could I find you in this tomb but to smell you out?"

"I…don't know what you mean." He snarled and it was not the utterance of a man but similar to the canine species. I began to realize the scent of wet dogs atop the fetid pool.

"Admit it. You've always despised me, loathed my presence, judged me on your own standards without regard…without regard." He became silent. I could actually *feel* him staring down from above.

"I know…" I said.

"You admit to it?" he said with a tone of astonishment.

"Yes, but not because I loathe you."

"What then?!" he demanded, and the walls echoed.

"Fear. I'm afraid of you," I said and waited for what seemed an eternity of silence. Suddenly I could sense him closer, I could hear his voice nearer.

"You agree to pay for my sacrifice?" he whispered in the dark. I agreed. "Then stretch yourself man. Reach! Reach until *your bloody bones crack!*"

I could hear scratching, clawing, upon the rock just above me as if some wild animal where frantically pawing the stone. With every ounce of energy left in my body I forced my frame, legs and limbs to extend upward toward the sounds issuing forth and this time I felt a hand. I grasped *at the mane on the back of the hand* and clutched with all my might. Like lightning, I felt him twist his hand about and the nails slice into the flesh of my wrist. I stifled a cry of pain and grabbed at his sleeve slamming my other arm hard against the rock above, securing more of the arm and–holding on for dear life–I felt him raise me from the grip of that damnable pit like a man extracts a drowning child from an icy river.

I recall several nightmarish dreams. In the first dream I was riding the back of a large beast (a horse?) as it galloped through an ebony night. I remember digging my fingers painfully into the creature's mane and holding on as it bounded, the darkness closing in all around me. The horse galloped wildly through the darkness; knocked me at every turn; the sound of baying hounds at our heels pushing us wildly on.

In the second dreaming–and its relentless repetitions–I was on a dark windy hillside. Below me I watched in horror as Mr. Corbeau engaged *several dark and fierce Samurai warriors* wielding long silver *katana* swords and brandishing them in the moonlight. The blades reflected the silver light of the moon as they cut and sliced at his ebony torso.

Anton raged forth, fighting fiercely, a wild half-animal, with outstretched claws and fangs he would bury into his assailants, his mighty fists scattering them like ragdolls; yet try as he could to elude them, they continued to hound him relentlessly; like a pack of wolves attacking a grizzly bear, remorselessly pursuing the larger animal's every step, attacking singularly or in carefully choreographed groups.

I watched this nightmare unfold, unable to make my body move. As if caught in a quagmire, I watched helplessly as they parried back and forth across the hillside slashing at him mercilessly. This unsettling dream did not diminish but returned to haunt my sleep repeatedly, night after night, each time as intense as the night before. I became fearful of its ferocity and utter strangeness.

When I finally came to my senses, I was in a deep sweat and feverish, lying on a white tufted futon. Sunlight (sunlight!) filtered in through an open shoji door and small birds–sparrows–piped about the balcony, picking at seeds scattered across a fine wooden surround.

In the distance, above the tops of green trees, rolled large billowy white clouds. A soft cool breeze wafted through and tickled a small iron bell that hung just outside the shutters.

I wondered for a moment *if I were possibly dead?* Perhaps this was the fabled afterlife? It was certainly serene enough. I tried to lift myself and instantly a pain shot through my head forcing me to lie still. I realized that both my hands and head were heavily bandaged. I wasn't dead. I had survived my ordeal and the details of my subterranean adventure slowly crept back into my consciousness.

I sensed I was being watched. Ever so slowly I turned my head in the direction of the hall and there stood a small Japanese boy, no older than three or four years of age, watching me. We stared at each other a moment. He poked and prodded his nostril with a grimy forefinger. His soiled shirt had a small picture of a yellow bear in a red shirt with the word *'Pooh'* written beneath in Roman. I lifted my bandaged hand towards him to gesture and this caused an immediate look of alarm upon his face and he screamed and ran out of the room shouting down the hallway at the top of his lungs:

"Gaijin daiyo! Gaijin daiyo!" Soon an elderly Japanese woman entered and upon seeing me shouted back out the bedroom door.

"Oide, oide...hayaku, hayaku!" An aged man in a rich *yukata* robe entered and quickly took my side. They attended to me carefully inspecting my bandages and mopping the moisture from my face and arms; all the while conversing softly in their native tongue. He checked my pupils with a small light and said something with intent, upon which she bowed. *"Hai,"* she exhaled loudly and instantly left the room. He gazed at me through his wire spectacles.

"Daijobu desu ka?" He was asking if I felt all right. I feebly nodded. He smiled, felt at my bandaged wrist, apparently checking the pulse of my heart, then rose and left the room. Soon after, Lucien and Mori joined me by my bedside.

"How are you holding up young man?" Lucien asked, a genuinely rare smile upon his face.

"Where am I?"

"The local healer's home. You've been unconscious for two days."

"Two days?" I echoed incredulous.

"You were chilled to the bone and shaking like a rattle when we found you."

"You found me? Where is…?"

"Anton?" Lucien answered my half question. "Gone. We searched and searched the tunnel you had taken but you must have deviated dramatically. When night began to fall, we had no recourse but to arrange a search party while Anton remained behind. When we returned to the tunnel entrance, you were lying on the ground with his coat over you in a fevered delirium; *looking like the devil had had you."*

"How he found you…" Mori said solemnly unable to finish his sentence. "I am so happy," he said bowing, obviously feeling the bitter dregs of his decision to separate. Lucien asked if I might take some soup. I agreed feeling a great pang of hunger inside me. Mori excused himself to retrieve it and Lucien drew up close to my ear and whispered.

"Do you remember anything?" I recounted the entire story to him from the moment we separated to the moment Anton pulled me from the pit like a rag-doll.

He listened in silence, his eyes intent, with an inner gleam. When my narrative was over, I questioned him about my rescuer; he seemed reticent. I pressed him. Just as he was about to answer Mori, and the old woman, entered with a tray of miso soup, pickles and rice and the subject was dropped. It was later when I was more myself that I learned he had travelled back to Shanghai, but there was an aspect of the story not addressed that I believe was on Lucien's mind.

One thing that continued to haunt me was that same recurring dream–or nightmare–for the subsequent several nights during my convalescence. Though aspects of the dream changed, the basic premise remained night after night.

In the dream I was walking under the moonlight across the plains somewhere on the island when I became aware of a commotion upon the hillside. Upon further inspection I realized to my horror that Anton was engaged in an on-going battle with the same group of fierce samurai warriors. The dream was always in black and white, or dark muted tones, except the distinct red of blood. The group slashed at him viciously with their swords shimmering under the moonlight and Mr. Corbeau was *fury incarnate, garish, half man half wolf.* He pounced upon them *baring long hideous claws and gnashing yellow teeth.* However, fight as he would, their pursuit of him was relentless. Backed up against a rock face on the hillside he would leap into their rank and file and maul one or two of their number, wildly tossing the body aside like paper only to be chased again to some other cleft or tree-lined hillock *and the whole ordeal commence over again.*

It was awful to watch. Try as I might to join him, I was always impeded by some great force, some great form of *gravity* that held me in check as if I were trying to tread thick viscous water clothed in heavy wool. Each time this dream appeared to me–and it was every night since the mishap–I awoke in a pool of sweat, breathing heavily and weary as if I had been engaged in some extraordinary endeavor.

It was a few nights after my near fatal evening underground when Lucien knocked at my bedroom door one evening.

"I need to leave tomorrow," he remarked casually. "I've asked Mori to look after you and he's agreed to have you stay on here as long as you need."

"What do you mean?" I asked surprised. "I'm fit to travel. My hands are healing rapidly." He stared at me in the twilight and his piercing eyes were rather uncomfortable.

"You don't intend to return to the cemetery and remedy the situation?" I was quite shocked by this sudden admission. I looked at him with surprise.

"Do you realize what you're saying?" I asked.

"Implicitly," he said not wavering. I stared at my hands, deep in thought.

"What can be done?"

"Well, if I were you old chum, I'd go back and see the grave-keeper, follow his advice." I stared at him dumbfounded.

"You believe in this…this curse business?"

"I believe in *omens and what they portend*," he said pulling the shoji open and lighting his pipe.

I watched as the thin smoke, silhouetted against the waning moon, circled and formed strange patterns against the deep indigo of the night sky.

"It is less, primitive superstition than intelligence to comprehend the invisible qualities inherent in life," he expounded. "For after all my friend, what is life but energy, and what is energy but consciousness?"

"Why didn't you speak of this with me sooner? You know I respect your opinions deeply."

"How can you learn, become the Adept you have the potential to be, with me constantly critiquing your processes?" he exhaled. I shrugged.

"I had no idea you considered me in this light," I said, and he laughed softly.

"You think I keep you around for your bookkeeping? Tut tut..." he said and returned his gaze at the sliver of moon that studied us from its place above. "Office management is hardly your calling Willem." I could hardly conceal my disappointment. He tapped the ash of his pipe into the ashtray on the rail and commenced to return downstairs.

"Lucien," I said, detaining him. "What happened to Mr. Corbeau? Is he all right?" He looked at me and his expression although not dark, was neither light.

"Anton saw the omens gathering about you. This is an ability of his, to perceive these things so many of our kind regard as fancy. He knew something would happen at the caves as he knew something would happen at the shrine. How he knows this *I cannot tell you*."

"But, in the cave...in the darkness with no light or..." my voice trailed off.

"*His affliction, was your salvation* my friend," he said. "We got him well off the island a-right, let's leave it at that. He's with Madame Houri, in Asia for the time being."

"Lucien, I've been having strange dreams about him." I began to elaborate when he held up his hand.

"To a psychologist, dreams are the machinations of the mind's restless nature. To an *initiate*, they can sometimes be the ethereal voice of the higher self, consider wisely." With a warm handshake and slight nod of his head he exited the room.

It was a challenge to my overtly rational self–and its unbending grip upon my attention–but the simple fact had always been there, that I too had become aware of the rather ominous events subsequent my visit to that lonely graveyard. Thus, it was that the following morning, I rented a small vehicle from the local station and retracing the quiet meandering road, skirting the ancient volcano, found myself standing in that same solemn place.

It was a balmy morning, having rained very early. I fanned the humidity from my brow–perhaps it was nervousness–and peered about; all was quiet. Oddly, there were no birds tittering about the foliage and nary a soul could be seen or heard. I retraced my steps to the site in question and stared at the monolith. It was extremely old and quite grand. Although I could not decipher the Kanji characters inlaid upon the stone, it was obvious to me that this monument marked the burial site of a distinguished person. I studied it a moment before following the same tiny path the old man had taken over the hillock.

Some thirty or forty meters further on, I spied a small shack made of wood shingling. I surmised it to be a work shed; all about it was littered with tools; shovels, rakes and brooms, many made of bamboo. A multitude of stone slabs, some monuments, others for retaining walls, were piled about in controlled chaos. I also noted lots of fresh wood shavings, poles and stumps and newly fashioned *toba*. Underneath a makeshift canopy of palm fronds, a *tatami mat* was in the process of being stretched.

As I gazed about the retreat, I heard a familiar, '*Oye,*' and turned to see the bent old man ambling along the soft curving path that snaked on into the recesses of the jungle. He greeted me genuinely. His face shone brightly as he bowed his head in a series of quick jerks.

"Anata- ka?" he said pointing at me.

"Hai, watashi-desu," I responded and bowed deeply. He spoke vigorously in his native tongue and I asked politely, "Yukuri, onegaishimasu. Nihongo, wakarimasen," I said asking him to talk slower; that I wasn't fluent in Japanese. He slowed his conversation and looked me over intensely, his eyes agleam.

"Genki desu ka?" he asked directly, and I shook my head.

"*Tatari,*" I said, and he nodded, his eyes shining.

"Ah, so neh," he said emphatically, ushering me to a wooden bench, then the odd old bone disappeared into his shed. He soon re-emerged carrying a small iron kettle and two hand-made ceramic cups without handles. The kettle contained green tea and rice and we sipped tea together. His demeanor was relaxed but attentive. He seemed to be considering me deeply without being rude.

After a while I began to wonder if we were just passing time. He continued to speak to me–sporadically–in his native tongue. I did my best to decipher his words and meaning but I must admit most of it was beyond my comprehension.

My lack of ability with his native tongue seemed of little concern to him as we continued our tea. He seemed to be a genuine sort of spirit, amicable and friendly. When the pot neared its bottom he again disappeared into his shack, returning promptly with a small cloth bundle and a small white scroll, wrapped with a silk thread, which he handed to me and we set off *in the direction of the grave.*

We prostrated ourselves before the monolith in traditional *seiza* style–the technique of sitting upon the back of the calves with the soles of the feet facing upwards–and commenced to bow our heads low to the ground with the palms of both hands resting upon the earth underneath the forehead.

After the initial genuflection, he withdrew from the bundle a thin white candle, perhaps five inches in length and a box of matches. He placed the candle in a small clay holder and lit it, placing it on the ground between the grave stone and where we kneeled. He clapped his hands together three times and held the palms together, before his forehead, addressing the grave. He seemed to be uttering a prayer, his eyes closed tightly; the hands held rigidly.

After a minute or two, he again retrieved the small silk package and produced a bundle of incense sticks, perhaps thirty in all, and split the load in two and handed me one half.

"Thank you."

He held the ends of his sticks in the flame of the candle catching them on fire and gestured for me to do the same. Shaking the flame out with a quick efficient jerk, he placed the bundle of smoldering sticks horizontally upon the stone base of the monument and implied I do likewise. Once the sticks were neatly laid and smoking, we again bowed deeply, his head actually making contact with the earth. Returning to the upright position, he once again clapped his hands together sharply and held them in supplication and began to chant with a deep rich intonation that quite surprised me, coming from such an aged person. We repeated this several times–without a break–for several minute intervals. It was a long drawn out process, methodical and time-consuming.

The pain in my legs, that I initially felt so acutely, slowly subsided due primarily to the warm tones of his chanting. I became light and unencumbered. The quality of the intonation was impeccable. I could feel the vibration touching every part of my inner body.

We repeated this process a countless number of times. I must admit the concept of *time itself,* was lost to me; in fact, I felt strangely free of it, and this feeling imparted a symbiotic sense of joy within me. I could feel the soft breeze expand my sense of self and the tired old bag of bones that I referred to as *'me'* was simply not available for its incessant commentary.

Then abruptly, the chanting ended. I opened my eyes and was surprised to see my acquaintance with his arm extended toward me, the palm open. At first, I was utterly confused; what was he doing?

His eyes shone brightly, and his demeanor was smiling. He continued to hold his palm toward me, nodding at the grave with a small gesture of his head.

I realized–to my embarrassment–that he was asking for an offering, a gift to the spirit against whom I had trespassed. I was taken aback; I had not anticipated–nor prepared myself–for this moment, although it seemed obviously natural. I reached into my pocket and withdrew my wallet and procured a respectable amount of yen notes. When I attempted to give this to him, his demeanor changed radically. I realized, abashedly, that the offer was coarse and vulgar. I felt awkward and stupid. What possible aesthetic value would money have *to the spirit of the dead?* This demanded a real gift, something given from the heart…but what?

My attention wandered to the ring on my right hand. I carried a most special silver and onyx ring, that had been given to me as a gift from a Navaho man, on one of my journeys to that remote area of the American desert. It was a very special ring to me; something I treasured. *Before my mind could prevent it*, I slipped the large silver piece from my finger and handed it to him. He received it graciously as if attuned to the loss I felt upon its departure.

He placed the ring upon the headstone and returned to his supplication and chanting, which–remarkably–went on for no less than thirty, possibly forty more minutes; only taking time out to light more incense. I recall floating between thoughts of discomfort and awe at what the old bone was attempting to accomplish on my behalf. However, I was resolute not to *succumb to my mind's chattering and complaining*.

Finally, near my point of exhaustion with the whole affair, he broke off his resonant mutterings and became absolutely still and silent. I quieted my breathing and listened. The old man cocked his head off toward our left in the direction that was west of us. I instinctively followed his manner, remaining still and attentive. I studied the thick pervasive jungle that engulfed us. What had caught his attention? I could see some of the gray sky that hovered above the distant western horizon; was it storm clouds or the advent of twilight?

How long had we actually sat there staring into the twilight, I couldn't fathom to guess. I studied my odd host; without doubt *something had drawn his attention to the trees.* I gazed about but nothing, save the wind, stirred amongst the branches. What on earth was he staring at?

Then I saw it, something flitting deep within the umbrage; a momentary dark flash within the shadows between the leaves and boughs. Suddenly–quite unexpectedly–an enormous raven, with huge penetrating black eyes emerged from the upper canopy and perched, rather impertinently, upon a large limb staring down at us. Its eyes were piercing, as it studied us for several minutes. Slowly, but not necessarily cautiously, it advanced closer, flitting from branch to branch, ever resuming its inquisitive posture. I looked over at the old man, expecting him to resume the mantra but he continued to stare intently at the ebony fowl.

The bird teetered about limb to limb, always drawing just a little closer. What was he so mesmerized by? Perhaps the chanting had attracted him? Again, the dark fowl stretched its massive wings and hovered closer to us. Yes. I was quite certain it was *ourselves* that the bird was inspecting.

Like some inquisitive old soul, his deep black eyes darted about, scrutinizing us with obvious intent. It was at this moment that the old man tossed a look my way. His face shone with great emotion, pleasure, amusement, and yes, perhaps surprise!

We three soldiers three–as the old rhyme goes–considered each other for several minutes when the great bird let out a terrific sound; a loud and meaningful *'Caw.'* Was it a question, or a statement? However, before I had time to decide upon an answer, the incredible beast swooped down, snatched the silver ring from its place on the stone, and like that, was gone!

The old man gazed about then looked me square in the eye and laughed, a laugh from deep within the center of a person. We both stared after the crow for a few minutes–laughing together–when, abruptly, my patron got back onto his tottering old legs, dusting the dirt and twigs from his trousers and retrieving his small bundle, and as suddenly as the bird, bid me farewell and withdrew down the path. I was astonished, watching his bent old form retreat into the darkness of the jungle and an abrupt and profound sense of sadness–mixed with an odd sense of joy–rocketed my mind like a boat on a windy sea is tossed about to-and-fro. There was nothing else to do but to climb back into my vehicle and quietly return to town.

When I returned to the Mori's home, I asked them to read the elegant *Shuji* calligraphy on the scroll the old man had given me. Yuki-san was first to take it. Her eyes were wide with excitement as she carefully unfurled it.

"It is a poem," she said. "Haiku," her fingers gently caressing the paper. "This is magnificent," she said and recited this poem:

"'What is death, but a thin veil
The spirit burns like fire in the night
Lights on a distant ocean'"

A year later I revisited Mister Ushihara at the graveyard on Hachijojima. Mori-san accompanied me to serve as interpreter. We burned incense at the grave much the same as before. I expressed to Mister Ushihara my interest in knowing more about the person whose bones the monument had been bequeathed. He was very obliging, and we met together later that evening at his modest but comfortable dwelling.

It turned out that what I thought was his work shed was in actuality his humble abode. Like a jewel in the rough, the exterior belied little of the country elegance of the home's interior.

He was quite a packrat, with books, papers and boxes– all stuffed to the gills and wrapped with string–occupying nearly every available space except the living room with its marvelous authentic *kotatsu*. It smelled of burning wood mixed with the wonderful cooking of his meek round faced wife, Noriko, who never quit smiling the entire time we were in her house.

After a delicious traditional *Nabe* dinner, Mr. Ushihara conducted an exhaustive search through dozens of shelves and boxes and–after several consultations with his wife–finally managed to procure a very old and delicate scroll wrapped in a fine silken cloth and bound with gold embroidered thread. He then commenced to tell the story about the gravestone with Mori-san acting as translator.

"It is the grave of a nobleman, samurai...Asayama Mitsuhide. He was a good man, who was betrayed and banished to Hachijojima. He was accompanied by four vassals...oh, the vassals were self-imposed exile to remain with their lord. Asayama was a respected leader and warrior. Honorable. He led the defense of the island against Chinese and Japanese pirates...pirate raids.

"He always believed he would one day return to Mikawa, and his beloved wife...her name...was Tomo. He refused her to come to the island...its harsh environment. In those days, men had to work hard...to sustain enough food and material, from the island's meager resources. This man was betrayed by his daimyo, his lord...oh, the great Ieyasu himself! Tokugawa Ieyasu. Some sort of political maneuver. Asayama was banished. He was young, thirty-seven years, when he died here on Hachijojima...killed fighting a man...who wanted to..." He scratched the whiskers on his chin and looked directly in my eyes. "He killed a man who wanted to be...what's best word? Dictator...a man who wanted to become dictator of the island. Asayama killed him...then committed seppuku to answer for...the crime of murder." A flourish of words from Ushihara. "He was what you say in English...um...? I'm sorry, I don't remember word but, it remind me of the word *mother*."

"A martyr?"

"Hai, so...good word Willem-san. Lord Asayama killed this dictator...in exchange for his own life...then...all the vassals, each one, commit this act...what we call *hara-kiri*. Here, this very spot...never having returned to his ancestral home." Mr. Ushihara glanced up from his reading and rubbed his eyes while Mori lit a cigarette and stared into space.

"Who was the ghost who was haunting me?" I asked pensively and Mori translated. Mr. Ushihara shook his head and spoke rapidly to Mori in Japanese.

"There is no way to answer," Mori repeated. "Asayama Mitsuhide had four vassals...Yamana, Tsuseki, Nakamura and Ohno. You prayed to the spirits of these men, each, one year ago...and of course, Lord Asayama." Mr. Ushihara again spoke to Mori, who nodded and addressed me.

"He doesn't know too much about these other men, but there is public record about Asayama Mitsuhide's burial." The old man nodded and smiled broadly, his eyes growing misty as if seeing very far away, and each man took a moment to silently reflect.

He then engaged Mori in a lengthy conversation. Eventually my host grunted softly before turning to me, gathering his thoughts.

"What is it?"

"There were some visitors...long time ago, he thinks from Nagoya. Family maybe. He's not exactly sure. It was a long time ago, when he was very young...still a boy." They exchange another lengthy series of syllables, words cloaked in the mystery of the human tongue. Mori was obviously questioning him on some point and a look of surprise crossed his face. "Oh, his father was caretaker then." Mori seemed quite impressed. "His grandfather and great grandfather too." He listened further to the words of the old man, puffing on his cigarette down to the butt before tamping it out in the ashtray on the table. "This is a very old haka."

"*Haka?*" I repeated.

"Grave."

Eventually there was nothing more to say, and after passing on Noriko's offer of more tea, we bid adieu our aged informer. Mori bowed deeply, shaking Ushihara's hand with a deep show of respect. Once we were back at the Peugeot, I apologized formally to Mr. Mori, for his time and patience with the whole ordeal.

"Not at all, Willem-san. It is not a problem. This experience is very good thing for me. This graveyard you see here is over five centuries old. Only certain people know it. Mr. Ushihara's family have been the caretakers from the very beginning. It is an incredible story. I will come back here many times in the future Willem, to speak with Mr. Ushihara and collect data. I intend to write a book about this very place, *and its people*, before it disappears."

"Disappears?"

"The jungle. It grows deeper each day, swallows it more every day, just look." He waved his arm and indeed the entirety of our sight was like a tunnel of verdant green plant life. "You cannot stop it. Earth will take back all things in the end. Mr. Ushihara is the last. The last surviving caretaker. Once he dies...well, I would think Nature takes it all back, probably forever. Only families keep the traditions going...from disappearing from the earth, forever." He then actually bowed, rather formally, before me. "Thank you for this opportunity to meet Mr. Ushihara and to find this incredible place hidden away from the world. Arigato Willem-san, arigato."

I'm happy to say that my string of bad luck rapidly subsided and my dreams improved tremendously. However, I admit that I don't look at crows, and especially ravens, in quite the same dismissive way.

As it turned out, the old man's leads proved fruitful; Mori conducting quite a thorough research into Asayama Mitsuhide's past–and those of his relations–and the startling things they accomplished. Perhaps someday we'll be able to tell the story, about their time spent on this very tiny place nestled in such a very large ocean.

Chapter 5: The Burning Man

To the best of my knowledge, *Karras and Corbeau: Investigators of the Strange and Occult*, never solicit themselves as *ministers to the justice*. I've witnessed a general reluctance of the firm to delve in the forensic arts. When petitioned to do so, their position is to redirect the inquirer to the proper professional resources. There have been, however, occasions where the firm's talents have been sought by various agencies, regarding strange and inexplicable oddities surrounding *certain homicides of note*. Of course, Mr. Corbeau shuns these relations intrinsically, remaining quite obdurate about engaging with agents of the law, barristers or any such authorities; relegating this interface solely to the care of his more erudite companions.

One such circumstance was quite markedly sinister. The occasion was a chance meeting–or so we thought at the time–with K, of the San Francisco Police Department. A mid-level inquisitor with SFPD homicide, K, is a person Mr. Karras has known for decades.

I had travelled with Lucien to the beautiful *city by the bay* to visit Emerald Montaigne when a chance meeting with K occurs near the Embarcadero. We were to find out later that this *meeting* was, in effect, premeditated. In a downtown establishment near Market and California streets the men reacquaint themselves over drinks.

The gentlemen share each other's professional accomplishments to date when in a casual tone K, elaborates on a current unresolved situation he is deeply preoccupied with. Lucien inquired into specifics, as per his nature, whereupon K responds by taking us to an address on Clay Street at the periphery of Chinatown and the Western Addition.

The bleak tenement house is a depredated Edwardian structure painted a drab gray–or perhaps deplete of color– that sits like a corpse on the periphery of the neighborhood. We ascend a dark narrow flight of stairs that seems to take us nearly to the roof. Once we make the door of the uppermost apartment, K engages his torch to see about the proper latchkey. I take note of a marker issued by the SFPD forbidding entry of any *unauthorized persons* with threat of imprisonment. After several moments in the stagnant darkness, K procures the appropriate key, unlocks the portal and enters whereupon a fetid air greets our senses. I hold a silk to my nose and let my olfactory adjust. K switches on the light, a feeble yellow glow illuminates a very bleak interior.

"How long was the body dead?" Lucien inquires.

"Well, no *body* was recovered, exactly," K murmurs.

"Are you purposely being obtuse?"

"Follow me." The inspector directs us down a dark narrow hallway and the feeling is not unlike entering into an abyss.

We pass two doors both on the right. The immediate possesses an antique toilet with the cistern above– activated by a draw chain–and an old marble washbasin. The second door, which catches Lucien's attention for he stops before it momentarily, leads to a disheveled bedroom dim in the light from the hallway.

We follow K as he takes us to the rear of the apartment into a large austere kitchen deplete of foodstuffs; merely a scattering of cheap pre-packaged remnants.

From the kitchen, two doors leading back remained ajar. The left ends in a sort of storage room full of a variety of boxes and junk. The right leads through a narrow vestibule with a wash tub and mounds of moldy clothing, to an exterior door which K is quick to open allowing fresh air to enter the apartment. The door opens out onto a small rickety deck with a precarious set of steps descending down into a wild tangled and disused rear garden full of litter and debris.

As we make our way through the apartment, I begin to notice the unsettling detail that all the windows and doors are fastened shut *with locks and bars*. I comment about this to Lucien and K concurs emphatically. "The place was locked up tighter than a nunnery, all the windows and doors heavily barred and bolted." He points out several serious handmade bars with heavy locks on the rear doors and windows. "They were obviously trying to keep somebody out."

"Or *something*," Lucien whispers under his breath. "The entire apartment was completely secure, from the inside?"

"Entirely, all locks fastened. In fact, the front door had to be forced."

"Odd," Lucien whispers. "Nothing ajar?"

"Everything locked tight with deadbolts," K says. "Front, back, even all the windows were locked and barred. A little over the top for a third story apartment."

"Curious," Lucien says stroking his beard. "And the body, where was it discovered?"

"Well, like I said...there wasn't *a body*, exactly."
Lucien looks at him strangely.

"You speak in riddles my friend, I thought it beneath your métier. I know a dead body when I smell one."

"No riddles Lucien," he says with the utmost seriousness. "Follow me."

We retrace our steps back down the flat's long darkened corridor to the same bedroom Lucien had noted earlier. At the door I hear my employer whisper to K.

"Yes...of course."

K pauses at the portal. It was obvious to me that *he was reluctant to enter the room*, taking in a breath then switching on the light; it casts an even duller luminosity than the previous room's dull pallid glow. I squint in the feeble light and carefully follow my companions into the macabre chamber.

What struck one's attention immediately–other than a feeling of morbid reserve–was an enormous black patch in the middle of the floor; a large and ugly burn that *distinctly resembled the human form.*

A foul air gripped the room in a stranglehold and an unsettling feeling of dark and ominous activities presses in upon my psyche. A foreboding sense of dread, in fact the feeling of a kind of *evil*–for lack of a better word– saturated the ambiance of the place. I become acutely aware that a horrid murder by fire has been committed.

K kneels down beside the abysmally blackened shape, muttering in a muted tone usually held at obsequies in reverence of the dead. He extracts the penlight, using it as a pointer.

"Here, we bagged two shoes, definitely male...*with the feet still inside them.*" He moves to his left not bothering to look up at us. "Here," he continues, now pointing midway further along the burn, "*we found three fingers*, one with a man's ring still attached...thoroughly scorched." He adjusted his position slightly, now pointing toward the end of the burn, opposite the shoes. "Here we found burnt human hair...and small fragments of skull."

He returns his gaze to us and his eyes reveal the horror of what he had witnessed. I can make out the distinct sense of awe captured–probably to the end of his days–within his mind's eye. I stand there without removing my attention from the floor, making out clearly the rough human form portrayed by the burn, like black paint on a dull ochre canvass.

Lucien kneels and studies the area, searching, taking in the essence of the story hidden there, K loitering above his shoulder.

"No traces of gasoline, kerosene or any other flammable. It's as if the body burned from within."

"Are you suggesting human spontaneous combustion?"

"I'm not suggesting anything Lucien, just that our team analyzed everything for cause, the remains, the carpet, everything. They were completely stymied as to what substance was the catalyst."

K, rose from the spot as if unconsciously wishing to put distance from himself and the event; or perhaps knowing intrinsically Lucien's methods, putting some distance between him and the man as he attempted to *see* the story hidden there.

From the proximity of the door we watch as Lucien studies the area. He calmly and methodically moves about the room staring from time to time blankly into the dark. I knew he was *seeing* into the past; for I had learned from him and his exotic associates that all actions are locked in the *energy stamp* of the event and under certain conditions viewable *as if watching a movie*. In fact, this was probably what he *was* doing, for twice he walked from the bedroom back into the kitchen and studied the environ as if watching some invisible drama play itself out. The process was fantastic and mystifying.

We silently follow him from room to room and from spot to spot noting as he did so, the entire contents of the shabby apartment; an obvious second-hand mattress and bedspring mounted on cinderblocks, and milk crates for bedside tables. Candles–scores of them–throughout the apartment, were especially prevalent in the bedroom and their arrangement gave the unsettling appearance of a makeshift altar. With amazing synchronicity in reference to my thoughts, Lucien suddenly questions the inspector.

"What materials were removed from the apartment besides the man's ring and remains, in particular this room?" K hesitates, engaged by this question.

"Well, everything still remains except...well..." he searches for words, whereupon Lucien looks at him squarely.

"Sacrificial accoutrement would be the tactful answer."

"Yes, a lot of it," he says grimly.

"Human?"

"Doesn't appear to be."

"What then?" K puffs out his cheeks and scratches his head.

"Well, cats…rats…dogs, I'm not exactly sure what all Lucien, but it was pretty damn disgusting." He studies his friend, an abhorrent look upon his face. "Our man was pretty damn sick," he states emphatically. Lucien holds up a finger and taps at the air.

"He was afraid, in terror I would say." He gazes about taking in a wide sweep of the environment. "The animals were a placation. *The fear* still resides, you feel it?" K gazes about as if half expecting to see something and says nothing. We canvass the rest of the room, I, taking detailed notes in my ledger. I observe that Lucien seems to be listening to something, some sound, or is he thinking and reacting to his thoughts? I follow him to a ramshackle dresser in the far corner. He gazes at the contents strewn across the top before reaching and plucking up a thin gold lapel pin, commencing to scrutinize it closely.

"Careful about handling anything, the case is hot," K, says from the door, I believe he wished to leave that dreadful chamber.

"Yes, indeed," Lucien interjects, holding the pin before the inspector. "K, look at this pin a moment." He does so, engaging his torch. He twists the shaft between his thumb and index finger.

"Mean anything to you?"

"I believe it to be of eastern European origin. Slavic perhaps."

"You suppose our man was Yugoslavian?"

"I'm making no such assumptions, just that this is a very particular object."

"Perhaps he was a pin collector?"

"Have you found evidence to support such a theory?"

"Not at all."

"Do you realize there's not a single book in this entire apartment? Not one volume. Not even a magazine," Lucien says, and K looks about.

"No. Weird huh?" he says below his breath.

"Not if he couldn't read English," Lucien says, and K looks at him squarely.

"Lucien, I've known you long enough. You've been walking around this dump, taking it in. I need to know what you know." Lucien looks at him long and hard then studies the pin between his fingers.

"May I hold onto this for a short while?" he asks and K nods.

"Okay, but I need some kind of read on this mess. I've got nothing Lucien, not a damn thing."

"Alright, but not here in this loathsome place where the dark enterprise still hovers." We look about and I sense what I believe Lucien could actually see.

"A pub?" K is quick to inquire.

"Capital," Lucien says and carefully places the pin between the leaves of his notebook.

Soon we are sitting in *Churchill's Pub* on Irving Street sipping pints of Guinness while K pounds down a double Dewar's, quickly ordering a second.

"Artificial entities…" Lucien says absently staring into the wall, as if it didn't exist.

"What the hell is that?" K asks.

"Yes, *hell*…that's an appropriate word my friend. Man-made hells. A subject of deep and exhausting parameters. Knowing your tenacity all too well, that you'll not let the subject drop, I'll say this much. Just outside the material plane resides *the inchoate realm*."

"Inchoate? What does that mean?"

"Without going into overly taxing detail, this *realm* is the depository of mankind's restless nature, *entities form.* Certainly, the majority of mankind unconsciously, bring to life–and I use that word in the relative–what has been referred to, since antiquity, as *an artificial entity.*" He studies K intently who shrugs, apparently not following his train of thought. "This *realm* surrounds our world and is susceptible to the influences of human thought, so imagine how it is affected by determined purposeful thought and evocation."

"Lucien, I'm just a cop...what are you talking about?"

"Crudely, a man's wish, or more appropriately his desire, takes on an aspect of his consciousness. I know this seems incredible but this *effect*, can actually take form. You might imagine a type of being referred to as an *elemental* that fulfils this desire. However, an entity, once created by this life energy, *is by no means under the control of its creator.* It can live, feeding upon the host's thought-force, which sustains it, holds it together. Thus, a repeated thought, or desire, can form an *elemental* whose existence may extend to days, weeks, sometimes years in fact and remains hovering about him like a shadow."

"So, this, *elemental* thing, takes over the man?"

"Since repetitive thought, repetitive desire, serves to strengthen it, the creature takes an ever-increasingly definitive shape, takes form in fact and may gain more and more strength and influence over him. If the desire be a wicked one, the effect upon his moral character will be odious at best." K, stares at him blankly but the words Lucien speaks makes me involuntarily shudder.

"Then, this...this entity...is the burnt remains we've recovered?"

"Not in the least. K, this poor devil whose last moments on earth were beyond horrific, was undoubtedly an attendant, and certainly not the only one in this grim drama who was preyed upon by what I fear is *something quite out of control.*"

"Out of control? Explain that."

"It is extant that he had gone to great lengths to escape it, relocating thousands of miles...even attempting–pitifully–to bar its exclusion from the premise with crude but useless locks and rods." Lucien shook his head grimly. "As the *imp* grows stronger, it influences others it comes into contact and subjects them to the same moral contagion." Lucien withdrew his pipe. In the process of lighting the bowl, he's set upon by the waitress.

"Excuse me sir, there's no smoking allowed inside the bar."

"My apologies," he says politely, returning his pipe to his pocket. K prods him.

"Why the animal carcasses, what's that all about?"

"Appeasement...*a libation of blood,*" Lucien whispers gravely. K's expression goes rigid.

"Lucien, I'll be honest with you. That place goes through me like an ice pick."

"As it should. Sinister machinations my friend, sinister." Lucien sips his ale. K studies him, his expression an amalgam of concern.

"What do you think? What do you *feel?*" he asks.

"Feel? *Horror.*" The following silence is deafening. K takes several sips of his whiskey, deep in thought.

"That word isn't in my vocabulary pal. I need more than that."

"Malevolent energy, in whatever lexicon K, is a distinction, as love is a distinction, or fear."

"You think the place is haunted?" he asks, and Lucien's eyebrow rises sharply.

"*Haunted*, is hardly the word for it my friend," Lucien says. K downs the rest of his drink neat, sits on the edge of his chair, closing the distance between us and whispers.

"You said *murder* earlier. HQ is calling this a suicide. All the doors and windows were locked and bolted from the inside. You think he was murdered?"

"Unquestionably."

"How?"

"There's no way to tell…physically."

"What do you mean?"

"K, you're a man of physical means and processes. You follow a trail of physical fact that piecemeal leads you down a path to an end result. Our methods are often the reverse. We're given an end result and must divine a path back to a progenitor."

"Can you please be more specific?"

"My dear sir, physical existence is subject to physical laws. Energy cannot be destroyed; all action suffers equal and collateral reaction. Therefore, energy given is energy retained." At this point K leans back in his chair and runs his hand through his greying hair, exhaling loudly.

"Lucien, I'm just a hack investigator on city payroll. I can't go into my briefing and talk about…*energy* or whatever. I need facts, and this…is just freakin' weird. Can't you tell me anything? Anything at all?"

"K, you recall our previous work together, the process I employ? Apparitions at the spot of the crime are usually thought forms projected by the criminal, perpetually obsessing over again and again the details of his actions. This is what I mean by *energy*."

"But this isn't just any ordinary murder…is it?" There's an extended silent exchange as K struggles to hold Lucien's gaze.

"First, there were two deaths, are you aware?"

"Two? How do you figure?"

"The burned man and another."

"Another? Where?"

"In the kitchen, the back hallway leading to the fire escape."

"How do you know that?" K asks incredulous.

"The energy stamp. The shock and horror of the man's demise."

"But…then, *what happened to the body?*" K inquires and Lucien says not a word but stares with piercing eyes into ours. K quickly changes his questioning. "Go on."

"Near simultaneous deaths. First the man in the bedroom was dispatched, then the second immediately afterward in the kitchen as he tried to escape."

"How was the man burned alive?"

"I cannot be certain, but *something not human* was concerned. It's left its mark, the windows and doors all shuttered. Fear is everywhere…*death a release from it.*"

"Who were the men?"

"I cannot tell, there's a shroud over the whole affair."

"A shroud? What do you mean?"

"A veil, like a mist obscuring a landscape of its detail. This, this problem requires someone of more ability than myself. Might I suggest we contact Emerald Montaigne? I believe this is right in line with-"

"We already have. She's declined."

"Declined? For what reasons?"

"She seems…reluctant, to get involved."

"Hmm," he mulls quietly. "Perhaps we might persuade her to help." Lucien falls deep into thought staring into space. "Yes, quite," he says aloud to no one in particular. He then turns to our resolute detective and nods. "K, we better call it a night." The inspector raises his arm and our waitress saunters over.

"Put all the drinks on my bill," he says handing her a credit card and dons his overcoat.

K offers us a ride, but Lucien declines in lieu of the tram. Neither of us speak the entire trip back downtown, Lucien in a near trance-like meditation over the day's grisly events.

I watch the foggy evening roll by through the tram's dark pane of glass. I see them, the city's people walking the bleak streets like phantoms in mist. We eventually transfer to the cable car, which conveys us up the steep incline to the top of Nob Hill. A loud group of tourists get on and the dark thoughts in my mind gives way to their words and laughter. Lucien sits in silence with the contingent of late-night revelers while I'm content to stand on the board and hold onto the brass rail as the old car shakes and rattles its way up the hill.

At the *Mark Hotel* we disembark but Lucien strolls past our solemn and ornate hostel taking a bench in the park across from the beautiful Grace Cathedral to smoke his pipe and muse over the day's proceedings. He becomes quintessentially silent. I leave him to his thoughts undisturbed. The beautiful cathedral is engulfed in mist, its twin belfry towers reminiscent of her famous Parisian sister, Notre Dame. I watch the taxis line-up before the Fairmont then one by one disappear into the foggy San Franciscan night.

The following morning Lucien is up very early, before dawn. I can hear him busying himself in the common room of our suite. He's ordered room service and there's a cart with fresh fruit, wheat-cakes and coffee. When I join him, he is already donning his long dark overcoat and instructs me to meet him in the lobby when I finish with breakfast.

The Mark is a beautiful old hotel and part of the city's heritage. I gaze about the suite's splendor and its interior design mimics the hotel's outer halls and vestibules. There are a series of old photographs on the walls and I realize the ancient monolith has been host to many illustrious personages and many years of human activities and dealings.

In the lobby, Lucien is reading an early edition of the Chronicle. I hurry to join him and attempt to arrange a cab. He declines, preferring to stroll the distance from Nob Hill to Emerald's Victorian on Sutter Street. Soon we are knocking on the front door of her beautiful antiquated home.

Emerald Montaigne answers the door, greets us with a broad genuine smile and entreats us to enter, embracing Lucien. Her deep azure eyes gleam with an inner vividness. She extends her long graceful hand–richly jeweled–and her handshake is frail and warm as if holding a bird or a small delicate animal.

"Willem, so very nice to see you again." Her gaze penetrates mine; studying me intently. She smiles but her eyes are piercing, searching. I fight to hold that gaze and actually feel relief when she returns her attention to Lucien and the sensation dissipates.

We sit in the drawing room partaking of black tea from a silver tea service. I gaze about the room while Emerald and Lucien talk. An enormous scarlet macaw within the breakfast nook sat listening, craning his head, the eyes darting back and forth between us *as if listening in on the conversation.* There is a plethora of artwork and sculpture including many well-mounted Japanese *mokuhanga* prints. Several large walnut bookcases line the entirety of two walls and an impressive collection of old books, many in piles, permeate the environ. A sleek orange tabby cat enters the room and leaps into Emerald's lap and purrs loudly as she absently strokes his chin. She wears a long flowing black dress with a black shawl adorned with bright colorful embroidery, flowers, vines and interlacing patterns. Her long ebony hair flows into the fabric creating an exotic effect and as I look at her, her eyes slowly turn and catch mine and the keen intelligence in her cerulean gaze creates a mild sensation within my chest.

Eventually the conversation turns to the business at hand–the bleak proceedings on Clay Street. Emerald rises abruptly, gently dumping the feline to the floor and peers out the bay window overlooking Sutter Street.

"No," she mutters shaking her head. Lucien withdraws his meerschaum from a pocket in his tweed jacket, tamps and lights it, exhaling a stream of gray smoke into the room. She turns and crosses her arms. "I know what you're thinking," she alludes. "No."

"Your unique talents are quite necessary my dear," he says resolutely. She looks away and her brow knits fiercely.

"I refuse to go back there," she says.

"You've already been to the property?" he queries. She collapses back into her chair.

"I'm sorry Lucien, but that's why you're here."

"Meaning what?"

"Meaning that's why I asked you to come. The excuse of the old manuscript was a ruse," she says. "A blatant lie in fact...how horrible," she says to herself. Lucien puffs on his pipe.

"Hmm...I see," he mutters.

"Forgive me," she asks graciously, her eyes emphatic. He dismisses her comment.

"It's immaterial, the problem however is not. It is, unfortunately, all too very real. This is completely within your sphere of expertise." They exchange a long deep uninterrupted stare. Finally, Emerald breaks the silence.

"You know as I, this was no ordinary murder Lucien, this was...*horrid*." She seems to visibly shudder and buries her chin into her shoulder.

"I realize that Emerald, it's more than evident. However, we mustn't be remiss. It's essential we-"

"Lucien I've told you countless times. I do not wish to be involved in police matters of this sort. Anton should deal with this, if we must, he's more...resolute. This is simply...horrific." Lucien sets down his pipe and takes her arm.

"Exactly why K needs our help. This is beyond their capabilities. Em, it's impossible to walk away at this point. What is happening here is a violation against God and mankind." She refuses to look at him. He shakes her softly. "Emerald, this is vile, it behooves us to assist in its coming to light." She turns back and I'm shocked; her expression is one of utter sadness, tears welling within her dulcet eyes.

Lucien gestures for me to join him outside. He instructs me to a local Japanese restaurant to purchase meals. When I return, I'm greeted by a tall attractive woman, perhaps in her early thirties, with a vibrant shock of dark hair. She introduces herself. *Morgan*, Emerald's eldest daughter. She indicates that Lucien and Emerald *are in seclusion.* I don't ask about the details but question her about the food I've brought for them. She investigates the contents, laying the packages out neatly upon the dining-room table. She takes relish in the items I've bought and begins snacking on the sushi rolls.

I clearly see the resemblance between mother and daughter. Both are rather attractive with dark hair–nearly black–and possess very handsome facial qualities. The only striking difference, other than their age, is Emerald has vivid azure eyes whereas Morgan's are a deep green hue, the gaze more distant and aloof than her mother's intense engaged properties. They both seem to have the propensity of wearing black, with silver jewelry upon their fingers and wrists.

She pokes through the fare with long delicate fingers. The ring, on the left hand, is a beautiful ornate setting with a solid black stone; Jet I surmise. The ring on the right hand carries an elegant purple amethyst. This ring has an attendant–a small silver band embossed with a tiny skull–and the wrist carries a splendid silver bracelet that I recognize as Hopi Indian design and craftsmanship, quite authentic. I'm somewhat mesmerized as she snacks on the various flavors, savoring them. She gazes at me without speaking. I decide to open some sort of conversation. "Do you live in San Francisco?" She shakes her head, taking time to finish her bite before answering, dusting her palms together.

"New York. I live in Manhattan."

"Oh, you're visiting then?"

"Working. I just popped over to have a look at the pin." I'm shocked; she holds up the golden pin from Clay Street.

"Is that the pin from the crime scene?" I inquire with more than a modicum of surprise in my voice.

"It is. It's from a Czech photographer's guild."

"Are you a photographer?" I ask and her eyes search mine.

"I am," she says and studies me intently. "I'm here shooting a fashion set for *Perle* Magazine."

"Oh? Interesting," I say. She continues to study me.

"Do you read fashion?" she asks. I wonder if she's having fun at my expense.

"Not at all." She smiles, the corners of her mouth curving softly.

"I didn't think you the type." She returns to eating Lucien and Emerald's lunch. "What do you do?" she asks without looking up.

"I'm a business manager for *Karras and Corbeau*." She looks at me strangely.

"You work for my mother?"

"Indirectly." There's a sudden commotion at the stairs and a lovely young woman with long golden-brown hair, perhaps in her early twenties and wearing pajamas, emerges from the stairs yawning. She joins Morgan at the table and begins poking through the meal.

"How's the shoot going?" she eventually asks Morgan.

"Good. Slow. Really slow," Morgan says between mouthfuls. "Try the salmon roe...to die for."

"Yuck," the blonde girl says and looks at me. "Hi," she says without really engaging with me, pulling a vegetarian hand-roll from the plastic tray.

"Hello," I respond and watch as these two women begin to completely devour the lunch I've brought for my companions.

"Oh, this eating machine is my sister Audrey," Morgan says and the other waves her hand in my direction without looking at me. They begin to converse on very personal, esoteric subjects. They are obviously two very sophisticated young women. I notice Audrey has no jewelry upon her person but several hemp wristlets and two turquoise earrings.

Eventually Lucien and Emerald emerge from their exile, their expressions rather serious. Emerald approaches the table and looks over the devastation. Audrey gives her a hug, but Emerald seems more absorbed in finding anything left to eat. Lucien stands with Morgan who extends the pin in his direction.

"Maestro…this pin is from the IKP, the *International-Kamera Praha*, a professional cinematic guild in Prague. Extremely rare," she says. "I can't imagine there are many of these knocking about." She hands it back to Lucien who studies it closely.

"Can you get me contact information about the guild?"

"I'm quite certain of that," she says placing her hand upon his arm. "In fact, I'll do you one better Uncle. I'll look into securing a member's roster. There can't be too many members. This is a very exclusive organization."

"Excellent my dear, thank you." She then takes her mother in arm.

"I have to go mum." She kisses her cheek while Emerald scavenges for something to eat, she pats Morgan's cheek.

"When do I get to see you?" she asks absently.

"You *just* saw me."

"I mean quality time dear-heart, not all this coming and going," Emerald says. Morgan sighs, pulling a long black jacket from the hook by the door.

"I've got to get back. We're shooting at Fort Point in an hour. I'll send you and Uncle Lucien some info soon."

"Morgan, I'm serious."

"About what?"

"You know *what*, your incessant over-working. What's good for *the career* isn't necessarily good for *the girl*. Look how thin you've become. Don't those people feed you?"

"Mom...I'm '*those people*' you refer to, and yes I feed my crew. I'm sorry but I don't have time for this."

"Well, we need to talk dearest. I'm worried about you." This doesn't stop her from heading out the door.

"I'll stop back, after we wrap." She leaves.

"I'm worried about her Lucien. I feel that it's starting all over again with her." Lucien holds the small gold lapel pin up to Emerald.

"Morgan confirmed my suspicions about this pin, very rare, very out of place," he states, and Emerald takes it gently in her grasp. Something transpires instantly that proves to be quite unexpected. I notice an immediate change in Emerald's face, her eyes dilating into large dark pools. I reach out and take her by the elbow.

"Are you all right Emerald?" I ask. Everyone stops to watch the transformation.

It is an amazing thing to witness someone with the ability to *see into the invisible*. Even now it's difficult to explain in words the look of awe–or terror perhaps–that comes over Emerald's beautiful face so abruptly. When her eyes turn toward me, I feel a shaft of energy bristle the hair at the nape of my neck. What happens next is quite astonishing as Emerald, apparently, goes immediately into trance.

"I see them," she whispers, "I see the man. Very dark... *from Europa*."

"What is his name? Do you have it?" Lucien asks.

"He's Slavic. R-A-D...Radic. Radic is his name."

"Continue please." There's a pause. She seems to be peering.

"He's waiting, many nights. *Fear* sits in the room with him." She cranes her neck. "Oh...a door," she says pointing nowhere.

"Which door?" Lucien queries.

"No...not of this world...wait, something comes...*the shape of man, but shadow only*. It is not a man...no light." She squirms, disturbed. "It's unwinding," she says and squirms in Lucien's grasp. "Oh, how dreadful! Oh, dear God."

"What is it? Emerald?"

"It's got hold of him...*his eternal soul*." She falters as if in pain. "Oh dear God!" I hold her thin frame from falling, her eyes dilate wildly. "He's on fire! Fire from his mouth, his hands burn, the skin burning. Lucien help him! For God's sake someone help, he's burning alive!" She screams and collapses. I carry her to the velvet sofa. As we administer to her, she slowly returns and looks into our eyes.

"Are you all right Emerald? What on earth is it?" She looks into each of our eyes and I see the horror.

"*The Lover of Souls...*" she whispers and the way she says this sends chills through my body. "It's infernal. Oh Lucien, it must be hunted down and *annihilated*. Help me up." We help her sit then escort her to the table where she asks for a pen and paper. Audrey returns with a large glass of water. Emerald writes on the paper handing it to Lucien. "This is the name and directions to an Apache medicine man in Arizona. Ask K, to contact him and fly him here. He'll clear the apartment on Clay Street. Should we fail to do so Lucien, the next tenants will be contaminated."

"Are you saying this thing still resides within the apartment?"

"*It* does not, but its ruinous effects remain. They'll seep into a person of weak character, contaminate them morally. We mustn't take chances."

"Understood. Why not contact Hennepin?"

"No. This is not for her. *This requires a warrior...*a fight will most surely evolve, a psychological and spiritual struggle. This has become a very dark place Lucien...*the imps abound.*"

"Very well," he says. "What are we to do?"

"If Morgan is correct, and I'm certain that she is, we go to Prague. It returns to its source."

"What is it? What do we pursue?"

"This thing...this entity, is *the Lover of Souls*. It is quite ancient and truly evil."

"I've heard of this thing somehow...somewhere."

"Once, many years ago, Seamus spoke to you about it. Something that happened just before his death."

"Of course, *the Lover of Souls*. I recall it now."

"It has been the harbinger of ill fate upon the planet for centuries. It feeds upon the life pulse of the individual, possesses him and ultimately consumes him." They exchange a long intense look. "It has existed in this way, precariously from life to life, for over a thousand years."

"Astonishing. This is the reason for the veil cast over the murder site."

"It is insidious, a survivor, it has fought many battles. Lucien, *it intends to survive*." They share another long silent exchange. "The *incubus feeds upon the life force of the living,* in direct violation of the laws of God and Universe. We're in grave danger pursuing it." Her expression is hard, but her eyes have an inner gleam that emits a strange feeling of hope.

"Agreed," Lucien says and looks directly toward me. "Have our things brought over from the hotel. We'll work from here until the flight."

"The flight?"

"Arrange three seats to Prague, leaving in three days." He returns his attention to Emerald. "Are you sure you are all right?"

"Yes, yes I'm all right."

"I'll need the use of Seamus' study," Lucien says.

"Yes, of course. I'll arrange both of your rooms."

"Don't bother over me, I'll sleep in the study," he says.

"As you wish." She closes her eyes, sitting motionless. I sense the horror she has just witnessed.

We remain at the house in San Francisco for two more days. I can't remember Lucien leaving the upstairs study except for an occasional stroll down the block–to stretch his leg–or our nightly nocturnal car ride through the city.

I'm kept busy running errands and dropping Lucien off at various quiet nondescript homes of friends and acquaintances, including visits to the Goethe Institute and the Zen Center, for a period of usually no more than an hour before returning him directly to the Sutter Street house. I notice late every night, light streaming through the smoke-filled crack of the study door as he pours through the large collection of old texts that once belonged to Emerald's esteemed first husband, Seamus MacIntyre, Morgan's father.

My room is a cozy mother-in-law apartment on the ground floor, just off the back garden, with its own egress opening into a sizable backyard, wild with native Californian plants including several young redwoods and a small dwarf lemon tree filled with fruit.

Morgan joins us for dinner the evening of the first night. Emerald has prepared a variety of exquisitely smelling vegetarian food, arranging the dishes atop the large oak dining table. While Audrey helps her mother prepare and set the meal, Morgan engages Lucien and I in a detailed conversation about photography, the Cinema and Prague. She sips red cabernet from a crystal goblet and extends a blank white envelope toward Lucien.

"What's this?"

"Your coveted roster Uncle."

"You've already secured a member's roster for the guild in Prague? Caliber. Once again Morgan, your ability supersedes your illustrious skillset. I'm indebted."

"As I said Uncle Lucien, it's a very small, select group. The *name of the murderer* you seek is somewhere in that list." Her dark eyes wander to mine and I'm lost within the expanse of her pupils.

"How'd the shoot go today?" Audrey interjects, setting an eggplant ratatouille in the middle of the table and adopting a rather dramatic chic pose. "Miss me?"

"It's going slow. Dumb and stupid. We wasted a lot of valuable time covering basic stuff. Where do they dig up these new girls? I swear it gets worse year after year."

"*Girls*?" I inquire.

"The models. They become more vacant every year. It's like shooting an Instagram meme. What are they thinking? What are they eating?"

"They're not. It's called tranquilizers," Audrey adds.

"Certainly not anything healthy," Emerald says placing a bowl of Kalamata olives next to a plate of hummus and glaring directly at Morgan. "A person doesn't look so thin and frail if they eat right," she says pointedly. "Right?" Audrey drapes an arm around her mother's neck and kisses her cheek.

"Right Mum. As usual."

"Lucien, I've bottles of Guinness in the refrigerator. Would you like me to pour you a glass?"

"Please. Thank-you Emerald."

"I'll get it," Audrey says. "You don't pour them right," and she disappears into the kitchen.

"*I don't pour them right*...what on earth is that supposed to mean?"

"Never mind," Morgan interrupts. "So, Mom are you coming to visit my set tomorrow?"

"I'm sorry Morgan but there isn't time. I've too many things to get ready before the flight in two days."

"Perhaps Willem would like to go?" Lucien inquires from behind the roster; chancing a quick furtive glance in our direction. Morgan's eyes change, studying mine intently.

"Well?"

"*Well* what?" I ask.

"Would you like to visit the set tomorrow?"

"Yes, if it's alright with Lucien?" and we both scrutinize his eyes panning the list before him.

"Take the rental. I shan't be needing it until tomorrow evening," he says without diverting his eyes from his study.

"Don't bother driving," Morgan says. "I'll pick you up tomorrow say, oh, around six AM?"

"You guys start early."

"When I shoot on location *Mother Nature* is always my gaffer. *She* gets up early."

"What on earth is *a gaffer*?" Emerald inquires, arranging the silverware.

"The *head* electrician."

"That's nonsensical," Emerald huffs.

"Alright," I say. "It's a date."

"Hardly *a date*," she laughs. "We're behind schedule. I'll be shooting my *tush* off. But it'll be fun having you along."

"Thank you. I look forward to it."

Audrey enters carrying two glassfuls of dark Guinness beer and gives one to Lucien. When I raise my hand to receive the other, she frowns.

"Get your own," and she proceeds to empty the pint glass by half.

"Audrey really. Willem is a guest in our house," Emerald informs her.

"I didn't put up a sign saying *keep out*," she says and Emerald scowls, poking her daughter's rump.

"Would you be kind enough to put the fennel bread on the table? Everyone, dinner is served."

On the morning of the second day I attend Morgan's fashion shoot on location at the Palace of Fine Arts, a large expansive stucco façade reminiscent of ancient Byzantine architecture. We park her car in the rear lot and make our way into the grounds. She breathes in deeply.

"You smell that?"

"What?" I ask.

"The Pacific Ocean. It smells completely different than the Atlantic don't you think?"

"Oh? How so?"

Before she can answer we're assailed by a bearded young man in a thick woolen sweater.

"Good morning Morgan," he says taking her camera bag from her shoulder. "The grip truck just arrived. I'm having them park next to the shooting set as you asked."

"Will this is my manager. Laz this is Willem, a friend. He's here to watch us shoot." He cups my fist in his.

"Solid. I'll get him a laminate so no one bothers him."

"Have all the models arrived yet?"

"Trickling in…about half. Claudia and Nina have already set up their stations under the rotunda."

"Perfect. Take us straight there."

The head makeup stylist is a vivacious British woman named Claudia with orange hair wrapped in a knot atop her head and held in place by two lacquered chopsticks. Her lead hair stylist is an Asian woman named Nina who doesn't say much; a gaggle of hairpins in her mouth and a model's hair in her fingers. She wears glasses that appear to be bifocals although she looks to be only thirty years of age. There are several assistants who all manage to stay busy and a police officer munching on a granola bar and sipping a cup of coffee at the craft service.

"Good morning Love," Claudia says embracing Morgan, kissing her on both cheeks. "You look smashing." I clearly see the affection they share.

"Ready to rock-and-roll Claude?"

"Born ready. I pitch, you catch. Do try to keep up."

The entablature of the palace is crowned with lifelike effigies of Romanesque women, their backs facing outwards and draped in long flowing dresses clearly conveying the exquisite female form. The *palace grounds* encompass a large aquatic pond, a fountain shooting water to a height of perhaps fifteen feet. Sitting at the foot of the enormous rotunda is an impressive domed structure, open on all sides, that serves as the centerpiece of *the temple*.

There's a five-ton grip truck and four grips. Two of the grips, secure large sheets of white translucent muslin, twenty-by-twenty-foot squares on aluminum frames, that serves to diffuse the direct sunlight. A third grip holds a four-by-four white-board *bouncing* light back underneath the model's chin. Standing about is a plethora of beautiful women, models in an amazing array of costuming and expressive makeup. We shoot in a variety of locations beneath the ornate structure–that seems to serve no discernable function other than its beauty and grace.

I'm surprised by the transition of Morgan's personality. It's nearly as if watching an entirely different person. Here, she is clearly the master photographer and artist, firmly in charge of this entire *pantheon* of outlandish characters. She seems deeply respected by the models and crew. Her black t-shirt, with the sleeves rolled up onto her shoulders, reads: *Paul's Boutique* on the front and *The Beastie Boys* on the back. She wears boots and a pair of old blue Levis, blown-out at the knees. The shoot grinds on into the afternoon.

Eventually we settle on the large grassy lawn between the street that frames a southern border of the palace. The pond, to the north, reflects the sun's golden rays, behind us to the southwest.

They have lined up a series of shots and the models, done up in brilliant creative ways, file through one at a time, each taking her place in the blocking Morgan has set for the series. She is shooting hundreds of photographs. At a certain point she gestures to the lanky tattooed camera assistant wearing a New York Knicks jersey.

"Zig, I'm tired of this techno-pop, it's been techno-pop all day."

"Well what do you want?" he asks, forearms raised.

"Where's my ipad?"

"On the mag-liner."

"Stick that in and put it on shuffle," she says. He hustles over to one of the carts that hold a player and speakers that pump music to the set and an older *Sonic Youth* tune is the first song to erupt. She gives him the thumbs up and gestures for more volume and returns to the shoot, passing on the model she's been shooting and beckons the next girl; a willowy brunette with vividly colored eyes steps into the light and immediately begins striking exaggerated but chic poses. Morgan clicks away several dozen photos. The girl blends with the intense rhythms of the tune, tossing her hair about and engaging with the lens.

"Some hip," Morgan says gesturing, her hand on her hip. The model responds immediately doing so in a variety of poses and angles sometimes looking into the lens sometimes toward the sun hidden behind the muslin over our shoulders.

"Dickie let's try some air," Morgan says to the older grip–standing opposite the guy holding the bounce card–and the fellow scrambles for a hand held wind machine and begins intermittingly fanning the model's almond colored tresses creating beautiful windy patterns. "Nice," she says from the eyepiece firing away. After about fifty photos she says, "Okay lose it, thanks." She waves the next model over. "Zig, let's go back to the fifty." The assistant instantly hands off another camera with a slightly different lens. I watch as she adjusts the framing and focus snapping a couple shots. "Pout for me," she says from around the camera and the model does this. "More," she says from behind the eyepiece and the model instantly exaggerates the look. "Little less…good." About twelve more pictures. "Next please, thank you."

The next model, a tall sultry young woman takes the exact spot and begins striking a variety of poses. Morgan immediately begins shooting what she's doing without saying a word until she stops abruptly and shouts over to the camera team. "Ziggy, the card's full." He jumps as if someone were having a heart attack. He checks the camera, shouting an expletive. He doesn't change the card but immediately retrieves another camera. Morgan begins to frame the shot then stops, handing the camera back toward him.

"Zig, I'm on the fifty," she says calmly. He swears again, grabbing a different camera and jumps–knocking over a case–and hands this off to her.

The model is doing very interesting things, more fluid than the previous model's wilder dramatics. "Who's your favorite band?" she asks from the eyepiece.

"I don't know, I'm kinda eclectic," she says and laughs. More photos. Morgan stops and gestures for another camera, but Zig is busy chewing out the second camera assist for not formatting the card in the other camera. Morgan waits for him until he turns.

"I want to go with the wide please," she says with no great urgency and waits as he grabs another camera. When he arrives with it, she looks it over a moment. "Do we have the super-wide, the rental?"

"Of course," he says.

"Get that on, and kick up the ISO two stops," she says handing the camera back.

Like watching a brain surgeon at work, he has the camera upon his portable table and quickly and efficiently swaps out the lenses and filters taking care to dust them. *Dickie* sides up to her.

"I know we're losing light. Do you want us to prep the flash system?" he asks. Morgan shakes her head.

"No thanks Dick. Let's stay with *the big ball* until she goes to bed. I love the orange we're getting…it's beautiful don't you think? The west coast gets that little extra pink in the orange, it's very different than back east. Not as rich as the Italian sunsets but…nice." He nods returning to his spot, the remaining grip takes his side.

"Prep the flash Dick?"

"Put it all to bed. Strike everything that isn't working."

While Morgan waits, she scans the sidewalk behind us. I realize there's a small group of people forming, watching the spectacle. We're like some modern version of a renaissance fair, with the models in exotic costume and the crew and production vehicles in tow gathered around the set like a carnival train.

The camera soon arrives and Morgan checks something on its screen returning to the model. The music moves on to some French techno-beat as Morgan gets closer and more intimate with the model, setting her frame and focus from different angles, whispering with her all the while. She takes a few quick snaps, another adjustment, a few more pictures.

"How old are you?" Morgan asks the model.

"Eighteen."

"Oh really?" Morgan says obviously being coy and the model laughs; Morgan snapping another dozen pictures. "How long have you been doing this?"

"Since I was five." More pictures.

"Your mother's dream?" she asks and the girl laughs, a flurry of photos.

"Exactly. You got it. Just like *Mommie Dearest*."

"So…you like it or what?"

"Yeah, I like it." Several more shots from different angles the model getting reflective.

"You're good at it," Morgan says, and the model looks deep into the lens, striking a dramatic pose, good for another dozen pictures or so.

"Thanks, so are you," the girl says which makes Morgan grin.

"Have some fun," she says, and the model strikes a series of carefree poses. Morgan slams out at least fifty shots before she stops and asks, "What's your name?"

"Angie," the model says. I had noticed earlier that Morgan kept a small Leica camera hanging at her hip. She slides the Canon onto her back and takes up the Leica snapping a few more shots of the model, the last few very coquettish.

"Thanks Angie, take a break…nice work." The model heads to the makeup table. Claudia is looking squarely at Morgan who answer's *that look*. "Claude, let's wrap gold and move on to the blue set."

"Smashing darling," Claudia says and there's instantly a flurry of activity in the Hair and Make-up departments. Morgan walks to where I'm standing near the camera gear. Zig and the second assistant are engaged in a verbal row that's getting personal. Morgan calls him over.

"Knock it off Zig, it's not a big deal," she says.

"Not a big deal?" he says indignantly. "Yeah, it is a *big deal* Morgan," he responds loudly, "a very big deal."

"It's just a full card, it's not-"

"I'm not talking about the f'ing card," he interrupts, "or the f'ing wrong lens or how goddamn frickin' slow he is! It's everything…his incompetence, his frickin' pissy attitude."

"Zig, just calm down. We're doing pretty good. We're almost caught up."

"Whatever," he says annoyed. "But next time, *if*, there is a next time, I'm bringing Diesel. Why hire a local Morgan? *My* second…a local, really?" She turns, taking my arm and we stroll in the direction of the sidewalk. She's fuming.

"You got a cigarette?" she asks pinching her temples.

"I thought you said you quit?" I tease her and she smiles.

"Moi? I think you have me mixed up with another woman?" We smile together. Two, very contemporary, young women approach us holding books and magazines.

"Ms. MacIntyre?" the brunette asks, and Morgan shades her eyes, squinting in the thin golden band of sunlight that sneaks through the tree line.

"Yes?"

"We're students from the San Francisco Art Institute. I wonder if I could get your autograph?"

"Me too," the bleach-blonde says and Morgan laughs.

"You want my autograph?"

"Hella yeah," the first girl says and extends a black covered book toward her. Morgan seems to freeze, taking the book in her hands and caressing it, almost adoringly.

"Where did you get this?" she asks the girl.

"From one of my instructors." The girls exchange a strange look then laugh out loud.

"Ha. Right," her friend chides.

"Well…maybe I borrowed it."

"Maybe you stole it." More laughter. Morgan looks at me and I see a distinct change in her demeanor.

"What is it?" I ask. Her eyes search mine, moving back and forth between both pupils.

"It's a copy of my book."

"Your book?" I say bewildered, reaching down and opening it.

"Yeah. It's out of print now." Inside is a collection of the most stunning photography I have ever seen. It ranges from bright colorful fashion shots to stark black and white portraits. We spend a moment paging thru it, the girls commenting on certain photos.

"Why don't you republish this digitally?" the girl asks, and Morgan tosses the cigarette away.

"Yeah, I suppose that would be a good idea."

"Hell yeah," the girl says. "Your work is the shit man. I want to shoot like you…real people in their real worlds." Morgan looks at her and smiles, but the smile seems laced with concern. As she stands there with the sun, golden on her face, I see a subtle yet profound sadness in her eyes.

She returns her attention to the book, gently leafing through it until she reaches a full-page black and white portrait of a young barefoot girl on a New York street. She stares at the photo then abruptly closes the cover and apparently, I'm the only one who seems aware that this photograph pains her deeply.

"Thank you," she says to the girl. "Thank you for bringing this." The two exchange a smile. Suddenly Zig is at her shoulder.

"Hey, we're ready. Claudia is lining up the blue set now." The smile vanishes from Morgan's face. There's a small pensive glance back at the set.

"Zig, do you have a sharpie on you?"

"Of course," he says. It's the same *'of course'* I've been hearing from him the entire day.

"What's your name?"

"Beatrice," the girl says, excitement in her eyes. Morgan writes something to her and returns the book. "Wow, awesome. Thank you!" The other girl hands her copies of two fashion magazines–Morgan's photography on the covers–and she signs these too. As we leave, Beatrice extends her hand. "A pleasure to meet you," and the smile returns to Morgan's face for a fleeting moment.

"You too. Take care." We head back toward the set.

"What's up first, you want to stay on the wide?" Zig asks seemingly unaware that this chance encounter has pained his employer.

"I don't care," she says softly.

"What the hell Morgan?" he says abruptly. She flashes a hard look at him. "What?" he asks defensively. "I'm supposed to make this shit up?"

"Ok then, put on the *twenty-four to seventy zoom* on, the F-two-eight," she says, and he acts nonplussed.

"The *zoom* lens, not a *prime*? Are you serious?" he says, and she stops and glares at him.

"Maybe I want to play around a little Ziggy, you know? Have some fun. This used to be fun, remember?" He throws his arms up in the air and heads toward the camera cart. "And cue up some *old school* on the playback…the Chemical Brothers!" she shouts.

"Whatever," he snaps over his shoulder. When she looks at me, it's not a happy look.

"He's a wound-up guy," I say. We watch as he shouts at the second assist again; she sighs deeply.

"It's not his fault," she says and looks into my eyes. "It's mine. It's my fault the way he's become." I'm shocked by this sudden admission.

"How is it possibly your fault?"

"I did this to him," she says, and I laugh out loud.

"I doubt it.". She fathoms my expression.

"He's been with me ten years. Those were tough years. He's biting back at me now, for those days when I was-" She stops mid-sentence, and as if shaking off the past. "…less conscious." She smiles, a thin fragile smile.

"I don't get you."

"Now that I'm no longer shouting and screaming…he sees it as weakness."

"Why don't you just get a new assistant?" I ask, and again I see that near invisible look of pain.

"And that would be the final irony wouldn't it?" After those crazy years, being too hard on him, putting the work before the human being…to just let him go. It would kill him. He could never work on this level. No one would hire him."

"Why? He seems to know the equipment." She turns, her body close to mine and looks deeply into my eyes.

"Because to do this sort of thing, to photograph people on this level Willem, you have to care about them, in front and behind the camera," she says her gaze growing misty. "You can shout and scream but you have to have compassion for them, despite whether they're egotistical or insecure…as long as they know." Her eyes grow deep and intense, as if looking into another world and I find myself transfixed by the emotion welling in her delicate, beautiful eyes. "Like those photographs in that book just now…you have to see yourself in them, *walk in their footsteps*…does that make sense?" she asks but before I can respond, Claudia strolls up.

"I'm sorry to interrupt my darlings," she says endearingly, glancing between us, "but I need you Love, just a wee bit." They instantly turn toward the Hair and Makeup station. "I'll have her right back," Claudia says to me graciously and that's the last I talk to Morgan the remainder of the shoot.

That night, back at the house on Sutter Street, I find it impossible to sleep. Thoughts about my time with Morgan and the upcoming trip to Europe fill my mind. Eventually I decide to stroll the house and it's during my nocturnal sojourn that I surprise Emerald's daughter Audrey silently descending the stairway. After her initial shock, we commence a quiet conversation culminating with an invitation to join her in '*a walk to the park*.' Perhaps due to my anxiety, I find myself agreeing. I quickly change and meet her outside on the front stoop where she smokes under the streetlight. We begin a slow pace into the quiet misty evening. The houses and shops are all quiet, only the buzzing of the halogen lamps, and the low hiss and rumble of the city, permeate the evening.

"How come Morgan doesn't stay at the house?" I eventually ask, more to break the silence. She stares at me with an incredulous look on her face.

"Are you stupid?" she asks. I don't know what to say. "She's in the Saint Francis on Union Square. You'd stay with your mom instead of taking a suite in a five-star hotel?"

"I guess that *was* a stupid question," I admit, and her quiet reaction indicates she agrees with me fully. Perhaps to take the edge off her response she begins talking about her sister.

"How was your visit to her set today?" she asks.

"Good. Your sister is a pretty good photographer." She looks at me with a sudden disdain.

"I doubt you even realize how ridiculous that comment is."

"What?"

"That's like saying Rembrandt was a *pretty good* painter. She's known around the world man, she's on top of her game. Well...at least she was."

"*Was?* What do you mean?"

"Exactly how long have you worked for my mother anyway?"

"I don't really work for her. I'm employed principally by Mr. Karras."

"Okay then, how long have you worked for Uncle Lucien?"

"Not very long," I say obliquely.

"What's your job anyway?" she asks and it's as if I'm suddenly being grilled.

"I'm one of their business managers...the one that travels."

"What business school did you go to?"

"I didn't. I went to school for Cinema." She looks at me curiously.

"I don't get it. Are you trying to be flip?"

"Not at all. I was in Paris working as a production manager on a French television project, which shouldn't have happened really since I don't speak French, but I'd worked with the Producer on a documentary production in America and-"

"I'd like to work on a film someday," she interrupts. "Is it fun?" she asks warming somewhat.

"Well, depends upon a lot of things, the cast and crew, the location where you're shooting, how intense the schedule is…there's a lot of parameters."

"I bet it beats Fashion," she says, and I puzzle about her meaning.

"What do you mean?"

"Never mind."

We stroll on several more blocks when she gestures toward a large stand of eucalyptus trees and we disappear into the darkness beneath their boughs. Suddenly I'm standing within a group of young people smoking cigarettes and drinking beer.

Eventually she introduces me to two of the young fellows nearest us. They offer me a beer, which I decline. She leaves me standing there while she talks quietly with several other youths. Just at the point I'm thinking of heading back to the house there's a loud sharp whistle from the hillside and I see a young woman waving us to join them.

"Hey Manella, up yours," she shouts extending her middle finger and Audrey pulls my arm.

"C'mon."

I follow her back under the moonlight–painting everything in surreal indigo tones–to a picnic table on the crest of the hill where two young people, a guy and a Goth looking girl with too much mascara, sit quietly conversing and drinking. Audrey embraces and kisses the young man. He wears a sleeveless white t-shirt, oily jeans and heavy motorcycle boots. His dark hair stands on end and his ears are pierced with a dozen or so earrings.

"Hey Manella-Prunella, who's your new boyfriend?" the girl says and laughs. Audrey gazes at me with a purposefully bland expression.

"The loudmouth is Sara, that's Teague," Audrey says. "This is mom's business manager." They all look at me. He reluctantly holds out his hand and we shake.

"You work with Audrey's mom?" he asks in a sort of ramshackle voice.

"Well, sort of, I work for Mr. Karras." He looks at Audrey then back at me and in total sincerity asks:

"You see ghosts?" I'm caught off guard, thinking this is some form of amusement however there is no sense of levity in his question as they all wait for my answer.

"I beg your pardon?" I ask. He looks at Audrey who shrugs.

"Um...I asked if...ya know...you see ghosts," he repeats. I look at Audrey who also seems to be waiting for a response.

"Uh...no, I haven't," I say. They exchange quiet unassuming looks. "Why did you ask me that?" He seems to mull over this question and shrugs.

"Well...because...you know..." He looks at Audrey who is taking a drink from the girl's bottle of beer. "They all see 'em...so I thought...that's maybe why you work for them?"

The Goth girl stares at me and hangs by one hand from Audrey's shoulder.

"Just because he works for the firm doesn't make him a ghost hunter," Audrey interjects. "He's a filmmaker...a production manager." Teague runs a hand through his spiky black hair.

"Oh," is all he says, then to Audrey, "so...are you coming over tonight?"

"I can't...they fly to Prague tomorrow."

"Prague? Why?"

"Ghost hunting, what else," she says coolly. They all quietly mull this over as if it were just another everyday conversation.

"Are you going?" he asks her.

"Why should I?"

"So...are you coming to the concert tomorrow then?" he asks. She takes a long drink, thinking.

"Like I said, it depends." He takes her hand gently in his, playing with her thin ivory fingers. I notice that his hands seem large and strong.

"C'mon," he whispers, "I want you to come." Audrey *thinks* this over.

"I better get back...early morning tomorrow." They kiss and he stands, tossing a beaten leather jacket over his shoulder and looks at me.

"So...you really don't see 'em?" he asks, total sincerity in his tone.

"Ghosts you mean? No." He ponders this a moment.

"Then...be careful," he says and heads off down the hill, Sara close behind. Audrey turns back toward the house on Sutter.

"C'mon, let's go."

A heavy fog has begun to settle on the city and a cold moist breeze blows in from the dark Pacific Ocean. I tighten my collar. Audrey seems oblivious to the night's sting, lost in her thoughts. After walking several blocks in silence, I decide to break the quietude.

"Is he your boyfriend?"

"Seriously? That's a stupid word...meaningless."

"Is he in some sort of rock-and-roll band?"

"*Rock and roll?*"

"*The concert tomorrow.*"

"He's training to be a pianist. He's playing with the San Francisco Youth Symphony tomorrow in Golden Gate Park."

"Oh," I say, surprise lacing my voice.

"What's the deal man?"

"*Deal?*"

"You think my friends are a bunch of low-life dopers? It surprises you one of them can play Rachmaninov?" I look at her, surprised by her sudden expostulation.

"No, no I don't mean that," I stammer and study her. "Being in a rock-and-roll band doesn't infer you're a low-life. Some of those people are the wealthiest persons on the planet."

"Oh really? And why does the quality of a person's life have anything to do with money? Does money mean everything to you?"

I'm dumbstruck. "What? I'm not-"

"I really don't know you, but I think I know what your problem is."

"My problem?"

"Yeah, you judge things, people, by their wrapper, that's a mistake," she says. "I'm surprised Uncle Lucien hasn't hammered that out of you by now."

We walk on for several minutes in complete silence. I'm completely dumbstruck and somewhat irritated when we make the stoop of the house on Sutter Street. She heads up the stairs while I wait on the sidewalk looking at the streetlamp glowing in the mist, lost in my thoughts. She stops and looks at me.

"Hey, don't get all pissed-off about what I said. I'm just winding you up," she says quietly unlocking the door. Then suddenly she stops, turns and stares at me. "Hey man…when you get to Europe…can you keep an eye on my mom please?"

"What do you mean?" I ask, total confusion.

"Just…watch out for her." Long pause. "Think you can manage that…*manager*?"

"Okay," I say shrugging my shoulders. She continues to stare at me for the longest time before slowly stepping down the stairs.

"They can't hurt you you know."

"*They*?"

"The spirits of the dead. They're no longer of this world, so they can't hurt you. But what mother and Uncle Lucien are searching for isn't a ghost, it's worse than that, much worse." Her eyes become black pools cast in shadow from the streetlamp's shallow glow.

"What are you getting at?"

"It's something Uncle Lucien said to me…a while ago. When they brought me back from Los Angeles." She stares waiting for me to respond.

"What did he say?"

"He said: '*It isn't the ghosts you need to fear, it's the demons that masquerade as ghosts that are the mortal dread.*'" She looks at me in the darkness and her words strike an odd sensation.

"That's rather ominous."

"Does that mean anything to you?" I'm somewhat shocked by this sudden and unexpected question.

"I don't know. I've never thought about something like that before." She stares unmoving.

"Well you better start," she says and something in her tone sends a spike of energy down my back. She shakes her head. "Man, I give Uncle Lucien a lot of credit for not giving up on you. I would." She turns and enters the dark and quiescent house. I sit outside on the stoop for a long time thinking about the meaning behind these words.

The following morning is cloaked in a steady persistent rain. Morgan arrives early and parks the white SUV she's renting at the curb. An excitement arises within me when I see her again, to be near her. We load the satchels and luggage taking pains not to get our feet wet in the rivulet that's formed in the gutter. After she's satisfied with the pack, we have a cup of coffee together while Lucien and Emerald remain sequestered in the study.

I realize, while sitting within the dark muted warmth of the Victorian–the rain pouring down outside–that Morgan has begun to intrigue me deeply. It's almost a kind of déjà-vu but more profound as the sensation continues to build instead of dissipating. As she talks about yesterday's photo shoot I'm acutely observant of small details about her; the rain droplets clinging to the laces of her hair and eyelashes, her fingers in the way she holds her cup; the clothes she wears–as black as space– with tapering sleeves that accent her arms and wrists. Mid-sentence she stops and stares at me.

"Am I boring you?" she asks, a hint of sarcasm.

"Not at all," I insist.

"I don't feel you're listening to me."

"You were talking about technical problems with the lenses you rented, and cropping." She smiles. I realize those green irises are perfect, and unique.

"Go on," she challenges me.

"Well, you were unhappy with some of the models because they weren't focused on their *craft* as you call it."

"That's right. What else?"

"Um, you talked a lot about hair, clothes and make-up, stuff I really know nothing about." She laughs softly, looking into me intently. "How long have you been a photographer?" I ask to change the topic. She leans back to pet the orange tabby that rubs at her boot, crying to be picked up.

"Since I was seven," she says, and I surmise there's more to that story. The feline suddenly jumps onto her lap and the conversation dissipates.

"Rufus, no. I can't have your hair all over me before my meeting." She places him back onto the carpet and he whips his tail, displaying his discontent. She dusts off her arms and legs. I fear our conversation slipping away.

"You've a meeting today?"

She rolls her eyes. "Yeah. With the boss. She's flying in from New York. I don't think she'll dig the proofs from yesterday either." She rises and stares out the window at the falling rain, her slender form like a dark shadow in the muted light silhouetted against the panes of the bay window.

"Are you shooting this afternoon?"

"We were supposed to shoot this afternoon but…looks like Mother Nature cancelled that." She turns and studies me. "That's who's in charge. She's the boss *on location*."

"Can't you use the rain creatively?" I ask and she laughs loudly.

"You're right, I guess you don't know anything about hair, makeup and wardrobe. Oh, I'd just love to see the models roll with that." She laughs softly to herself.

"In film production, we work in the rain sometimes, sometimes with rain effects." I say and she becomes contemplative.

"We never work in the rain...unfortunately...it's so beautiful. But these girls would just melt, like little witches."

"Little witches?" I say and she laughs.

"Okay, sorry I said that...some of these chicks take this stuff seriously...but it's not like Europe." She returns her gaze outside. "That's what I mean about models and casting. Don't send me chicks out of high school because they're tall and have a pretty face...you need *a woman,* who has experience and knows herself," she says. "The European female has that over the American...they didn't grow up being cheerleaders." Her dark silhouette standing before the rain-spattered window, sends me to another place, another time.

"What do you mean?"

"How else can you capture the moment? That single frame, single increment of time if you're not *here, now*? A good photograph, a winner, all rides upon two things...the model's inner moment and the photographer's ability to get it, immediately or through a slow meticulous process." She gazes at the street. "A good model understands that. the process, and that it's *now*. She becomes more than just herself in front of a camera...she becomes *Woman,* in all our mysterious guises." She turns and her dark eyes push me further into somewhere timeless.

"Yes…I think I know it when I see it."

"The problem with too many models is they're not in *the now*…they're thinking about yesterday or tomorrow. I tell these chicks–only a handful ever get it–I'm not paying you for yesterday or tomorrow, I need *you*…right now. Not your body or your face, I need *you*…not thinking about your date tonight or whatever." She sips her coffee. "Maybe it's exactly that, *thinking*. They're always thinking. That's the difference. A great model doesn't think…*she just is…look at me…Woman.*" She sits down and looks deeply into my eyes. "Does that make sense to you, or am I babbling?"

"It does," I say with conviction and our eyes lock.

"You should come sometime…next time we shoot Europe. You'd see exactly what I'm talking about," she says not breaking eye contact. We stare at each other in the dim light. "It's all about the eyes…all the best cinema, the best photography…it's in the eyes…that's where *the moment* comes from."

She looks deep into my pupils and I've no problem keeping her gaze, her eyes are tranquil and alluring. We sit this way silent and unmoving until the arrival of her mother and Lucien. The women immediately interact but I notice Lucien looking at me oddly.

"Are you ready?" he inquires. I stand and nod. He doesn't break-off eye contact and I squirm a bit under his stare.

"Where is Audrey?" Emerald inquires. She seems pensive and preoccupied.

"Asleep, you can hug her when you get back."

"But she's driving us to the airport," Emerald says, and Morgan seems abashed.

"Mom, I'm driving you to the airport. I blocked out the morning for you."

"But your *shoot* dear, I don't want to interrupt your work."

"Mom, look," she says pointing out the window. "It's raining! The shoot's been cancelled," she says, a harshness permeating her voice. Emerald stands looking at her and her soft azure gaze suddenly clouds and a thin line of tears stream down her cheek. Morgan instantly embraces her, wrapping her arms around her. "I'm sorry. I didn't mean it to sound the way it did," she says in her ear. "I'm sorry."

She holds Emerald tightly burying her face into the mother's neck. Lucien quietly steps to where I stand, extracting the car keys from the tabletop and hands them to me. "Willem, would you mind warming up the car?" he whispers. "We'll be along in a minute."

I exit the confines of the house, skirting the puddles pooling the concrete, and take the driver's seat; starting the engine. The encapsulated vacuum of the vehicle is absolute. I watch the rain falling across the windshield, create strange undulating patterns bending and contorting the dim light of morning. The interior of the automobile is disheveled; a chaotic state. There are production forms, call sheets and printed photo proofs littering the seats. A large three ring binder filled with resumes and the headshots of models' faces, placidly staring back at me, lies open upon the dash. Morgan's purse, wallet and mobile phone sit atop the center column in plain view. A half-empty coffee cup congeals in the holder next to what appears to be a battery charger for a camera and another for a mobile phone. The vehicle's ashtray is overflowing with burnt cigarettes; many hardly consumed.

Something about the chaos distresses me. There's a pack of Marlboro's on the column. I take one, exit the confinement of the car and stand outside to smoke. The street seems vacant, everything in gray; the houses, the sidewalk and street drenched in water like a coat of gray paint. The immense sky above drops rain upon my head saturating my shoulders. I pull the collar of my jacket up around my ears and cup the tiny burning ember of the cigarette within my palm as if it were something precious.

The following afternoon the three of us are seated in the lobby of the hotel in Prague. I watch people pass through the marbled colonnades of the stately old building that once housed the Communist leadership of former Czechoslovakia. A young man in a bellman's uniform approaches.

"Madame Montaigne?" he asks in fairly clear English. Emerald answers and he hands her a slip of paper. She tips him and we are immediately on our legs exiting onto the broad boulevard swarming with people. It's a fine clear morning, the trams trundle up and down the length of the old thoroughfare.

"Our colleague, Doctor Kucera, will meet us for coffee in the Malostranska in one hour," Emerald declares. "This allows us more than enough time to walk the Karlmost. Is your leg up to the journey Lucien?"

"Quite," he responds, tapping his leg with the boot of his cane. "I'd like to see the Staro Mesto Square again…in particular the old clock." He winks at her.

"Splendid!" she beams taking up both our arms. "Imagine, back in lovely Prague with a handsome gentleman on each arm, I'm in heaven," she laughs, her face glowing.

We turn off the boulevard and stroll down the narrow winding cobblestone streets of old Prague, making the square within, what seems, a matter of minutes. The *old clock,* as my intrepid employer understates it, is an architectural–and astronomical–masterpiece, the center of the Staro Mesto Nameste.

"*The Orloj is an astrolabe,*" Emerald says to me her eyes beaming, "and quite magical, look, see the rooster, *our symbol,*" she says pointing toward a golden rooster. I don't connect with her meaning and she doesn't elaborate, becoming transfixed with the enormous mechanism on the face of the building. "It's over six hundred years old," she says. I gaze about the clock-face and its Gothic characters as Lucien and Emerald discuss the astronomical dial in detail. I become completely lost to their words and their meaning, advanced concepts about space and time.

My attention wanes and I look about the old town square. I'm impressed by the mix of tourists throughout this enormous open plaza that must have seen so many amazing and incredible moments of the past. Eventually– probably on time–the old wooden figurines emerge from their ticky-tack doors and play out a small drama. A garish skeleton figure emerges.

"What is that?" I ask and my colleagues both look at me.

"Death," Lucien says matter-of-factly.

"Oh." I watch as the withered effigies interact with the bell, *and another hour of this century is sounded.* The exhibition delights Lucien and Emerald, I sense there's some history here. I watch my friends, arm-in-arm, seeing the smiles on their faces, like children around the tree at Christmas and a deep feeling of empathy for these persons reverberates through my being.

The old clock sends its plethora of characters–apparently all crafted by hand hundreds of years ago–in a slow methodical circumference; the witches and goblins, the farmer and his wife, the old King and his buffoon, the menacing Cardinal and the glorious but pensive apostles. When the enormous machine once again grows still, we resume our slow methodical advance toward destiny.

As we meander westerly along a narrow curving street, we stop before a tiny archaic church sandwiched between two residential buildings. It is an old venerable building, richly adorned in trappings of religious history. Lucien and I watch as Emerald genuflects and lights a tiny candle in the foyer placing it amongst a throng of others. She then approaches the rich ornate alter, again genuflects and sits motionless before the cross. She's silent, in prayer, or meditation; we wait patiently as she spends a moment with herself–or her God–before rejoining us and proceeding outside. I sense that this process is not new to her and that her familiarity with the ancient city is not a novice one.

I find myself wondering about her; puzzle over the mystery that I perceive in this woman. I know she's older than her countenance bears–her lovely face–for the eyes are deep and knowledgeable, they emit the type of *knowing* that only comes with time and experience; eyes that see much deeper into the illusion of the material world. They possess a rich mixture of wisdom and inner intensity that gives off a strange amalgam of light and darkness both. Deep inside me I know those eyes have held witness the joys of existence as well as the awe–undoubtedly the horrors–of physical reality.

Soon we are at the banks of the Vltava, its dark turbulent waters flowing to join her gentler sister, the Elbe, to the South. Spanning this mighty river is the *Karlmost Bridge* named after the beloved king Charles who built Prague in the sixteen-hundreds into the centerpiece of Europe.

One realizes immediately the importance and grandeur of the structure. The ornate and decorative bridge elegantly connects the old city center with the *Malostranska* district nestled on the opposite side of the river. The majestic spires and gothic belfries of the *Hradzany* castle tower above this historic center of political and spiritual leadership. As we stand staring at the castle in the hazy mist I look into Emerald's eyes glittering in the sunlight and she looks into mine. For a moment I sense the joy, the history, she and the old city have shared together.

"Magnificent," she says, and we step out onto the ancient structure.

Magnificent is barely adequate a word to describe the bridge and the *Hradzany*. The bridge's entire length–both walls–are adorned with life-sized effigies of past kings, queens and saints. When one stands before these figures, they are so very life-like as to give the impression that they are in fact *alive or possessed of some kind of awareness*. The thought that a kind of consciousness is present and looking back at you is so distinct that I find myself staring back over my shoulder at a few of them as we make our way across the structure.

At the extreme center of the bridge stands *the Christ*, gilded with a golden aura, he stands open palmed bearing witness to man's penchant for separation from *Universal thought.*

As we approach the Malostranska on the western bank, the ancient castle's gothic cathedral stands tall and majestic in the morning light, the spires and belfries piercing the ether above. We make our way through the thick stone archways and for a fraction of an instance I feel myself here, this very same place, centuries prior. In the distance we spot a thriving restaurant with a large white marquee with red lettering.

"There's the *Kavarna* just ahead," Emerald reports and we follow her up the winding street.

It is an old and weathered place with a warped wooden floor smoothed and sanded by years of human shuffling. We take a small table, deplete of paint, near the front window and order coffee and pastries. The café is peppered with antiquated wood and metal tables and a motley array of chairs all uniformly mismatched. The pastries are delicious, but the coffee is less to my liking being the type where the grounds are added directly into the drink. After fifteen minutes Emerald points inconspicuously out the window.

"Here he comes, Dr. Kucera." We watch as a lean slight man dressed in an old-fashioned brown suit makes his way across the street. He enters the Kavarna hanging his hat and cane upon a coat rack near the door and joins our table. He embraces Emerald warmly and kisses her hand.

"Emerald, how long has it been? Much too long."

"Hello Vilos." She kisses his cheek. "These are my travelling companions, my business partner Lucien Karras and his assistant Willem Furey. Gentlemen, this is Doctor Vilos Kucera, my mentor." He cordially greets us taking a seat only after helping Emerald with her chair. He studies her closely.

"My word, you've not changed in the least since I saw you last," he says. "In fact, you still look as you did when you were a student in my class. It's...rather uncanny. *How is it that Time has not touched you my dear?*"

"You are a great liar Vilos," she says laughing. He chuckles softly and withdraws a pair of gold pince-nez eyeglasses and sets them upon his nose as if to *actually see a clearer picture of her.* With the old-fashioned cut of his suit and the pince-nez on his nose the man looks as if he has just stepped out of the late eighteen-hundreds. After his perfunctory study he leans back in his chair pulling the glasses from his nose and commences polishing them with a silk handkerchief.

"So, what brings you back to Prague this time?"

"Something quite serious."

"So I gather from your communiqué." He leans in. "What has happened?"

Emerald conveys him the entirety of the situation. He ponders deep in thought all the while polishing the spectacles, a nervous habit I surmise.

"Radic, you say? Extremely common name in these parts. I should fear your search is not going to be an easy one." Lucien leans forward opening a small pen box revealing the gold lapel pin taken from the Clay Street apartment. Mr. Kucera replaces the pince-nez upon his nose and studies the object with a distinct fascination. "Why, I haven't seen a pin like this in many years, where did you get it?"

"From the murder site," Lucien says grimly.

"The room of the burned man?"

"Precisely. My question Dr. Kucera...is this the genuine article? What can you tell us about it?"

The old man retrieves it, turns it about in his fingers several times, examining it closely. He looks over the rims of his glasses, his eyes gleaming with renewed energy.

"Distinctly original, look closely. See where the pin meets the placard?" Lucien eyes the pin closely. "This tiny dab of solder? Most probably Czech, a facsimile nowadays would certainly be fabricated as a solid piece." He smiles and points. "The coloring is ceramic instead of paint, also common here. I would imagine if you took pains to have the clay analyzed it would most likely come back as Czech in origin." He holds the pin up between his thumb and forefinger. "There are impressions still within this object…did you take care to note?"

"Quite," Lucien responds, deferring to Emerald.

"This will certainly aid you in your enterprise."

"So we believe."

Kucera leans back in his chair continuing to scrutinize the pin when he suddenly grips it tightly in his fist, closing his eyes. He sits in a state of abject silence without moving for several minutes before coming back to life.

"Give me a few hours, I believe I'll have something concrete for you. Can you loan me this?"

"Most certainly," Lucien says. "And here is a current roster of the organization we've managed to procure," he says handing Dr. Kucera a plain envelope.

"Very good, this should help as well. I'm sorry but I have to be going," the old doctor says rising. "I've a student arriving in twenty minutes and it will take me exactly that to get there." We all stand. He takes Emerald's hands. His vibrant smile quickly gives way to a darker expression. "Of course, this is very serious business…your endeavor."

"Yes, we do know it," she whispers. "But we mustn't be remiss." He pats her hand quickly regaining his previous demeanor.

"You've not changed, not in the least," he says warmly. "And personally, my dear, I'm quite very pleased about that." They embrace, a warm loving embrace. "Come to my office tonight at closing."

"Thank you Vilos," she says still holding his arm. He waves as if to scatter her words.

"No...no need. The thanks is ours," he says, the sudden look in his eye pricking the hair at my neck. He turns toward Lucien and extends his withered hand. "Mr. Karras, my regards sir. A pleasure to finally make your acquaintance."

"Mine to you Doctor," Lucien says shaking the old man's hand. He then looks at me for a brief moment a gleam in the dark of his pupils, then turns and is gone.

At ten o'clock that evening we are standing outside the *College of Paranormal Psychology Praha*, a nondescript building located several blocks from the Andel tube station. There is nothing but a corroded bronze plaque–staining the beige brick a lustrous shade of blue–that denotes the building's occupation.

A thin gaunt man, with an amazingly bland expression, bodes us welcome and escorts us up two flights of wooden stairs to Dr. Kucera's office where we find him in deep discussion with an incredibly rotund woman well into her seventies. We are introduced to *Madame Linhardt*. She remembers Emerald fondly, the two women speaking together in Czech.

Mr. Kucera produces a bottle of *Becker* and pours each man a shot, *'to warm ourselves'* as he puts it. We toast and the liquor is rich, sweet, and powerful. We take our place around a large round wooden table, the top polished and lustrous.

"We've scrutinized the names from the guild's roster which you gave us. We then correlated the possible persons selected and applied *cognitive resonance*. This is the person you seek, undoubtedly." Kucera withdraws a slip of paper from his breast pocket. "We phoned the guild. He's not been in attendance of late. I took the liberty of taking down his last known address." He slides the small scrap of paper across the table towards Lucien, who studies it, handing it to Emerald.

"Vilos, this address is in the Sixth isn't it? Near Barandov I believe?" she asks.

"Yes, you are correct."

"Barandov?" Lucien inquires.

"The motion picture studio." Emerald returns the paper to Lucien who places it in his notebook.

"Interesting…very interesting," he murmurs.

"Hopefully this information isn't too much out of date," the old doctor says.

"Let us hope," Emerald agrees.

"And let us also hope you are prepared for what you may find," he whispers, and his words tingle my nerve endings. "Madame Linhardt, would you be kind enough to reiterate our previous conversation?"

The queer old woman with intense beady eyes, shuffles in her seat, actually dimming the table lamp and taking in the moment before starting her remarkable recitation.

"The story of *The Burning Man* is well over thirteen centuries in the telling. Over the course of time, the entity's manifestations have been documented due primarily to the gruesome effects it perpetuates upon its living hosts."

"*Effects*?" Emerald whispers.

"What your modern science refers to as *spontaneous combustion,* or in the mystic what is referred as *the Blue Flame*, is in fact the direct results of the creature's *involvement with human hosts*." We all sit there, rather transfixed. "What in antiquity was attributed to the process of witchcraft or sorcery are, in our belief, the results of this entity's *continuation* upon the planet. As mentioned, we trace the elemental's premiere on Earth back over a dozen centuries."

"Good lord…"

"Witness accounts claim, seeing brilliant flashes of light followed by a bright blue flame, then naught but the charred remains of the person. Some are apparently consumed in whole, other records report bits of charred flesh, or feet and hands that remain. In most cases, the torso, head, arms and legs *are entirely consumed by fire*."

"Incredible," Emerald whispers, lacing her fingers across her slender neck.

"There are reports encompassing several hundreds of years in England, France and Germany of people bursting into flame in daylight while in the company of friends and family. However, much more common are reports of the passing of individuals during the night, whilst alone, asleep in their beds or while sitting reading a book or supping, in some instances, a private study or office. Rarely does a conflagration occur; as if the body burns out instantaneously."

"Fascinating," Lucien says quietly. "You're alluding the home or building is almost never destroyed by fire?"

"In very few cases."

"Is it possible the body combusts to such a degree as to rob oxygen from the immediate environment? This could explain such a phenomenon," Lucien says, and the woman stares at him with beady black eyes.

"A very astute observation Mr. Karras, and considering the narrative, quite accurate I should think."

"Go on Clarisse," Kucera interjects.

"I'll have you note the odd and disturbing constant that while people from all walks of life, gender or ethnic backgrounds seem subject to this monstrous affliction, we have never witnessed evidence of it in the animal kingdom, as if the enigma *were prey to the human species alone*. Science offers us no explanation save to say that the inferno is sparked on the sub-molecular level."

"Indeed," Lucien mutters stroking his beard.

"Of course, those of us within the field of study, of the paranormal, disagree in a purely scientific explanation. Emphatically. In fact, we trace a consistent and uninterrupted pattern since the seventh century. This is not mere fancy nor whimsical conceptualization but case fact. We've documented well over two hundred cases of *the Burning Man* since the time of *Charlemagne*. Contained within this meticulous study is a clear and consistent timeline." The old gal finishes her diatribe. You could have heard a pin drop.

"Madame Lindhardt, has there ever been record of an attempt to intervene?" Lucien eventually inquires.

"Intervene?"

"To…interrupt the timeline, shall we say?"

"In antiquity it is impossible to say, however, late eighteen-hundreds, London, the Douma School assigned two doctors and two orderlies to an estate in Dartmoor. The case is highly classified, but the results speak for themselves."

"What happened?" Emerald queries.

"Three dead bodies, two burned beyond recognition, one individual committed to an insane asylum outside of London." We exchange dubious expressions.

"There was another attempt soon after, near the turn of the century in the Banat region," Kucera interjects. "That attempt involved this very organization."

"One of our very earliest advocates, Dr. Marcus Buehler, was apparently *killed* when the home he was occupying caught fire under extremely questionable circumstances while researching two burn victims in the region. As recently as 1928 your fellow countryman the esteemed researcher Dr. E. Noel Petterson disappeared without trace while investigating two burns in New London, Connecticut, and Glen Cove, New York."

"Tell me Dr. Linhardt," Lucien interrupts, "does your group have a suspect, or suspects, in mind?"

"We have been tracking a series of incidents on the continent since the nineties, until a break occurred."

"A break you say?"

"Would *lull* be the more appropriate word?" she asks and Kucera nods. "We lost the thread and feared our objective had slipped away."

"What then?" Lucien inquires.

"*Then*?" she asks and looks to Dr. Kucera and back to us. "Why…*you* called."

This effectively terminated our meeting. After a prolonged silence, Kucera informs his companion that Emerald had been one of his most promising students at which point Mme. Linhardt engages Emerald in a lengthy conversation in her native tongue. It was obvious that all had been said for the moment. Lucien became reticent, sinking into one of his silent and detached meditations. I was certain he was ascertaining the gravity of the situation. I excuse myself and retire outside to smoke.

The night air is cool and refreshing after the confines of the upper chamber and its macabre conversation. I watch the ancient city narrowly from the recesses of a small garden, an innocuous courtyard open to the avenue, as the last hackneyed old tram trundled down the desolate landscape of the street carrying its last human occupant of the night.

As I sit in the solitude of the quiet garden my thoughts shift from the dark business at hand to thoughts about Morgan. I see her clearly in my mind, her handsome face, her mysterious eyes, the soft melodic words and I drift off into a kind of reverie, not asleep yet neither entirely cognizant, and *Time* disappears, for the moment, and the moment extends itself into an hour.

It is nearly midnight when my friends join me, the streets derelict, forgotten, only the wind and dust remaining. We say our solemn goodbyes to Kucera at the door and leave to walk the austere and complacent night in silence. Neither of my companions seem anxious to disturb the quiet solitude the city has wrapped around us like a velvety blanket; mist swirling at our feet as we retrace our steps back toward the Andel subway station.

A cab loiters at the curb and we all solemnly take our seats inside, I in the front, Lucien and Emerald in the back. She exchanges conversation with the driver in Czech, the car lurching forward into the bleak night. Not a word is spoken the entire trip back to the Staro Mesto.

We do not return to the hotel at all but to a subterranean restaurant just off the square. We descend a flight of stone steps leading under the street into a dimly lit and smoky underground room lined with thick wooden tables and benches; a relic from the communist occupation I surmise. Emerald orders for us: '*goulash, cyr, knedlicky and pivo*' (shredded-pork in gravy, cheese, bread and beer.) She eats only the bread and cheese with a glass of regional wine, not to her liking. The beer is from Plzen and excellent. Lucien and I drink several flagons of it.

My companions whisper together from time to time, but it is plain to see that no one is much for conversation. I look upon my friends, in particular Emerald with her tiny exiguous meal; the light joyous air of the day now replaced with a kind of melancholy, perhaps it is nervousness. After a half dozen pints of beer, the three of us stride quietly back to the hotel to await the coming morning and the next day's arduous task.

Arriving in *the Sixth* early the next morning by tram, the three of us stroll approximately seven blocks from the platform to the address written on the piece of paper in Lucien's notebook. We peer up at the derelict old building, a rather decrepit plasterwork full of cracks and without paint. Someone has half-heartedly erected a series of makeshift rusty scaffolds apparently in a feeble attempt to recondition the weathered and beaten exterior, yet no work was in evidence anywhere about the building.

We find the door–the number painted by hand–and knock, each of us straining to hear any sound, any form of reaction from within. Dead silence.

Lucien raps on the door, several more times. Again, there is no response. When a final attempt brings no answer, he does a rather shocking and amazing thing. Pulling a small device from a hidden fold in his coat lapel, he bends to one knee and *commences to pick the lock.*

"What are you doing?" I whisper. He gives me an odd look and commences his effort to raise the lock. "Are you mad?" I question him further. "You're going to break in? Lucien, we're in a foreign country."

"Shhh," he hisses resuming his task. I look to Emerald. She only watches Lucien work. Suddenly the metallic click of the mechanism sets us all on our toes. Lucien turns the knob and the door quietly opens. I can feel the blood pumping in my veins as we slowly step into the darkened apartment, a fetid smell greeting our noses.

The place is as dark as a tomb, the windows apparently all blocked out much the same way as the apartment in San Francisco.

Emerald's hand grips my jacket sleeve as Lucien leads the way, following his cane, proving the darkness before us. He stops abruptly and my mind swims with a variety of possibilities; caught-up in the sickly odor of the chamber. Suddenly a brilliant flash of light fills the room as he turns on the overhead light.

What confronts our senses is beyond monstrous. Propped before us in a chair, as you or I might recline after a day's work sits *the charred remains of a human body*–less perhaps a body than the blackened outline where one once sat!

Emerald gasps and buries her face into my shoulder. I take her to my chest, covering my nose with a handkerchief. Lucien leans forward onto one knee and examines the grisly sight.

"Check the other rooms," he whispers to me pointing toward the bleak interior. Dread instantly courses my body. I am not a timid or squeamish person by nature, but it takes all my resolve to do what I'm directed. Slowly, painfully, I seek out the rest of the apartment, room by room, mentally preparing myself for whatever horror I might find yet there is nothing but the usual collection of human debris; articles of bedding and clothing, books–all in Czech–etcetera. Eventually I rejoin my comrades hovering over *the corpse*. It's a ghastly visage.

"Willem, write this down," Lucien instructs, and I quickly procure the notebook from my coat pocket. "Body charred beyond recognition, entire torso deplete. Right hand and lower right arm intact, left hand partially missing. Both legs charred to the shoes." He moves to the top of the chair. "Fragments of the occipital bone adhering to the chair-back...*hello*..." He bends down onto one knee withdrawing an ink pen from his breast pocket and spears into the darkness of the floor re-emerging with a gold ring dangling from it. "Looks like a gold wedding band, completely unscathed." We all study it a moment before he does the incredible and *drops it into his lapel pocket* before resuming his study. "Emerald, I think it advisable to contact Dr. Kucera immediately. He'll contact the proper authorities. There's a telephone on the desk in the corner."

Shortly after, while standing outside on the street watching the police come and go, I chance to question Emerald about Lucien's behavior.

"What exactly do you mean?" she asks.

"Well, breaking and entering for one…and of course the ring, you saw him place it in his breast pocket?"

"Yes, of course."

"Isn't that illegal, withholding evidence?" I ask bluntly.

"What possibly do you mean?"

"Why did he take it?"

"That will become quite evident very soon," she says tersely. I sense her studying me but cannot bring myself to look into her eyes. She continues to scrutinize me until I make eye contact. "Why do you work for Lucien?" she asks. I pause, unsure how to respond.

"Because I answered a solicitation for an office manager," I say. She shakes her head.

"No."

"No?" I echo, incredulous.

"No," she reiterates. I stare at her dumbfounded. "You work for Lucien Karras because the universe dictates that you do so."

"I don't know what you mean." Her expression becomes unfathomable, her eyes piercing, and I have to release their hold on me, staring off dead-pan into the teeming street. After a moment she takes my arm and we begin to stroll the boulevard.

"You've been to Japan?" she questions, knowingly. I can't imagine what Japan has to do with the topic of my employment.

"Yes, you know we were there recently, not too long ago."

"Did you walk any of the gardens?"

"Yes, I suppose we did," I mutter.

"The Japanese people plant the plum and cherry along the brook that flows to the pond. During the winter the trees are cold and barren but when spring arrives, from nothing but the bare limbs come the glorious white and pink blossoms. They sit magnificently upon their branch, yet all too soon fall. The brook takes them, each one regardless of how uniform or unique, inexorably gaining the pool. Some may meander in the eddies, but most will cloak the entirety of the pond in a brilliant pink or white brilliance." She stops and engages my attention.

"What is your point Emerald?" I ask and her eyes relentlessly fathom mine.

"We are very much like these tender delicate blossoms and the universe is very much like the brook and the pond. Inexorable. We can only flow where these forces take us."

"What does this story have to do with my working for Lucien?" I ask and her brow knits severely.

"Willem, you work for Lucien because Universe decreed it. *What we perceive as free will is the delicate balance of our uniqueness coupled with the inexorable quality that is life.* And what is this thing we call *Life* but that flowing? And the quality of our lives is the ability to respond, to move within this universal constant. If we struggle and fight with it, with ourselves, the world around us, we create the turbulence of conflict. Within all of us resides the potential for conflict. Some choose a contentious life. It is this contention that results in things of the nature of which we now struggle. All we need do now is follow this turbulence to its source. At the terminus of this train of repercussions and echoes writhes a living moving thing."

"I understand that but…what does this have to do with Lucien then, his breaking into the apartment?"

233

"Willem, I accept what Universe has given me and I accept what it takes away. This is the essence of the warrior. Lucien is such a man, in his quiet unassuming way he is of the *warrior persuasion*, fearless, relentless. We must not be weak in our resolve Willem but *possess the heart of the lion. We will devour our prey or be devoured by it in turn. No quarter given, none asked.*

Later that night, well after ten o'clock, so as to lessen the impact that human electro-magnetic activity creates, a strange meeting takes place in the upstairs offices of the *College of Paranormal Psychology Praha.*

Seated around the circular table sits our consistory of Doctors Kucera and Linhardt and our intrepid trio. The only object upon the table's dark lustrous surface is *the burned man's ring*, taken that morning by Lucien from the crime scene.

We have been instructed to sit as still as possible, to breathe steadily, clear our thoughts and not to take our attention off the object. Only Emerald sits with closed eyes. It is a simple gold wedding band. It radiates no light or warmth but appears dull and listless.

I do my best to keep my mind clear of all except the ring, however as the minutes drag on, I find my mind wandering back to the horrific scene that morning; as if I'm back in the bleak and grisly confines of the death house, walking aimlessly about the midden left by *the burned man*, as if I were reliving his final morbid days. My mind fights to free itself of the oppressive atmosphere. I peer at the others, as still as stone, their eyes fixed entirely upon the object, and the effect gives the moment an eerie quality.

A sudden inhalation breaks the silence and all eyes inadvertently shift to Emerald. She writhes as if in pain. We all stare at her unable to remove our attention while she seems to struggle with some unseen force when suddenly she speaks out in a rather unnerving voice.

"I see. I see them." She jerks her head slightly to one side. "The man...no longer of use," she winces. "Discarded like clay. Horrid. Blasphemy." She then becomes surprisingly calm, serene, her voice becoming low, nearly a whisper. *"Back it has gone. Back underground, all the faster, back to stone, brick and plaster. Silent, ever unseen, from whence it came into being."*

"Emerald, you mustn't go to the higher realm. Come back to us here. Where are you now?" Mme. Linhardt says, breaking the quietude with her assertive voice. "Emerald, stay within the astral. Tell us where you are, describe what you see." Emerald seems to regain her prior composure as if the strong commanding voice of Dr. Linhardt grounds her.

"We are here, where the two mighty rivers meet. We are here." Emerald seems to struggle anew. "It knows we seek it."

"Describe what you see." Linhardt says again, loudly. "Be not afraid Emerald Montaigne, we are here with you." This seems to calm her. "Now, orient yourself...tell us what you see."

"The ancient castle," Emerald whispers, pointing at nothing. "See, the ancient battlements...dying...how sad...the great castle...fallen...the great Prince...fallen."

"Quickly, where are you Emerald? Describe the view from the castle."

"We are here…above the valley, the river flowing, forever…on and on…into forever. The great family has fled this place…our home…oh these evil people…stop before you've drowned us all!" she nearly screams. "How dare thee violate this holy place."

"Go to the castle," Linhardt commands. "Go now." Emerald seems to struggle.

"No…so cold. Night has fallen cross't the great kingdom." She clasps her arms, her shoulders congealing. "It is come…it is here…the great horror…devourer of souls. It is upon us. Flee. Take the women and children far cross't the mountain."

"Emerald, we are here with you. Go to the castle…tell us what you see." Emerald pauses for several moments then tenses in her seat, her eyes dilating wildly.

"It knows we've come." She pauses, then inhales sharply. "It knows I've come!" She screams violently and collapses onto the floor. Moments later we're reviving her with brandy. We gently prop her head with Lucien's overcoat.

"I'm sorry to have fainted Vilos, forgive me. I've such a long way to go I'm afraid; hardly worthy of your mentorship," she whispers as she sips the amber liquid, coughing.

"You did fine Emerald," Dr. Kucera says smiling. "Quickly my dear, while the impressions are strong with you, what did you see?" he asks, and she becomes very reserved, as if peering into the distance at something very far off and unclear.

"I…I was travelling…with my family…on a winding road, through a verdant countryside, when I saw a very old, old castle sitting high upon a hill…overlooking a broad valley where two large rivers intersect."

"The intersection of two large rivers you say?" Lindhart questions her.

"Yes…very large…the two became one…proceeding south far into the distance."

"Go on Ms. Montaigne."

"I entered a large grassy courtyard, surrounded by the castle's bulwarks, what was left of them, then, a wide flight of stone stairs leading underground." She pauses deep in thought. "That's all I remember." Kucera looks at Linhardt and his corpulent companion is smiling and nodding profusely.

"What do you make of it?" he inquires and Lindhardt laughs, smiling broadly, taking Emerald's cheek between her plump thumb and forefinger, her eyes glittering.

"You are a truly accomplished young woman Emerald Montaigne. Bratislava is where you go next. Your journey takes you to Slovakia and the thing's birthplace."

That night when we arrive back at the hotel a most peculiar event transpires. As we pull up, Lucien requests I remain in the car. There's a short conversation with Emerald at the curb followed by her speaking in Czech with the driver. Lucien gets back in and the automobile speeds off into the night.

As we roll down the boulevard, I ask Lucien about our destination. He merely gestures for me to be patient. It is an odd feeling, speeding through the darkened foreign city at the midnight hour, *destination unknown*. Everything seems quiet and shuttered, only a few late-night revelers walking the bleak suburban streets beneath the pallid glow of dull yellow sodium lights.

After a period, we arrive at the high ground to the north overlooking the city. It's nearly pitch black as the cab ascends a narrow curving road to what appears to be *a long concrete structure void of windows.*

As we exit the cab, I raise my collar to the brisk cold breeze nipping at our faces. It's a lonely desolate spot, void of light or activity; a nearly surreal landscape, *like walking within a dream.* Lucien begins ascending a long series of broad massive concrete stairs flanked on both sides by thick stands of juniper. Oddly, there's not a single lamp shedding light. As we slowly make the crest of these large, broad stairs–gazing into the darkness at the low concrete façade–an eerie feeling envelops me.

"What is this building Lucien?" I whisper from my collar. He peers intently into the darkness. I repeat my question. He looks at me strangely in the thin moonlight, obscured by clouds.

"Stalinoff," he whispers. I echo his word in wonder. "The Stalin monument," he says. I look at the austere building seeing nothing like a monument at all. Lucien withdraws his meerschaum and lights it in the darkness casting a glow within the oppressive night that engulfs us.

"The great murderer," he says under his breath. "He built the enormous monument of himself here," he whispers softly as the wind buffets the flame of his butane causing strange shadows to dance about the periphery of the glow. "The Czechs destroyed the statue decades ago. This was the base for the statue of the great megalomaniac."

"Where are we going?" I ask. He looks at me oddly in the dark.

"Inside," he mutters, and a very unsettling feeling instantly engulfs me. "Hello…" he whispers pointing the stem of his pipe. In the distance, nearly invisible in the oppressive darkness, is what appears to be a tiny feeble light at a distance of several hundred feet, perhaps a lighter or small torch. Lucien pockets his butane. "There's our man," he states and begins to prod with his old briar stick in the direction of the light like a moth attracted to a flame. Suddenly he says: "It's imperative you remain absolutely silent and attentive. I don't anticipate any trouble but be prepared."

"Prepared? For what?" I ask. He looks at me hard in the darkness.

"*For the unexpected*." He then prods his way into the shadows.

At the entrance to the concrete *mausoleum* we meet a solemn dark stranger. Obviously Czech, the odd little man seems unable to speak English. I watch as Lucien pays him a small sum of Czech korunas. The man whittles through the thin stack of bills, grunts satisfaction then unlocks one of the towering old doors that shrieks in defiance as it swings open revealing the *dark gaping chasm of the unknown*. Lucien ignites a small penlight and enters guided by its soft luminance. I look to the side and am shocked by the sudden disappearance of our doorkeeper.

"He's gone!" I whisper and Lucien just huffs.

"No bother."

We slowly penetrate the gloom, following the tiny orb of his light as it bounces through the chaos of wrecked and decrepit debris–massive stone columns and marble blocks strewn about, helter-skelter.

The crypt is unbelievably massive. Everywhere is mounds of soot and shattered rock. Enormous cracked columns permeate the large stone surround, disappearing into the maw of darkness above and before us.

"What is this place?" I ask in awe as we slowly delve into the unknown.

"I told you, you're in the catacombs of the Stalinoff monument. The structure that supported the towering façade of Stalin, presented before the Czech people," he states. "This structure was designed to house military apparatus for the Soviet occupation of Czechoslovakia. Now it is acres of ruin. The remains of the statue were dumped in here. Be careful not to touch the debris, the Czech activists who blew up the statue used whatever variety of explosives they could muster including hand grenades and the rubble supposedly still carries some of those materials."

We press on into the bowels of the rotting vault. As we move amongst the large concrete columns that ascend into the blackness above us, I'm awed that such a structure exists. It is as if an entire complex has been hidden under the ruse of a political statement. I feel the sound and flutter of bats near my head and neck and it is an uneasy feeling to keep the push on into the abyss before us.

Eventually we spy a faint glow several hundreds of meters ahead in the solitude. We slowly make our way to the light amidst the omnipresent blackness. It is a feeble light that reveals a dark and mysterious *specter within the gloom*. This person–or visage–is robed, his face hidden from view, and completely dark. The feeling I get in *his* presence is uncomfortable to say the least.

"You have brought the *annuitas*?" he inquires with a raspy voice. Lucien hands the specter an envelope and the dark image bends over it as if examining it in detail. It looks, to me, to be a serious amount of money, several thousand Euros I believe. The ebony form then hands Lucien a small *alabaster vial*, within the vial is a yellowed scrap of paper. "The incantation *has not tasted the tongue of the living since before the Christ,*" the specter whispers with just a wisp of supplication. Lucien glances over the tiny scroll in brevity then carefully returns it to the cylinder.

"As it were," he says pocketing the vial and the being echoes his words. The *person* then becomes silent and this rapidly takes the form of a dismissal. Lucien turns and begins retracing our steps. I take wonder at what seems a hyper experience, an almost unreal feeling, *as if watching a play or movie* upon a stage or vinyl screen. We begin the slow trek back through the catacombs. When we gain the outside once more, I am nearly ecstatic to breathe in the night, clearing my lungs of the moldy stagnant air.

"What on earth was that?" I ask and Lucien shrugs.

"Merely a *weigh station on our journey*, nothing more, best not to dwell on it," he says grimly.

I'm enraptured when we return to the tiny cab that sits waiting to convey us back to the city. As we roll down the Czech streets within the womb of night, I'm suddenly overcome by the night's events.

"Why such a place Lucien?" He looks at me with that same mysterious expression.

"The incantation has *lived underground for two thousand years*. It will serve us in Bratislava." I wonder over these words the entire trip back into central Prague.

The following morning, we are southbound by rail for Bratislava, the capital city of Slovakia. Emerald, who had difficulty sleeping that night, is dozing in her seat; her soft radiant features, as she sleeps, remind me of the Madonna in a painting by Rubens. Lucien is deep in thought. From previous experience I know not to disturb his meditations. I entertain myself by gazing out the window, watching the Czech countryside pass. Small villages and towns, small farms, green and golden fields of wheat, old stone structures and modern houses all race distinctly into view, are there for the briefest moment then disappear into memory.

Upon our arrival at Bratislava Central Station we secure a cab and set out for our boarding. As we transverse the city–on route for the suburbs and our lodging for the evening–I'm struck by the difference between the two capital cities, shocked by the rows of concrete tenement housing left from the Communist era. I look at Lucien, as if reading my thoughts, he comments.

"Bratislava suffered severely under the boot of the Communists." We both stare through our dusty windows and I wonder about life under such austere conditions as that must have been.

Emerald engages the driver in a spirited conversation, not necessarily a pleasant one. Eventually he manages to find the bed-and-breakfast and Emerald pays him grudgingly, complaining that he had purposefully circumnavigated our destination to pad his meter.

"He thinks we're just a bunch of bloody tourists," she says snapping the clasp of her purse. "I know how to read a map!" I'm surprised by her outburst. It seems somehow uncharacteristic. Lucien calms her with a touch of his hand.

"Let's check in and get something to eat."

"Splendid. We absolutely must find fresh fruit and vegetables. I can't live on bread and cheese alone," she states rather tersely, and Lucien and I exchange a furtive glance.

Our choice of residence proves to be a fortuitous one, the proprietors cheery and friendly. We are shown to a clean modern suite with a comfortable common area and a fully functional kitchen, which delights Emerald, her mood brightening considerably. Mrs. Pavel, our efficacious hostess, is young and has schooled in England. She instructs Emerald where to acquire fresh produce. She then returns with various cooking utensils and she and Emerald quickly become intrigued with each other, carrying on a lengthy conversation in Czech. Mr. Pavel, slightly older and less social than his wife proves a valuable asset procuring a bottle of Scotch and two excellent cigars. Lucien and I smoke on the veranda while the women cook and converse together in Czech as the day slowly passes into night.

As I gaze at the newly risen moon, I sense the history and minacity of the region. My mind–or some aspect of it–conjures up a series of historic scenarios, events, war and pestilence alike; the suffering and joys of the people who have worked and toiled this land and its myriad of kingdoms, built and fallen, over the course of time.

The moon, radiant within the still of the night seems frozen within *her* effervescent twilight, everything in view painted a variety of deep aquamarine hues. I sense *she* has seen all these things come to pass since the very beginning of time.

"We're in luck," Emerald announces bursting through the door. "Mrs. Pavel has graciously offered her husband's services. He'll drive us to the Danube tomorrow. From her directions I surmise we should find the castle easily." Lucien only nods, deep in thought, his brow knit. I wonder what he is thinking about. When the meal is finished, I help Emerald clean up while Lucien takes what proves to be another of his extended nocturnal meanderings.

Before we turn in for the night, Emerald and I sit in the courtyard under a deep indigo sky that looks and feels surreal. The countryside rolls on into infinity cloaked in a dull blue light from the moon above. As we speak together, she sips tea from a china cup while I try to enjoy one of the Czech cigarettes I've brought from Prague.

She stares up at the moon high within the starry canopy above, the moonlight lovingly embracing the delicate features of her face. I clearly see her cerulean eyes, iridescent as they reflect the moonlight, taking in the splendor of the soft tranquil night. When she resumes our conversation, the eyes return to pools of darkness set within the pallid white face and a sense of timelessness engulfs me.

We talk softly together about our pasts. I'm more interested in hers than expounding about my own. She talks about New Orleans–an old traditional southern family of French ancestry, wealthy and eccentric–then about schooling in France and eventually London. I'm surprised to learn she is a published woman of letters, holding Doctorates in both Theology and Parapsychology. I learn she speaks seven languages.

"Learn Latin first," she advises, "and the Romantic languages will fall into place nicely."

"What will happen tomorrow Emerald?" I find myself asking. She becomes quiet and suddenly mysterious as if her brilliant mind has wandered to far distant places. I ponder what secrets she fathoms. She stares at me in the moonlight. *I feel she is peering directly into my being.* The black pools that are her eyes reflect a pinprick of light– perhaps from the moon–and the feeling is strangely familiar, the two of us sitting in silence within the starry world that engulfs us.

"Within the world, sequestered from the light of knowing consciousness, are those who choose to remain forever within *The Twilight Kingdom*. Like a dawn obscured by mist they live out their existence, concealed, preying upon the weak…*sometimes disguised as animals, sometimes priests."* I hold the dark pools of her eyes as long as I can bear. She suddenly lifts the silver chain with its simple silver crucifix from around her neck and hands it to me in the darkness. "This was made for me long ago, in New Orleans, it is a protective amulet." She places it in my hand. "Wear this tomorrow." I feel the warmth of her neck within the talisman in the palm of my hand.

The following morning after a breakfast of fruit, bread, jam and tea, we are trundling south toward the Danube. It is a magnificent sight, the mighty river. Broad and slow, it slices through the land unhindered. Mr. Pavel waves goodbye and takes the junction westerly as we set out on foot for what looks to be the remnants of an old decrepit castle sitting high atop a lush green hillside.

"Is it the castle which you saw in your dreaming?" Lucien asks Emerald. We pause on the side of the gravel road and she shades the sun, and her dark tresses, from her eyes.

"I'm not sure...I believe it may," she says. "Let's go there." We are not disappointed. The second we gain the crest of the ridge she gasps involuntarily. There it sits just as it had appeared to her in the vision, a derelict deprecated old castle, standing in utter ruin, the walls more a pile of rocks than a structure; centuries old.

My colleagues become eerily silent. I see clearly their trepidation as we begin ascending toward the precipice. When we gain the structure proper, I spy the large grassy courtyard so clearly described by our companion seer.

A cool and steady breeze blows across the broken castle ramparts, the highest point in the area. I survey the valley below, stretching for miles into a vague misty horizon. Just as she described it, two immense rivers converged to the south; the Danube winding on her course like an enormous indigo snake.

"Is this the courtyard you saw?" Lucien queries Emerald and she nods. "Off we go," he says, his eyes fierce.

We work our way down into the morass of fallen stone and brambles that choke the foundations of a once mighty fortress. We inch our way along so as not to slip on the loose rock. Eventually the journey eases as we make the courtyard and its thin patina of grass. Soon, we're standing before a series of cracked and weathered stone steps made from solid pieces of granite that must easily weigh several tons each.

The descent is blocked by gravel and fallen stone–the remnants of what was once the ceiling and walls of the structure. Our small group stares down into the morass of rock.

"This is it," Emerald whispers, *her eyes like fire.* "The door to the abyss."

"Let's get started." Lucien extracts the alabaster vial given him at the Stalin monument and carefully withdraws the thin piece of parchment, holding it before her. She begins to mutter the incantation written upon it, a tongue I don't recognize; old Czech I suppose.

Glancing about the ruins, I'm struck by the age of the place. It must be well over a dozen centuries old. There is just enough of the ancient structure to roughly make out the rectilinear shape. The north wall seems to have fared the best as it still stands approximately a dozen feet or so in height nearly its entire length. There is something of the eastern wall but almost nothing of the west and southern ramparts except a decrepit row of beige colored rock of varying sizes ranging from massive blocks to mere shards.

There is a length of wall extending south down the hillside toward the valley below. It terminates at a sort of platform that I surmise must have been a turret, perhaps a cistern for accumulating rainfall, it's not clear to me why this structure exists only that it was built of the same beige rock and well enough to have weathered the centuries.

As I gaze about this mysterious and mystical place, my attention is drawn back to our melancholy business at hand. Emerald is now deep into a sort of trance-like state as she recites the ancient magic formulae contained upon the parchment.

Whatever the words, or sounds, depicted upon the scroll I likely will never know. What I can tell you is that the power or purpose of this mantra, this series of magic syllables, this incantation and the vibrations they create, *instigates a terrifying event.*

What I first begin to notice is a thin noxious smelling air that seems to waft from the buried lower cellar, the breeze rapidly escalating into a rather potent wind, scoring the plain and creating strange sounds from its action between the rocks. Lucien takes hold of Emerald's lithe form and casts me a sideways glance.

"Brace yourself!" At this precise moment, a gust of foul wind explodes in our faces as if a subterranean fury had suddenly unleashed itself from an ancient tomb. We reel under the ferocity, dust, sand and grit blowing across our bodies and faces. I shield my eyes, in doing so, I see Emerald distinctly. I'm shocked by the utter frailty of her form against the maelstrom. I realize how thin and fragile she is, the clothes seared across her body by the intense wind.

Lucien shouts to me but I cannot distinguish his words. He clutches Emerald's miniscule form as she is rocked about like a blade of grass in a monsoon. I fear we are faltering. It feels as if we are being sucked into a vortex of unbelievable violence. I'm succumbing to a numbing sense of dread and despair. As I'm brought to my knees, losing my sense of balance and direction, I suddenly feel a vice-like grip upon my shoulder. Lucien stands rigid in the maelstrom like some crazed old Ahab at the wheel of his doomed ship, defying the monstrous beast set upon devouring us. He pulls me to my feet and shouts in my ear.

"Steady her! Steady Emerald!" I'm trying to clear the fog and confusion from my thoughts. He purposefully locks my hands upon the shoulders of our erudite colleague. I hear my mind think how could such a frail and insignificant person combat the voracious torrent we've unleashed? I distinctly hear my mind say: '*Run.*'

"Willem, steady Emerald!" Lucien shouts at the top of his lungs. I grip her fiercely her lithe frame feels like a willow frond in my grasp. I fear we are battling a monstrosity with a willow frond. Amazingly, I can hear her voice clearly through the storm; but what are the words she speaks? I strain to hear but it is an ancient tongue, words of a culture and people long perished from our earth; eloquent and vivid words, they are a tonal mantra that whips the entity into frenzy. The violence that rocks us contains an unworldly heat that defies my logic. We hold on and her voice gains pitch and strength. The words are clear and magnificent but unfortunately meaningless to my ears.

At the point where I fear we will be lifted aloft into the air and dashed across the rocks, it is over; just like the sudden cessation of a hurricane's wind, the sudden and inexplicable absence of the vortex leaves us standing in wonderment.

Instantly the world returns as it was, the sun reemerging, casting a warm glow upon our wearied and battered forms. I'm awed by the sudden absence of pressure, a deep resonant vacuum; nothing remains but a profound silence, peace and serenity, the tittering of birds under an electric blue sky. We gaze at each other. Lucien is the first to speak, steadying himself with the old briarwood that is his constant companion.

"Well…that's that," he says, his voice raspy. There is dust and debris in Emerald's long obsidian tresses, and she has a thin razor-like gash across her cheek that exudes a trickle of crimson blood. Lucien extracts a snow-white handkerchief from his pocket and takes the blood from her comely face and she lays her head into his shoulder and weeps. After a minute he looks at me with dark grim eyes.

"Let's get the hell out of here," and the three of us set off together *into the sun.*

I'm sitting at a café on Columbus Avenue in the North Beach district of San Francisco, enjoying a respite from the previous week's dark business when Lucien joins me ordering an espresso and focaccia for which the establishment is famous.

"You've tied up the loose ends of the affair with K?"

"And helped assist Grey. They've flown him in from the Southwest."

"The Apache medicine man?"

"He'll assist us in *clearing* the repugnant abode on Clay Street. I can't insist upon your help Willem. I leave you free to explore the beautiful *City by the Bay*."

"Thank you for that Lucien. I appreciate it. However, if you'll have me...tell me where and when."

Even behind his thick pervasive beard I see him smile and his eyes glint in the afternoon sun. People meander the North Beach sidewalks, the smell of pasta and coffee in the air; the press of cars on Columbus Avenue; the arms of Peter-Paul Cathedral hugging the square like an older sibling. He commences to explain some of the details of the dead man's life, a singular and lonely one; the history of an outsider who sought out the darker aspects of existence. Lucien finishes his recitation lighting his pipe with a cedar match.

"Did they fully take into account our experience in Bratislava?" I query. He looks at me curiously.

"Of course not Willem," he laughs under his breath, puffing on his bowl. "They're incapable of such thought. It's the tangible they react to, not realizing all this is in actuality consciousness."

"Speaking of the tangible Lucien," I say becoming thoughtful, "I don't really understand what happened in Bratislava. It seems...impossible."

"But you were there, you experienced it first-hand Willem."

"I was there...yet even now it seems unbelievable to me. How could words on a tiny scrap of paper cause such a reaction?" His eyes glow.

"Not the *written words* themselves but *the spoken word* and the spoken word's relationship to universal vibration, in particular *sympathetic vibration*."

"What do you mean?"

"It's immaterial that the word be in the form of a mantra, a prayer or in our case a spell or an incantation. It is the vessel that is of primary concern."

"The vessel?" I ask and his eyebrow rises sharply.

"The remarkable Ms. Montaigne," he says. "This is her praxis, this unique and yet universal ability."

"But I don't understand. How could what she said, cause such a tempestuous reaction...and the destruction of the demon?"

"You need to come to the understanding of a very profound yet simple fact...that the Universe itself is the result of the spoken word. Is *it,* in fact." I try to take this in.

"What is...*the word*?" I ask.

"The great mystery...and you ask it as if asking the time of day," he says and laughs softly, genuinely. "Such a direct and sincere question merits an equivocal answer. *The word...is the nearly infinite layering of universal vibration*."

"I'm not sure what you mean."

"How can I state it more clearly?" I shrug and he laughs softly. "You don't understand me?"

"No," I admit, and he grows reflective, spending a moment with his pipe.

"I'm referring to the *multiplicity of phenomenon*. Here in our miniscule *sphere* alone Willem…low frequency waves, sound waves, infra-red, the entire visible light spectrum, ultraviolet, mental vibration, extra-sensory perception…the cycles repeat themselves into the next realm, next vibrational state and beyond…on and on ad infinitum *and back again*. As the waves move outward, rarefaction occurs, the echoes reverberate back onto themselves, our words, our very thoughts, return to us." I think about this clear and concise metaphor realizing what he's talking about is immensely profound yet intrinsically simple and is all around me as we speak; the sights and sounds of the city, the sun on my face and the warmth I feel from its rays. Eventually I ask him directly:

"How was the demon destroyed by Emerald…exactly?" His eyes fixate and dilate.

"You do understand the question you ask?" he queries, and I find myself nodding. "What she referred to as *annihilation* might better be qualified as *disintegration*," he says.

"What's the difference?" I ask more out of a sense of confusion than inquiry. He pauses as if contemplating the question deeply.

"None really. More semantics than anything else I suppose," he says. "The science itself embraces the concept of *sympathetic vibration*. The inherent tendency of vibrations to synchronize and build upon one another, as the crest of one wave cycle will multiply that cycle twofold with proper *attenuation*."

"Attenuation?"

"This is the secret behind mantra, even prayer, and at the heart of Emerald's astounding ability. The concept of *attenuation*."

"What is *annihilation* exactly?" I ask and his brow furrows. He pauses studying me closely a moment.

"The action of focused vibrational patterns acting upon the cohesion of molecules of any given object being focused upon." He studies my expression. "The principles are similar to those used *in the concept of invisibility, the negation of manifest form.* However, with *annihilation,* it's taken to the extreme *and quite irreversible."* I must have a look on my face for Lucien continues. "The concept is not as abstruse as your expression would indicate," he says good-naturedly. "However, it does take a rigid application of principles and *absolute* focus; a deep encompassing study, verily a lifetime's worth of it."

The waiter arrives with Lucien's order and the morning edition of the Chronicle. I give my friend repose, content instead to meditate on his words and watch the procession of people come and go from the beautiful Peter Paul Cathedral across the square from the café. The park is filled with people at play, reading books, walking dogs or just loitering about under the shade of the eucalyptus trees. I wonder about their lives, reflecting upon my own.

"Will Emerald be joining us anytime soon?"

"No. She's off to New Orleans...*to see the Creole woman*, a kind of healing," he says. I feel a pang of remorse, oddly, more in my stomach than in my mind. He studies me over the top of his spectacles.

"What is it?" I ask as he stares into me.

"You were quite taken by her on this journey my young friend?"

"Not at all," I stammer, too defensively. "I'm only…amazed by her. She's quite extraordinary." His eyes gleam. He's laughing at me.

"Yes, yes indeed…a very exceptional woman," he responds and returns his attention to the news of the world. I gaze about, marvel at the exceedingly blue sky. It seems as if we have been living under a dark cloud for weeks.

"Shall I make arrangements for London?" I inquire. Lucien, as if sharing my sense of lightness, looks about at the beautiful city filled with people, laughter and light.

"No…I think we'll stay over for a spell. It's been a long rough road."

"Beryl will scream bloody murder. She's insisting on our return. Mine certainly."

"Of course," he says deep in thought. "It's more or less her job to do so. No lad, you work for me. I pay your salary not the company or our illustrious Ms. Collins."

"Well that's a relief. She actually threatened my job."

"Yes…I agree, wholeheartedly. We'll stay on awhile," he mutters as if speaking to someone else before he returns his attention to me. "I've some old business associates in this fair city Willem, I'm certain it's the same with you?"

"I'm sure I'll find something to do." He nods; studying me intently.

"You realize Morgan, is still here?"

"She is? She didn't go back to New York?"

"Apparently not," he says, sipping espresso from the tiny ceramic cup. "She's residing at the house. Do you remember the address?"

"Certainly but…" He waits as I search for words. "I'm sure she's busy." He looks at me as one might look upon a fool.

"Quite. I'm certain she is," he says folding the Chronicle and sticking it into the lower pocket of his tweed. "After all, why else would she still be here?" he says staring into the morning sky. I think about this for several minutes and I'm certain Lucien somehow is watching my every movement. "Sorry. Did you say something?" he suddenly inquires.

"No, I didn't." I stare at him fixedly.

"My mistake," he says and relights his pipe. "You don't believe a person can read another's thoughts, do you?" I sit in silence, taking this in.

"What do you mean exactly?"

"Exactly what I just asked," he says. I banter this about in my mind for a moment.

"No, I suppose not." He nods, puffing on his pipe.

"Yet, you agree with me?"

"Agree with you? About what?"

"That you were thinking about Morgan, just now," he says, and I realize indeed I *was* thinking about her, deeply; that I've been thinking about her ever since the first moment I looked into her eyes.

"A lucky guess," I say to fill the silence.

"Son, there are no *'lucky guesses'* in my line of work," he states flatly.

"Are you saying you can read minds?"

"The eyes," he says.

"*The eyes*?" I ask and he nods. "Can you explain that a bit more?" He closes the distance between us.

"I saw her in your eyes."

"How's that?" I ask, assuming a pun.

"Absolutely."

"I don't get you." He withdraws the meerschaum from his mouth and bangs it on the leg of the table.

"Look across the park, what do you see?" I gaze across the block of green grass and trees at the beige façade of the Peter Paul Cathedral.

"The cathedral?" I ask and he nods.

"What sees the cathedral Willem, the eyes or the brain?" I ponder this a moment.

"Both."

"Wonderful," he says. "The eye's retina takes in the light. The light information enters the brain which processes it into the concept of the cathedral."

"Yes...I suppose."

"So, then you agree the inverse would be in effect?"

"The inverse?"

"That the image of Morgan whom you were contemplating within your brain is reflected back in the eye's retina." He says this so matter-of-factly that I'm at a loss for words and the conversation goes stale.

"I imagine at some point in Vaclav Radic's life he could have followed a better path. A path filled with the energy of living and life. Somewhere along the line he chose *condensation*, the shadows; extreme materialism my friend. He probably suffered riches for a period of time in his life before a moral and physical decay...until the thing inside ultimately destroyed him." He lights his bowl, puffing away like a chimney; the young couple next to us indignantly rise and move to another table. Lucien sits staring at the blue sky, deep in thought when he suddenly addresses me. "You do understand we are energy beings?" he asks, less a question than a statement.

"So I'm starting to gather." He looks at me squarely.

"And apparently they're all quite wrong, as was I," he states mysteriously. "Incredible. Mistaken this long? Throughout antiquity…?"

"Mistaken?"

"The scientists and before them the alchemists of our world. Is it truly possible?"

"What?"

"That energy *can* be destroyed. That it can seep into the morass of the non-conscious, be dissolved into nothingness?" I've no answer to offer him and say as much. "*What other answer does She afford us Willem?* Such is the legacy back in Bratislava apparently." He puffs on his meerschaum, deep in thought, taking note of my confusion. "As energy-based beings we need the energy of life to sustain us, the sun, the trees and grasses, the wind and the rain, the joys and the tribulations of existence…the cosmos; the macrocosm and microcosm both. *The soul needs to see its reflection in life, within the eyes of others.*"

Fini.